NO LO
SEATTL___ ___ ___ LIBRARY,

D0466145

The Door at the End of the World

Also by
Caroline Carlson

The World's Greatest Detective
The Very Nearly Honorable League of Pirates series:
Magic Marks the Spot
The Terror of the Southlands
The Buccaneers' Code

The Door at the End of the World

Caroline Carlson

HARPER

An Imprint of HarperCollins*Publishers*

The Door at the End of the World

Text copyright © 2019 by Caroline Carlson

Map art by Virginia Allyn

All rights reserved. Printed in the United States of America.
No part of this book may be used or reproduced in any manner whatsoever without
written permission except in the case of brief quotations embodied in critical articles
and reviews. For information address HarperCollins Children's Books, a division of
HarperCollins Publishers, 195 Broadway, New York, NY 10007.
www.harpercollinschildrens.com

Library of Congress Control Number: 2018013449
ISBN 978-0-06-236830-0

Typography by Joel Tippie

19 20 21 22 23   CG/LSCH   10 9 8 7 6 5 4 3 2 1

❖

First Edition

for Kelly Wood,
who holds open the doors to a thousand worlds,

and in memory of Diana Wynne Jones

A VISITOR'S GUIDE TO ALL THE WORLDS

N

NW

NE

THE FABRIC OF TIME AND SPACE

W

E

SW

S

SE

THE SPACE BEYOND THE WORLDS

The Door at the End of the World

1

There's no signpost to mark the end of the world, so you need to know what you're looking for: a gatehouse, a garden, and a tall brick wall overgrown with flowering vines. The gatehouse bell is broken, but if you've managed to travel all the way to the end of the world, you're obviously persistent enough to knock on the door. You'll have to wait awhile, too, since the Gatekeeper likes to take her time. Traveling from one world to the next isn't something a person should do on a whim, and she wants to make sure you mean it.

While you're waiting, after you've checked your watch twice and wondered about the note taped to the door that says BEWARE OF BEES, you might happen to look through the window into the front room, where a girl sits behind a desk piled high with papers. That's me. My name is Lucy. I'm the one you don't quite notice as I stamp your passport, collect your travel papers, and wish you the best of luck on your trip. I'm not allowed to take you to the tall brick wall or push aside the vines or unlock the door hidden behind them—only the Gatekeeper can do that—but I like my job. At the end of the world, it's important to be organized.

This close to the door, things tend to go missing. They're odds and ends, usually: gloves, keys, spare change, the occasional pencil stub, anything that might slip or squeeze or roll into the space between the worlds. "You'll get used to it," the Gatekeeper told me when I moved in. For the most part, she was right. I'd learned to stash extra gloves in my pockets and tie my pencils to the desk with bits of string; I'd started expecting to lose things. But I can't say I ever expected to lose the Gatekeeper herself.

It happened on an unremarkable Thursday. I'd cleaned the breakfast dishes and was sorting travel papers into stacks on my desk—pink customs declarations to the left, green returnee reports to the right, and blue applications for otherworld travel straight ahead—when the Gatekeeper stomped into the room. This was still unremarkable: the Gatekeeper always stomps. She has wild white hair that frizzes around her face when she's upset, or when it looks like rain, and she walks with a cane that she thwacks and thumps when she wants to make a point. She's not a witch, but some people think she might be, and she doesn't try to persuade them otherwise.

On this particular Thursday, the sky was blue and cloudless, but the Gatekeeper's hair was already starting to frizz at the ends. As soon as I saw the basket she was carrying, I knew why. It was full of rags and rolls of fabric, sewing needles and thread, wood polish and soap, and a screwdriver with a bright orange handle. "Happy Maintenance Day!" I said.

The Gatekeeper glowered. "*Happy* isn't the word I'd choose. I'd rather have my ears nibbled off by a thistle-backed thrunt than have to spend the day with Bernard." She set down her basket. "Well, maybe just one ear."

Bernard was the gatekeeper who guarded the other side of the door, keeping an eye on the travelers who passed from his world into ours and making sure no one smuggled out illegal otherworld goods, slipped past without their Interworld Travel papers in order, or stumbled through accidentally. He and the Gatekeeper had never been friendly—but then again, the Gatekeeper didn't like anyone from the next world over. According to her, Easterners were ignorant and impolite, and besides that, they smelled. Still, twice a year, the Gatekeeper went over to East for the morning to clean and polish the door between the worlds, tighten anything that had come loose, knot the stray threads in the fabric of time and space, and argue with Bernard over which of them got to hold the screwdriver. In the afternoon, both of them came back to Southeast and repeated the whole process on this side of the door. It was fiddly, tedious work, and at the end of the day six months earlier, the Gatekeeper had vowed to retire before Maintenance Day rolled around again, but both of us had known she didn't really mean it. I couldn't imagine what the end of the world would be like without her.

"Is Bernard really that bad?" I asked. I still hadn't met him. You might think that a girl living at the end of the world would have lots of thrilling adventures, but it wasn't quite like that for me. Even the Gatekeeper hardly ever went to other worlds, and in the year I'd been working as her deputy, I'd never actually been through the door myself.

"Bernard," the Gatekeeper said, "is always worrying about *irregularities*. Last Maintenance Day he swore there was something funny about the door hinges, and the time before that he was convinced the air near the worldgate smelled of lemon pie. He always wants to know if I've noticed any irregularities on my side, and of course I never have." She shrugged. "Have you noticed anything irregular, Lucy?"

I thought about it. "The bees seemed upset a few weeks ago," I said. "They found Henry Tallard wandering near the door without any travel papers. They told me they stung him twenty-three times before he finally ran away."

"Good for them!" The Gatekeeper cackled. "I don't care how famous an explorer you are; you can't go poking around my worldgate without my permission. Henry Tallard has been inconsiderate and nosy as long as I've known him, though. That doesn't sound so irregular to me."

I couldn't think of anything else unusual that had happened lately. A whirlwind had sprung up in a corner of the garden, right beside the zinnias, but that happened at least once a month. So did the lightning strikes that zigzagged down the side of the gatehouse; at the end of the world, the weather is always temperamental and usually dramatic. Three otherworld tourists had arrived the day before, passing through Southeast on their way to see the Great Molten Lagoon over in South, and two Interworld Travel employees from headquarters had hurried through the door on business just that morning, but none of them had been remotely interesting. They had all gazed over the top of my head as I took their travel papers, and people who find a vase on a fireplace mantel more fascinating than the human sitting in front of them can't be all that fascinating themselves. "If anything strange has happened here recently," I told the Gatekeeper, "it hasn't happened to me."

"That's exactly what I like about you, Lucy," the Gatekeeper said. "Nothing happens to you. At the end of the world, that's saying something." She stomped to the coat closet and threw on her cloak. "Unless Bernard finds some more irregularities to complain about, I'll be back by lunchtime. You know the rules by now, I assume."

I nodded. The Gatekeeper's rules were sensible, just the way I liked rules to be. "Don't open the worldgate, and don't let any-one through. Make travelers wait here until the maintenance is finished. Don't leave the end of the world for any reason, and eat my vegetables."

"And if there's an emergency?"

"Shout. Scream. Make a general ruckus." I frowned. "Are you sure you'll be able to hear all that through the door?"

"I've got two perfectly good ears, and you've got two strong lungs, which I trust you know how to use." The Gatekeeper smiled at me, which wasn't exactly a habit of hers. "Goodbye, Lucy." She thumped her cane three times, picked up her basket of cleaning supplies, and stomped outside.

I watched from the window as she went down the garden path, her hair throwing a tantrum around her face and her cloak swishing witchily around her ankles. When she reached the wall covered with vines, she drew a key out of her pocket, unlocked the door between the worlds, and squeezed through it. The door closed behind her, and I went back to work.

The Gatekeeper didn't come back by lunchtime. She wasn't back for dinner, either. By the time I washed the day's ink stains from my hands, combed the tangles out of my hair, and crawled underneath the quilt I'd brought from home when I came to live at the end of the world, she still hadn't returned, and I was starting to worry. It shouldn't have taken her and Bernard more than a few hours to work on the Eastern side of the door, and even if they'd found some extra snags to mend or bolts to polish, I couldn't imagine why the Gatekeeper wouldn't have stuck her head through the worldgate to tell me about it. In my nook at the back of the gatehouse, I lay awake listening for the squeak of door hinges or the thump of the Gatekeeper's cane.

By sunrise, I was prickling with panic. The Gatekeeper wasn't snoring in her bedroom or yanking weeds in the garden or calling out from the kitchen to ask whether we had any more milk for porridge. The gatehouse was eerily quiet, and there wasn't anyone else in sight. In my nightgown and bare feet, I ran down the path to the wall and pushed aside the vines, even though I knew the bees wouldn't be happy about it. Then I tugged on the door at the end of the world.

It was locked, as usual. At least *that* was as it should be. "Gatekeeper!" I shouted, using my two strong lungs as well as I could. "Bernard! Can you hear me? Are you all right?" I pounded on the door with both fists as hard as I could. Then I picked up a handful of stones from the garden and started throwing the stones one by one against the wall. "I'm making a general ruckus," I explained to the bees as they buzzed all around me, investigating the situation. "The Gatekeeper's been over in East for almost a whole day, and you know how much she hates it there. If that's not an emergency, I'm not sure what is."

I kept my ruckus up for a good long while, but if anyone could hear it from the next world over, they must not have been impressed: the door stayed shut. Maybe Bernard had been right after all, and there *was* something wrong with it. "This," I said to the bees, "is definitely an irregularity."

The bees huddled together over my head, humming to each other. After a minute or so, they spread out again to form foot-high letters against the backdrop of the sky.

SPARE KEY?

I'd thought of this, too. The Gatekeeper had taken her key with her, of course, but she always kept a copy tucked in a hat-box in the darkest corner of the coat closet. "In a place like this, where things tend to go missing," she'd explained to me when

I'd first arrived, "having only one gatekey would be extremely foolish. But you're never to touch the spare one, Lucy, or I'll make sure you won't find a respectable job again—in this world or any other. Just ask my last deputy what happened to him." The Gatekeeper had smiled at me as she'd said this, but I was sure she hadn't been joking.

"Do you really think that's a good idea?" I asked the bees now. "I'm not supposed to go anywhere near that key, and I'm definitely not supposed to open the door."

EMERGENCY, spelled the bees.

"I know, I know." The thought of breaking one of the Gate-keeper's rules made me uncomfortably itchy, but if she was really in trouble on the other side of that door, I wasn't sure what else to do. "Just out of curiosity," I said to the bees, "do you know what happened to the Gatekeeper's last deputy?"

The bees hesitated. They looked a little nervous.

I sighed. "Never mind. I'll go and get the key."

The Gatekeeper, I discovered, owned a lot of hats. By the time I found the right dusty hatbox, the one that held a small saw-toothed key instead of a bonnet or a bowler, the sun had risen above the treetops. This gave me something else to worry about. I'd been lucky so far, but eventually some explorer or trader or half-witted adventurer was going to arrive at the gate-house, waving their papers at me and demanding to go to the next world over. How would I explain what had happened to the Gatekeeper, or when she'd be back? How would I keep an increasingly large and grumpy pack of travelers safely inside? There wasn't that much space around the dining room table.

I crawled out of the coat closet and dusted myself off. "Stop worrying," I told myself, holding the spare key tighter. "The Gatekeeper will be home by then." It would be simple enough to unlock the door and let her through, I thought as I went back down the path toward the wall. I'd never opened a worldgate before, but it looked just like any other door; how complicated could it be?

FINALLY, said the bees.

"I'd like to see *you* search through forty-three hatboxes," I told them. They hovered around me as I pushed aside the vines and slipped the gatekey into the lock.

"I'm sorry, Gatekeeper," I whispered. I turned the key until something clicked. "Please don't fire me."

Then I pulled open the door at the end of the world.

2

Not many people get an opportunity to stand with their feet in one world and their eyes gazing into the next—and I didn't, either. As the door swung toward me, someone tumbled through it.

"Oh dear!" he said as he fell.

I didn't have time to think. I let go of the doorknob and leaped aside to avoid being squashed, and the door in the wall slammed shut.

It took a few moments for me to realize what had happened. A boy was lying on his back on the ground, and his eyes were wide. He looked older than me—I'd turned thirteen last summer—but not nearly as old as my brother, Thomas, who was twenty-three and extremely grown-up. "Bernard?" I asked, frowning down at him. The bees, who had zipped away in the confusion, flew back to get a better look at the boy. This made his eyes open even wider.

"Who are you?" he asked me. "Where am I? Bees!"

He sounded a little worried, but that was understandable. I was worried, too. "I'm Lucy Eberslee," I said, "the Gatekeeper's deputy. You're at the end of the world, of course. And you're not Bernard, are you?"

The boy shook his head. "I'm Arthur," he said, squinting up at me through wire-rimmed glasses. "Did you say the end of the world?" He blinked. "Does the world end in bees?"

Now I was sure something was wrong. The Gatekeeper would have been angry enough if I'd broken just one of her rules, but to open the door *and* to let an ignorant Easterner crash through it? Her hair would be frizzing around her face for at least the next ten years—not that I'd be working at the gatehouse to see it. "I don't suppose you have your travel papers?" I asked, feeling desperate. "Your passport? Your customs form? Your visitation fee?" I looked over my shoulder at the gatehouse. "Anything I could file?"

Arthur was still shaking his head. "I think," he said, "they're going to sting me."

He wasn't wrong. The bees were circling him faster now, and their hum had changed from curious to threatening. "It's their job not to let anyone come through the door without permission," I said. "If you don't have any papers, how in the worlds did Bernard let you come here?" The Gatekeeper had always said Bernard was useless at his job, but even for him, this was an unthinkable mistake. Traveling to another world without

11

documentation was dangerous, not to mention extremely illegal.

"Why do you keep asking about Bernard?" Arthur winced as he picked himself up off the ground. "I've never met a Bernard. My tutor is named Joseph."

"Your tutor?"

Arthur nodded. "I was supposed to meet him in the library. But I hadn't read the awful old book he'd assigned me, and I thought maybe I'd hide from him instead. I ran to the back of the library and leaned against a door to catch my breath, and right after that I was falling backward into this garden, which you say is the end of the world, even though it seems like a very nice garden to me, and I think I've sprained my ankle." He winced again. "If you don't mind my asking, why is it springtime on this side of the door and autumn on that one?"

The bees must have decided Arthur wasn't an immediate threat, because they stopped circling him and settled for hovering a few feet over his head. I wasn't quite as convinced. "Let me be sure I've got this right," I said. "You stopped to lean against a door, which just happened to be the door at the end of the world, and no one stopped you? Not someone named Bernard? Not a witchy sort of woman with frizzy hair and a cane?"

"I didn't see anyone like that," said Arthur. "I didn't see anyone at all, except for you!" He looked around the garden and adjusted his glasses. "I don't think Joseph will ever find me here. Would it be all right with you if I stayed for a while? Just for an hour or—"

"No," I said. "No way. You've got to get back on your side of the door, and I need you to do it right now." I was more worried than ever about the Gatekeeper, and I couldn't spend any more time taking care of an otherworld traveler, especially not an illegal one I'd accidentally brought through the worldgate. If anyone found out about *that* particular disaster, I'd be in at least ten different kinds of trouble, and not just with the Gatekeeper. The Interworld Travel Commission would be downright furious. What if they put me on trial in the House of Governors? What if they found me guilty? I tried not to think about all that as I walked past Arthur and went to open the door in the wall.

It wouldn't budge.

I jostled, jiggled, cajoled, and tugged. The key swiveled in the lock, and the knob turned on its spindle, but the door wouldn't open no matter how hard I pulled. "It's stuck," I said to the bees, trying to keep my voice low enough that Arthur couldn't overhear me. As a rule, it's not a good idea to give travelers any reason to panic.

"Stuck?" said Arthur. (I groaned.) "May I try?" Before I could explain any of the reasons why he shouldn't, Arthur strode past me, grabbed the gatekey, and twisted it hard. Then there was a sharp snap, and he stepped back from the door, holding the key in his hand. Or, rather, half the key.

"Hmm," said Arthur. "That's too bad. I think I might have broken it."

I stared at him in horror. "You *think* you *might* have?"

"I can fix it, though!" Arthur said quickly. "I'm sure I can!" He

13

went back to the door, fiddled with the lock, peered at it, took his glasses off, put them back on again, wiggled the doorknob up and down, said "Ah!" a few times, and turned back to me.

"It doesn't look fixed," I pointed out.

Arthur looked uncomfortable. "I can't quite see the problem," he admitted, "but I don't think you'll be getting this door open again anytime soon."

I could see the problem, and he was standing right in front of me. "You don't understand," I said. "I *have* to get the door open. It can't be stuck for good."

"Don't worry." Arthur smiled and handed me the useless half of the spare gatekey. "I'll just take the long way around."

I'd like you to know that I always try to be professional, even in a crisis. A few months earlier, the Gatekeeper had caught a woman trying to smuggle bags full of Eastern spices through the worldgate, and I was the one who typed out the whole incident report for Interworld Travel while the Gatekeeper shouted and waved her cane in all sorts of directions I'd never known about before. This time, though, I couldn't stay calm. "It's not as simple as that!" I snapped. "You've traveled into another world, and now you're stuck in it, and the Gatekeeper's stuck over in your world somewhere, and worst of all, *I'm* stuck here with *you*. Do you know what the punishment is for breaking the door between the worlds?"

"Um," said Arthur. He wasn't smiling any longer. "No?"

"That's because no one has done it before! It's not possible! But you've managed to figure it out somehow, and we'll

14

probably both be arrested before the day is out, and I'll never find the Gatekeeper, and it's all thanks to you!"

Arthur stared at me. Without blinking, he leaned against the wall and slid down it until he was sitting on the grass. "That's a lot to take in, Miss Eberslee," he said at last. "May I call you Lucy?"

I glared at him.

"All right. Miss Eberslee." Arthur plucked a handful of clover from the ground and held the little plants up to his face, one at a time. "Four leaves," he said quietly. "They've all got four leaves."

"Of course they do." I knew I shouldn't have shouted; I'd managed to make Arthur even more useless than he'd already been. "All clovers have four leaves."

"Not in my world." Arthur let the stems fall back to the ground. I could see his hands weren't entirely steady. "You're serious, aren't you? If this isn't my world, what is it?"

The Gatekeeper had told me that most ordinary Easterners didn't know much about the worlds beyond their own, but I hadn't realized exactly how serious the situation was until now. I sighed and sat down next to Arthur. We were going to have to start at the very beginning. "You're in the world next door to yours," I said. "This world is called Southeast. Your world is called East."

"It is?" Arthur frowned. "And East is just on the other side of that wall?"

"Sort of. Not really. It's complicated." If I started trying to

15

explain the fabric of time and space to an Easterner, we'd both be sitting there until we were ninety. "If you climbed over the wall, you wouldn't see anything but fields. The only opening between our two worlds is right behind the door. At least, that's where it *was*. Now there aren't any openings at all."

"Because I broke the door?"

"Well, yes."

Arthur looked so alarmed at this that I actually felt a little sorry for him. "To be fair, though," I added, "you wouldn't have broken the door if I hadn't opened it. And I shouldn't have shouted at you. I apologize for that." I stood up and brushed the dirt off my hands. "Anyway, I'm sure you have lots of questions, but they're going to have to wait. We're both in trouble up to our ears right now. You're not allowed to be here, I wasn't allowed to open that door in the first place, and the Gatekeeper, who *is* allowed to open it, is lost somewhere on the other side of it. If you didn't see her in your world, I have no idea where she might be, and now I've got no way to find out, and for all I know she's stuck over there permanently." I took a long breath. "Honestly, I'm not sure what to do next. What would you do if you were over in East and a person went missing?"

"I suppose," said Arthur, getting to his feet, "I'd call the authorities."

I shook my head. "That's no good. I *am* the authorities!"

Arthur squinted at me. "But you're a child."

"I'm thirteen," I corrected him. "I finished school last year, and I'm in charge here when the Gatekeeper's away."

"Well, I'm sixteen," said Arthur, "or I will be in a few months, and in my world, neither of us would be old enough to be in charge of anything. You're the Gatekeeper's deputy, and the Gatekeeper is missing?"

I nodded.

"Who's in charge of the Gatekeeper, then?"

I tried to imagine someone telling the Gatekeeper what to do. The idea of it was so preposterous that I almost laughed. "She'd probably tell you no one is," I said, "but we both work for the Southeastern Interworld Travel Commission. That's a government agency," I added when Arthur stared at me blankly. "Anyway, Interworld Travel can't find out what we've done. Their rules are the ones we've broken! Remember what I told you about getting arrested?"

"Right," said Arthur, but he sounded distracted. He scratched his mouse-brown hair and gazed past me. "Who's Florence?"

I blinked. "Excuse me?"

"Or where is Florence? I suppose it could be a place instead of a person. In my world, it's a place in Italy. Do you have Italy here?"

I had no idea what he was talking about. "Florence," I said, "is a person. An awfully important person, as a matter of fact. Why do you ask?"

Arthur pointed out into the garden beyond us. "The bees," he said. "They seem to have something to say about her." He lowered his voice to a whisper. "Did you know your bees can spell?"

Arthur was right. I'd been too distracted to notice, but at that very moment, the bees were spelling out FLORENCE and

17

getting more and more agitated about it; they didn't like being ignored. "You don't need to whisper," I told Arthur. "They know they're talented." Truthfully, they could be a little conceited about it sometimes. "They were a gift to the Gatekeeper from the next world over."

"Are you sure about that?" he said. "We don't have spelling bees in my world." He paused, frowning. "I mean, actually, we *do* have spelling bees, but . . . they're very different."

"Oh, the bees aren't from your world." I kept forgetting how much Arthur had to learn. Even his tutor hadn't managed to teach him a simple otherworld geography lesson. "Southeast has two ends. The near end, where we are now, is connected to East. And the far end is connected to the next world over on the other side."

Arthur looked dubious. "A world with magical bees?"

"Exactly," I said. "That world's called South. They've got lots of other magical things in South, too, but when they want to send a diplomatic gift of goodwill, it's usually bees. I'm not exactly sure why." I glanced back at our own colony. A few more bees had flown over to lend their assistance, and now they said, FLORENCE!!!!! After what had happened with the spare key, I wasn't exactly keen to take their advice again, but they were right: we needed help from an expert.

"Is there a door leading into South, too?" Arthur wanted to know. "A door like the one that's here?"

"Of course," I said. "And that door has a gatekeeper." I raised an eyebrow at him. "Her name is Florence."

3

I'd asked Arthur to wait in the front room while I packed for our journey to the other end of the world. He kept popping his head through my bedroom doorway, though, and each time he had a new question to ask. "I can see you don't have telephones here," he said, "but can't you send Florence a letter? Do we really have to go all the way to her house?"

There *is* postal service at the end of the world, but it's not reliable: In a place where things tend to go missing, the thing that tends to go missing most of all is the mail. A courier from Interworld Travel stops by the gatehouse once a month to pick up our paperwork, and the Gatekeeper had sent me out a few times to deliver her most important messages by hand. "We really do have to see Florence in person," I told Arthur as I stuffed my clothes into a rucksack. "I do, at least, and there's no way I'm leaving you here by yourself."

Arthur nodded and disappeared into the hallway. He was back three minutes later, though, brandishing one of the folded-up maps I always kept on hand for travelers on their first trips out of Southeast. It was a glossy, touristy thing decorated with illustrations of strange animals, historical figures, and famous otherworld sights. In fancy boldface type across the front, it said A VISITOR'S GUIDE TO ALL THE WORLDS.

"Miss Eberslee?" said Arthur. "*How many worlds are there?*"

I sighed. At this rate, I'd never finish packing. "There are eight."

"Eight!"

I set down the towel I'd been folding, unfolded the map, and held it up so he could see the eight circles, all different colors and sizes, arranged around the wrinkled fabric of time and space like points on a compass. "Yes," I said, handing him the map and turning back to my rucksack. "Eight."

The map stopped Arthur from asking questions, but only for a minute. "Who's the woman holding a pair of scissors?" he wanted to know. "Why is there a giraffe?"

"We can talk about it later," I said. "In the meantime, since you can't wait quietly, could you at least make yourself useful? You can go into the kitchen and pack up some food from the cupboard." I'd never traveled from one end of the world to the other before, but it seemed like a good idea to bring snacks.

"Of course." Arthur nodded. "Sorry." He folded up the map and disappeared again.

It wasn't poor Arthur's fault he was stuck in this world, I

reminded myself. He might not have been the traveling companion I'd have picked if I'd had a choice, but I would have to try to be more charitable toward him. At least he looked right at me instead of gazing over the top of my head. I didn't have many clothes that would fit him, but after a few minutes of searching, I dug out an old cardigan that might do in a pinch and a waterproof jacket that had been a hand-me-down from my older brother, Thomas. I tossed them both into my rucksack, along with a thick scarf the Gatekeeper had knitted for me—even in springtime, who knew what the weather would be like at the other end of the world?—and went to the kitchen to tell Arthur I was sorry for snapping at him.

He wasn't alone. A tall man with a graying beard sat in the kitchen chair, casting his eyes around the room while Arthur rummaged through the cupboard. The man was dressed in explorer's gear: the usual protective canvas pants, red-and-white-checked button-down shirt, and belt fitted out with compasses and map pouches and all sorts of other gadgets. "And the Gatekeeper," he was saying in a low, serious voice. "Is she on this side of the broken door, or on the other one?"

"The other one." Arthur stuck his head out of the cupboard and tossed three pears cheerfully into a picnic hamper before burrowing back inside. "At least, I think that's right. Miss Eberslee says she's missing, but I'm not sure where she—"

"*Arthur!*" I said as loudly as I could without shouting.

The man turned to look at me, and Arthur pulled his head out of the cupboard again. "Oh, hello, Miss Eberslee! I was just telling this gentleman about our troubles." Arthur pointed to the man with a stick of the Gatekeeper's favorite barley candy. "He says he wants to travel to another world."

"I'm afraid that won't be possible today." I glared at Arthur. He obviously didn't know who the bearded man was, but I recognized him from his dozens of trips through the gatehouse, and from his portrait in my old school textbooks, and from the commemorative postage stamp. "Arthur, this is Henry Tallard. He's a famous explorer."

Tallard grinned. "Discoverer of five Northern islands, mapper of the Ungoverned Wilderness, the first to take a dip in the cool blue waters of Lake Henry—I named it myself—and direct descendant of Arabella Tallard."

And inconsiderate and nosy, I thought. The Gatekeeper had been right about Henry Tallard, as far as I was concerned, but I didn't dare say it out loud. He was *very* famous.

"This end of the world is temporarily closed for business," I told him instead. "I'm sorry I didn't hear you knock on the door. You shouldn't have been let in." (I sent another glare toward Arthur.)

"Oh, I let myself in." Tallard leaned back in his chair and stretched out his legs, taking up most of the space in the kitchen. "I could see a small hailstorm springing up down by the wall, and the gatehouse door was standing open, so I thought . . . why not? Then I wandered around and found Arthur here. We've been having a fascinating conversation, Miss . . ." He scratched his beard and frowned at me as if he were waiting for my name to present itself in his mind. Unsurprisingly, it didn't.

"That's Miss Eberslee," Arthur told him. "I just mentioned her to you, remember?"

"Of course. The assistant." Tallard smiled at a spot somewhere over my left shoulder. "Eberslee, eh? Any relation to—"

"I'm not an assistant," I said. I wasn't sure which member of my family Tallard was going to ask about, but it didn't matter; I wasn't interested in talking about any of them. "I'm the Gatekeeper's deputy. As I was saying, you can't travel through the door today. Why don't you come back in a week or two? I'm sure the Gatekeeper will be happy to assist you." If I hadn't managed to bring her home by then, I'd have problems much bigger than Henry Tallard to worry about.

"So the Gatekeeper isn't trapped in another world?" Tallard asked. He looked over at Arthur, who he must have decided was the authority on these matters. "Or lost?"

"She went to East to make some routine repairs to the worldgate," I said firmly, "and I'm afraid I can't let anyone through the door until she's back from her trip." All strictly true, and all as much as any explorer needed to know. I put on my sweetest smile and the voice I reserved for our most difficult travelers. "Let me show you out, Mr. Tallard. I'm so sorry about the inconvenience."

He started to protest, but I happen to be very good at steering people to the exit. I opened the gatehouse door and propelled him through it. "If you ever *do* run into any trouble at the end of the world," he said as he went, "I'd be happy to offer my assistance."

"Goodbye, Mr. Tallard," I said, still sweetly. Then I closed the door between us and bolted it shut.

Arthur was still in the kitchen when I got back. "What was that all about?"

"I'd like to know that myself." Little balls of ice started to ping on the roof; the hailstorm Tallard had mentioned must have made its way over from the garden at last. So, he hadn't lied about everything. I was absolutely sure I hadn't left the gatehouse door open even a crack, though, and I hadn't heard anyone knock. Why had Henry Tallard been poking around the worldgate for the second time in a month? The bees didn't trust him, and neither did I. "Are you sure you didn't let him in?" I asked.

Arthur nodded. "He startled me when he came up behind me in the kitchen. Made me spill the jam." He pointed to a pinkish splatter on the floor. "Raspberry," he added helpfully.

"And how much did you tell him about our problems with the door?"

"Just about everything." At least Arthur had enough sense to look worried as he closed up the picnic hamper. "I wasn't sure it was a good idea, but he seemed so interested."

"I'll bet he did." I sank down in the kitchen chair myself. "Don't you remember what I said? That we could be arrested?"

"I did remember that!" said Arthur. "That's why I didn't tell him *we* broke the door! I just mentioned that it broke *somehow*." He took a white handkerchief from the pocket of his pants and swiped it across his forehead, as though that would improve our situation. "I'm sorry, Miss Eberslee. I wasn't prepared, and he asked where the Gatekeeper was, and I couldn't think of a decent lie. I don't know enough about this world *to* lie! And then, with the jam and everything . . ." He swiped his handkerchief in the opposite direction. "But I didn't tell him we were going to see Florence."

That was lucky. The door to East might have been stuck, but I already felt nervous about leaving it unguarded. The last thing I needed was for Henry Tallard to test the lock for himself or, worse, to run off and find twenty of his explorer friends to help him do it. The bees would have trouble fending all of them off. "Did you tell him you were from East?" I asked.

Arthur shook his head. "It didn't come up. He never asked about that, and it seemed like an awkward way to introduce myself—*Hello, I'm Arthur and I'm from another world*—so I didn't mention it."

"Good," I said. "You'd better keep not mentioning it, even if someone does ask, all right? We need to get you back home before anyone finds out you're here illegally, or you'll be in real trouble. And I wouldn't trust Henry Tallard to keep a secret like that. The bees don't like him."

"I'm sorry, Miss Eberslee. I'll be stone silent from now on, I promise." Arthur pantomimed locking his lips and tossing away the imaginary key.

"Well, you can talk to *me*," I told him. "In fact, you'd better, or I'm going to die of boredom on the walk to Florence's."

"Walk?" Arthur didn't bother unlocking his lips. "To the

other end of the world? Unless your world is much smaller than mine is, Miss Eberslee, it sounds like a long trip."

"It is." It had taken me days to travel from my parents' home in Centerbury out to the gatehouse, and that had only been half the distance. The nearest train station was miles from here; the closer the tracks got to the end of the world, the likelier they were to start changing direction without asking anyone for permission. Explorers like Tallard knew the local routes well enough to make good time, but for the rest of us, it could be a confusing journey, and no one who lived out this way relied on anything other than their own two feet.

I explained all this to Arthur, who didn't look particularly happy to hear it. "I should have packed more food," he said nervously. "Or less food, if I'm going to have to carry it all. I'd just assumed we'd have better transportation. A car, maybe, or bicycles. Even a unicycle might do us some good!"

I didn't know what kinds of otherworld devices Arthur was talking about, but he did remind me of something. "A rich tourist gave the Gatekeeper a strange gift last year," I said, "just after I started working here. The tourist was from South, but he'd bought the gift in East." It had been so large that he'd had to bundle it up in Southern shrink wrap to get it through the door; I remembered watching the gift expand in the back shed as he'd uncovered it layer by layer. "Anyway, the Gatekeeper hated it. She couldn't figure out how to use it, so she eventually swore at it and stormed off. I think it was supposed to be handy for traveling, though. I've got no idea how to use it, but if it's from your world . . . well, maybe you'd better take a look."

"I'd be glad to," said Arthur. "Even if it's a unicycle." He smiled at me. "I think the hailstorm has moved on, so please, Miss Eberslee, lead the way."

4

Arthur's eyes lit up at the sight of the Gatekeeper's traveling contraption. "You *do* have a car!" he cried. He ran over to peer at its gauges and prod its leather seats. "It must be ninety years old. That tourist gave you an antique."

I hadn't realized that. No wonder the Gatekeeper had had so much trouble with it. "Can you make it go?" I asked.

"Maybe." Arthur hopped into the car and began to tinker. "I've never tried to drive a car like this. I've read a few books about how they work, though. My father loves old cars, and I wanted to impress him. There's a chance I could make the whole machine burst into flames, but if I don't . . ." He bit his lip and wiggled levers and toggles in an experimental sort of way. I was sure Arthur would break the Gatekeeper's traveling contraption as thoroughly as he'd broken the worldgate, and I could hardly stand to watch it happen.

All at once, the car started to shudder and growl. I jumped and covered my ears, but Arthur was grinning. "Runs like a dream!" he shouted over the din.

I went back to the gatehouse to get my rucksack and the picnic hamper, and a little while after that, we were on our way to Florence's house at the other end of the world. Arthur wore a permanent frown of concentration as he maneuvered the car over the dirt roads, but whatever he was doing seemed to work well enough, and we bumped along at an alarming speed. Every so often, and for no reason I could fathom, Arthur squeezed a rubber bulb to make a terrible honking noise that sent squirrels and sparrows scurrying for their lives. I sat next to him, shouting out directions and hoping the whole contraption wouldn't fall apart underneath us.

LOVELY DAY FOR A DRIVE, the bees spelled out as they flew alongside the car. Most of the colony had stayed at home to protect the door in the wall, jammed though it was, but several of the younger and more adventurous members had come with us. I was grateful for the familiar company; it made the leaving easier. There'd been no time for one last walk around the gatehouse, one last whiff of the flowers in the garden, or one last glance at the door in the wall, where I'd hastily tacked up a sign that said Out of Order and hoped that would be enough to keep the likes of Henry Tallard away for at least a few days. I thought about how I'd walked down this same dirt road for the first time only a year ago, lugging the very same rucksack, anxious to start my new job and trying to ignore the sensation that I'd been wandering in circles for the better part of an hour. If the Gatekeeper hadn't come out to find me and introduce herself, I'd probably still be wandering.

"Haven't we passed that tree before?" Arthur asked now, squinting over the steering wheel. "The squat one with purple berries?"

I nodded. "Just keep going straight," I said. "The end of the world has a tricky effect on directions, but it's best to be persistent."

Arthur opened his mouth halfway, as though he wanted to ask more than a few questions about this, but to my relief, he thought better of it. We trundled along in silence for a while. Just after we'd passed the purple-berried tree for the fourth time, the road suddenly curved out of the forest, into a meadow, and toward a pond full of paddling ducks who seemed surprised to see us. Arthur's shoulders came down from around his ears. "Now we're getting somewhere," he said happily.

Once we'd passed the duck pond, the end of the world must have lost its pull on things, because the roads finally started behaving exactly the way you'd expect them to. They took us past tiny towns populated mostly with sheep, and then through larger ones where children ran outside to see our car as it rumbled by. DON'T MIND US, the bees spelled out. JUST PASSING THROUGH.

Arthur had plenty to say as well. "I still can't quite believe it," he told me. "This whole business about other worlds, I mean. This morning I was eating buttered toast and wondering where

I'd left my umbrella, and now I'm a traveler in a strange new land!"

I pointed out as nicely as I could that the land was really only new to *him*, and that the rest of us had actually been here for quite a while. "And it's not strange," I said. "At least, I don't think it is. Is your world very different from this one?"

Arthur looked around at the trees and fields and sky. "Our trees are taller," he said finally, "and our sheep are a touch more woolly, but other than that, it's remarkably similar. Do you have umbrellas here? Or buttered toast?"

"Yes," I said, "both of them."

"That's good news," said Arthur cheerfully. "What about the other six worlds? Are they similar, too?"

"Some of them are." We'd brought *A Visitor's Guide to All the Worlds* with us, and I pulled it out and unfolded it. If I could teach Arthur a few things as we drove, he might not ask quite so many questions at Florence's. "Each world has something about it that makes it different from the others," I explained, "and they all depend on one another to survive. Take Northeast, for example." I pointed to the little brown circle in the top right corner of the map. "It's famous for its farms. The government there sells meat and eggs and vegetables all across the worlds, especially to the places where people can't grow food of their own. It doesn't get much money from tourism, though, since the whole place smells like cows." I'd met enough otherworld travelers by now to know that Northeast was considered a pass-through: a place you were forced to pass through on your way somewhere else. More than a few travelers thought Southeast was a pass-through, too, and they hadn't been shy about telling me so when I stamped their passports and asked how long they'd be staying.

"That world looks exciting." Arthur took a hand off the steering wheel and jabbed a finger toward the big blue world next to Northeast. An illustrated ship sailed across the map toward it.

"That's North," I told him. "North's a maritime world. It's lots of islands, actually, spread around a huge sea, and the islands are usually at war with one another. Half the world population is in the navy, and the other half wishes they were." At the gatehouse, I'd met a lot of travelers headed to North: explorers planning to sail through its archipelagos, customers looking to buy fish or gunpowder, and tourists hoping to catch a glimpse of a thrilling battle at sea.

Tourists loved traveling to Northwest, too. It was a small green circle on the map. "Northwest is always sunny and warm," I told Arthur, "and it's got the Ungoverned Wilderness, which is a leafy old forest you can wander through for days. Next to that is West, which is huge. They've got a knack for technology. If you want a gravity-free skyzoomer or an encyclopedic brainchip, West is the place to get it."

Arthur maneuvered the car around a flock of wandering geese. "I'm not sure I do want those things."

The next world on the map was a pale yellow dot next to the vast gray circle of West. "Southwest is all a desert," I explained.

"It's very hot, and there's something special about its sand. It's not quite solid and not quite liquid, and you can make all sorts of strange things with it if you melt it down. West buys tons of sand from Southwest to use in their inventions. And then there's South." I pointed to the large purple world at the bottom of the map. "South has magic. They've got dragons and cloaks of invisibility and spells to make you fall in love and back out of it."

AND BEES, the bees reminded me. NATURALLY.

"What about my world?" Arthur asked. "What is East known for? What's our specialty?"

I'd been hoping he wouldn't ask. "East is . . . self-sufficient." It was a nice way of saying *standoffish*. "Easterners can grow or make almost everything they need, and almost none of you even know that other worlds exist. But you depend on us, too—for stories, mostly." The Gatekeeper had told me that otherworld tales had a habit of slipping through the worldgates, and most of them eventually found their way to East. On more than one occasion, an Easterner had overheard a tidbit of gossip from an explorer, written it down, and convinced herself she'd made the whole story up. "If East weren't connected to the other seven worlds," I told Arthur, "none of you would have any imagination to speak of."

Luckily, Arthur didn't seem to take offense. He was too busy trying to look at the map without driving us into a pond or a ditch. "I think I'd most like to visit the magical world," he said, "but I'd like to see all of them, really, even the one with all the cows. Which is your favorite world to visit, Miss Eberslee?"

The car rattled over a bumpy patch of road, and I squirmed in my seat. As a matter of fact, I hadn't been to any of the other worlds. It wasn't something I liked to talk about. Everyone assumed that someone with a job like mine would have visited all eight worlds herself—or at least a respectable number, like four or five. My work at the gatehouse kept me too busy to travel, though, and it was starting to make my job a little awkward. The people I met on their way to East always wanted to chat about which part of that world was my favorite, or if I'd ever been to far-off cities with names like Jakarta and Vladivostok, Sacramento and Pittsburgh. To tell the truth, I'd never even heard of these places. I wasn't about to let Arthur know it, though. "Oh," I said, trying to sound convincing, "I like all the worlds equally. It's impossible to pick a favorite."

Arthur nodded and kept driving, but I wasn't entirely sure he'd believed me. Even he had probably heard of Pittsburgh.

The road to Florence's house took us toward Centerbury, the capital of Southeast and the closest thing we had to a city, before shifting course and winding up into the mountains. Once we'd reached the outskirts of town, Arthur steered the car to the side of the road and fumbled with levers and pedals until it coughed to a stop. "I don't have any idea what time it is," he said, "but I'd like some dinner. Care for a sandwich, Miss Eberslee?"

I *did* care for one, as a matter of fact. Arthur had stacked a dozen paper-wrapped packets of sandwiches in the picnic hamper, and to my surprise, the first one I bit into was completely delicious. So was the second. I leaned back in my seat and dabbed tomato juice from my chin.

Arthur had climbed out of the car and found a place to sit on a rocky outcropping looking over the city. "I've got another question for you, Miss Eberslee," he said, "if that's all right."

I was used to answering questions from otherworld travelers, although most of them weren't quite as inquisitive as Arthur. "It's fine," I told him. "And you might as well call me Lucy. I don't really mind."

"All right. Lucy, then." He grinned. "Who's your famous relative?"

I sat up straight again, too fast. "Excuse me?"

"I've been wondering all day. That explorer wanted to know if you were related to someone, and you grimaced at him in just the same way you're grimacing at me now. I've got a few horrible relations of my own, so I recognize the look."

"Well," I said, "they're not horrible. That's the problem."

"Oh!" said Arthur through a mouthful of lettuce. "Of course. You're right. Wonderful relations can be even worse."

It was the sort of thing most people would have said as a joke, but Arthur actually sounded as though he understood. I didn't talk about my family as a rule, but I'd already broken so many rules that day; what was the harm in breaking one more? "It's my brother," I said, "and both of my parents. They're all extremely important, so I'm not sure which one Henry Tallard was asking about. My parents are retired now, but my mother used to sit in the House of Governors, and my father was a diplomat. He traveled all over the worlds, talking to impressive people about how their world and ours should be the best of friends. And my brother, Thomas, is a member of the Interworld Travel Commission. He's one of the people who's going to be furious when he hears we broke that door, by the way." I sighed. "My parents are very proud of him."

"I see your problem," said Arthur. "Being an Eberslee sounds like a lot of work."

"It is!" I hadn't meant to raise my voice, but even the bees jumped a little when I said it. "I love my family; of course I do, but they can be . . . exhausting."

"They must be proud of you, too, being a gatekeeper and all."

"*Deputy* gatekeeper." I hugged my rucksack to my chest. Getting the offer of work at the end of the world had been a huge relief. I'd done well enough in school, but I'd never really stood out much. Even my teachers had a habit of not quite remembering I was there unless they read about Thomas in the news or needed a favor from my mother or advice from my father. In the last year of school, when my classmates and I were finally old enough for apprenticeships, all the usual positions were given to students who actually got noticed once in a while, and I'd been the only one left without a placement.

Then Thomas had come home for the weekend with news about a spot opening up in Interworld Travel. It was a junior position, he'd explained, with not much salary to speak of, but if I was interested, he'd pass my application along. A few weeks after that, my parents were teary-eyed with joy that their little Lucy was going to make something of herself after all, and the Gatekeeper was teaching me where to put the pink forms, and the green forms, and the blue ones. I hadn't seen my family for ages, but I did hope they were proud of me. Of course, I couldn't help wondering just how many strings Thomas had pulled to convince the Gatekeeper to hire me, or how disappointed everyone would be when they found out how thoroughly I'd ruined things that morning.

"What about your family?" I asked Arthur. "Will they be missing you at home?"

Arthur laughed a little and tossed a pebble down the hillside. "If I'm not back in a few days, my tutor might get suspicious, and after a month or so it might occur to my father that I haven't come downstairs for dinner in a while. He's got eight sons, though, so he won't mind misplacing one." He frowned. "It's not going to take me a month to get back to East, is it?"

I sincerely hoped it wouldn't. "I'm sure Florence will be able to send you home quickly," I told him. I'd never met Florence myself, but I knew the Gatekeeper trusted her, and I trusted the Gatekeeper. "She probably fixes broken doors all the time. She'll know how to make everything all right."

"In that case," said Arthur, "I can't wait to meet her."

5

Florence's house was on the far side of the farthest mountain, where the ground was rocky, the wind was strong, and the trees were scraggly and stunted, as if they'd bumped up against the ceiling of the world. We reached it just after lunchtime on our third day of driving.

As soon as we did, I could tell something was wrong.

"I'm worried," I said to Arthur. He'd turned off the car's engine, and the quietness around us rang in my ears. The only sounds were the rustle of wind and the happy hum of the bees as they flew inside to say hello to Florence. "We got here too quickly."

"I thought we did." Arthur climbed out of the car and stretched. "Southeast must be awfully small."

It was, but that wasn't what I'd meant. "We didn't get lost," I explained. "We drove straight here, and we never got lost, or

38

even a little muddled; we didn't pass the same trees or streams or boulders seven times in a row. And we didn't run into any strange weather."

"We did!" said Arthur. "Don't you remember the snowstorm? My fingers are still a little numb from it." He wiggled them experimentally.

I *did* remember the snow we'd bumped into earlier that morning, but it had hardly counted; it had only lasted a few minutes. "That was an awfully feeble storm for the end of the world," I said. "We usually get blizzards. The Gatekeeper told me she once had to dig her onions out from under eight feet of snow."

Arthur shrugged. "Maybe your end of the world is different."

"Maybe," I said. But I didn't think it was. "Have you lost anything in the past few minutes? Spare change? Socks?"

We both checked our pockets, and I dug around in my rucksack. I couldn't remember everything I'd tossed inside, but I thought I might be missing a glove, and Arthur said his wallet felt suspiciously light. "That's a good sign, at least," I said.

"You and I," said Arthur, "seem to have different ideas about what's good."

Before I could explain that things at the end of the world were *supposed* to go missing, the bees came back. They were frantic. They swarmed around me in a panicky cloud, and it seemed like ages before they'd collected themselves enough to fly into formation. TROUBLE! they said at last. HURRY HURRY HURRY!

I took off for the house, and Arthur ran after me. When I got to the front door, I knocked—it was hard to break a habit—but then I pulled myself together and pushed the door open without waiting for an answer.

Stepping through the doorway felt, for a moment, like arriving home. Although the furnishings were different, Florence's house was laid out identically to the Gatekeeper's: there was the same front room with its fireplace and wide windows, the same coat closet under the stairs, the same hallway leading to what I felt sure was a kitchen.

Then I noticed the mess. It was more than normal untidiness—dirt tracked in from the garden, say, or laundry escaping its basket. Pink customs declarations, green returnee reports, and blue applications for otherworld travel were scattered across the room. The rug they'd fallen on was scrunched up in places, paintings hung crookedly on their hooks, and chairs were overturned. As I stepped inside, bits and pieces of something that might have once been a drinking glass made a crunching noise under my shoes.

"There's been a fight," Arthur said at once.

"Or a cyclone," I murmured. But even at the end of the world, bad weather never came inside the house. The bees were right: this was trouble. "Florence?" I called. "Anyone? Hello?"

There was another crunching noise, deeper inside the house this time. Then a girl came down the stairs. She had brown curls tied up in a blue bandanna, and she looked about thirteen, not any older than me. She moved carefully, as if she were

40

worried the floorboards might slip out from under her at any moment. When she reached the bottom of the staircase, she stopped and stared at us, taking us in: the rumpled clothes I'd been wearing for three days now, Arthur's uncombed hair, the rucksack, the sandwich crumbs, the bees.

"Who are you?" she asked

It was a reasonable question. "We're from the other end of the world," I told her. "I'm Lucy, and this is Arthur. I'm the Gatekeeper's deputy." I skipped over explaining who Arthur was, hoping the girl wouldn't think to ask.

The girl's eyes narrowed. "Are you really? I've been to that end of the world a few times, but I don't remember meeting anyone named Lucy. I *do* remember a plant, though. A fern, I think, in a big blue pot?"

"Well," I said, trying not to clench my teeth, "I sit next to the fern. And I only started working there last year. Are you Florence's deputy?" If the Gatekeeper had ever mentioned her name to me, I couldn't think of it, so I guessed we were even. "Where's Florence? Is she all right?"

The girl hesitated. "I wish I knew," she said finally. "I've checked every room, but I can't find her. If Florence is anywhere at all, it isn't here." She sat down on the bottom stair step. "I think something awful has happened."

The girl's name turned out to be Rosemary, and she was as confused as we were. "I wasn't here for any of this," she said, waving her arms at the mess around us. "I was visiting my pa

41

this week—he lives down in Centerbury—and I only got here half an hour ago."

"Maybe Florence just stepped out for a minute or two," Arthur said hopefully. "To the market!"

Rosemary and I both shook our heads. The nearest market—the nearest *anything*—was hours away. A gatekeeper would never leave for that long without warning, especially if her deputy was out. Besides, it didn't explain the mess. And Rosemary was upset about something else, too. "It's not just that Florence is missing," she said. "It's the door between the worlds. It's stuck."

I dropped my bag on the floor. My heartbeat started thumping in my ears, and I could feel my face flushing with worry. What was going on? What were the chances that the doors at both ends of the world would stick shut in the same week? Or that both gatekeepers would go missing? "We've got to see that door right away," I told Rosemary. "Where is it? Outside?"

Rosemary shook her head. "Upstairs. Here, I'll show you."

The door that led to South was built right into the side of the gatehouse, at the end of a short, dim hallway, and closed with a heavy padlock. "The lock's open," said Rosemary, twisting it to show us. "It was lying on the floor when I got here, actually. I hung it back up."

Gatekeepers aren't the type to leave their locks lying around if they can help it. "And only Florence has the key?" I asked.

"I think so," said Rosemary. "I hope so. But the lock doesn't make a difference one way or another, anyway, because the whole door's jammed shut."

She was right. I tugged on the knob myself, and then Arthur tugged, and then we both tugged together. Nothing happened.

Behind us, the bees were moving quickly. THIS IS BAD, they said. TERRIBLE. INAUSPICIOUS. CALAMITOUS. DIRE. CATACLYSMIC. They must have been panicking; I'd never seen them use so many synonyms before. And I didn't feel much calmer.

"This can't be a coincidence," I said to Arthur. "One broken door might have been an accident, but two—"

"Hold on." Rosemary pushed her way between us. "What do you mean, two?"

"The door to East is stuck shut," I told her. "It happened three days ago, and the Gatekeeper is trapped on the other side of it. We thought it was our fault. That's why we came here, actually—to ask Florence for help."

"Are you serious? That *is* cataclysmic."

Arthur had gotten down on his hands and knees to peer under the door. "I can't see Florence," he announced. "Actually, to be honest, I can't see anything at all."

Rosemary blinked at him. "You think Florence went through the door?"

"If she did," I said, "I don't think it was her choice. She wouldn't have left this house while her deputy was away, would she? If she's anything like the Gatekeeper is, you'd have to drag her out kicking and screaming."

Arthur sat back on his heels. "That would explain the mess downstairs."

"I can't believe it," said Rosemary. She looked from me to Arthur to the bees, as though one of us had played a prank on her and she couldn't decide who'd done it. "You do realize this sounds crazy, don't you? You think someone lured your Gatekeeper into another world, sealed the door somehow, came around to *this* end of the world, got in a fight with *this* gatekeeper, dragged her off somewhere, and sealed this door, too?"

It hadn't sunk in until Rosemary said it, but that was exactly what I thought. Both doors wouldn't have broken at once unless someone had made sure it happened like that, and they'd wanted the gatekeepers out of the way while they did it. No wonder the bees were upset.

"I don't know what's happening," I said, "not exactly, at least. But I think we need to get help. *Professional* help."

Rosemary winced, and Arthur looked worried. I didn't blame them; the last thing in the worlds I wanted to do was to bring awful news to the Interworld Travel Commission, and I'd come all the way out to Florence's house to avoid it. But the situation had changed. As far as I could tell, our world was sealed off from both its neighbors, both gatekeepers were missing, and none of it seemed like an accident. There was no way around it: Interworld Travel had to be told, and as the Gatekeeper's deputy, it was my job to tell them. It was Rosemary's job, too, even though she didn't look very happy about it. And we couldn't exactly leave Arthur behind. "We'll all go to Interworld Travel together," I told them. "We'll explain everything to them. The sooner they hear about what's going

44

on, the sooner they can do something about it."

Rosemary didn't look as though she agreed, but she nodded and went to get her bag. Arthur and I walked back to the car to wait. "I don't mean to be selfish," Arthur said once we'd gotten there, "but won't the people at Interworld Travel know I'm not supposed to be here?" He looked nervously back toward the gatehouse, as if he thought Rosemary might be able to hear him. "I'd really prefer not to be arrested."

I preferred that, too. "We'll go to see my brother, Thomas," I said. "He'll listen to us, and he won't get us in trouble." At least, I hoped he wouldn't. There were a few perks to being an Eberslee, and I was counting on that being one of them. "Anyway, we're doing a good deed. No one will want to punish us for it."

Arthur stretched his arms over his head and looked up toward the sky. "If that's true," he said, "then your world and mine are much more different than I'd thought."

6

No one ever asks for directions to the Interworld Travel building. That's because no one has to. It's impossible to miss: it's built all of glass and stands eight stories high in the heart of Centerbury, connected by a footbridge to the golden-domed House of Governors. At night, the Interworld Travel building glows with electric light, and during the daytime it buzzes with business as diplomats, explorers, scientists, cartographers, and government officials all make their way through the glass hallways. There's no sign at the entrance, just the Interworld Travel Commission's logo etched onto the glass panels of the revolving door: eight circles linked together by lines, representing the eight connected worlds. That same logo is printed on every pink customs declaration, green returnee report, and blue application for otherworld travel, but I'd never been so glad to see it before. "We're here," I said. "This is the place."

46

"Thank goodness for that!" said Rosemary.

We hadn't had the easiest trip down the mountain. Neither Arthur nor Rosemary had been in much of a mood to chat, and the bees kept spelling out words like UNFORTUNATE and GRIM until Rosemary finally snapped that she'd gotten the point, thanks very much, and they buzzed away in a huff. To make matters worse, we didn't get anywhere near as lost as we should have, and the weather near the world's end stayed stubbornly normal: a blue sky brushed with clouds, a warm breeze, and only the slightest hint of thunder. Even the forest flowers were blooming in season. All this was worrying enough to dampen the spirits of even the most optimistic deputy gate-keeper, so I was hardly surprised when our car let out a long, exhausted wheeze and slowed to a halt just outside the city limits. Arthur asked Rosemary and me if we had any automobile fuel handy, but we didn't, of course, so we gathered up our luggage, left the car by the roadside, and walked the final mile into Centerbury.

The bees, naturally, had reached Interworld Travel first. They hovered by the entrance, saying HELLO and HOW DO YOU DO? to everyone who walked by (but pointedly ignoring Rosemary). A few people stared at them, but twice as many people were staring at the three of us: we were all covered in a fine layer of road dust, my rucksack was practically bursting open, the scarf Rosemary had tied over her curls was slipping down her forehead, and Arthur was staring up at the Interworld Travel building with his mouth open wide, as though he'd never seen anything quite like it. None of us looked much like we belonged in the stream of starched and dignified businesspeople flowing through the revolving door, but we joined them anyway.

I waited until Rosemary was a few steps ahead of us before nudging Arthur with my elbow. "This is the world headquarters for Southeast's Interworld Travel Commission," I told him quietly. I didn't want him blurting out questions and letting the entire building know he was a helpless Easterner traveling illegally; even Rosemary didn't know that yet. "Each world has its own commission; they all talk to one another, but they're independent. And I'm not sure any other world has a building as grand as this."

The lobby was vast and open, with high ceilings, glass-paneled walls, and a marble floor that made your footsteps echo as you walked over it. Travel officers in white button-down shirts and smart red ties stood behind a glass counter under a sign that said Information, and long hallways radiated out like tentacles, as if the building itself was trying to reach every world we knew about and several more we didn't. Above it all, a huge glass sculpture of the worlds floated in midair: eight swirling, multicolored spheres joined into an octagon by thin lines of light. All three of us stared up at it.

"That," said Arthur, "is remarkable."

"It was a gift from South," I told him. "All those spheres are held up by magic." I'd seen the sculpture myself a few times before, but I still couldn't quite believe there weren't any hidden bolts or wires.

"Look, though." Rosemary pointed at the gold-and-green sphere closest to us, the one that represented Southeast. "Those two connections are out."

I squinted up. It was tricky to make out in the morning sun, but Rosemary was right: the lines of light that should have connected Southeast to East on one side and South on the other had both gone dim. None of the people bustling under the sculpture seemed to have noticed, though, or if they had, they weren't concerned. "It might be a coincidence," I said.

"If you believe that," said Rosemary sharply, "you're twice as foolish as I thought you were."

My face went hot. "I'm not foolish."

Rosemary raised an eyebrow at me. Then she pushed her bandanna back over her curls. "Do you think they've got a washroom here? I'm going to go and find one."

Arthur and I watched her go. "I'm not sure I like her," Arthur said quietly once she was out of sight. "She's a little . . ."

RUDE! said the bees.

Arthur nodded. "Exactly."

"Don't worry about it," I said. I would have liked to march after Rosemary myself and ask her exactly how foolish she'd thought I'd been, but it wouldn't have been professional, and anyway, her bad opinion was the least of my problems. "Let's go and find Thomas."

We walked across the lobby to the information desk, where one of the bored-looking travel officers waved us over. According to the pin on her shirt pocket, her name was JEANNE.

I smiled at JEANNE and cleared my throat, trying to sound firm and important. "I'm Lucy Eberslee," I said, "the deputy at the Eastern end of the world, and I'm here to see my brother, Thomas Eberslee. Can you tell me where to find him? It's extremely urgent."

Urgent or not, JEANNE didn't seem to care. She took her time studying us—me, Arthur, and the bees—as if she weren't entirely sure whether to call security. "Do you have an appointment?" she asked at last.

"Well, no," I said, "but—"

"All visitors need to have an appointment."

"But it's an emergency!"

JEANNE gave me a thin, bland smile. "I'm sure it is."

This was too much for Arthur to take. "She's his *sister*," he said. "And we've got *magical bees*." He pointed up at them. LET US IN! they said, before hastily rearranging themselves to spell PLEASE.

"I can see that, sir," said JEANNE. She didn't exactly sound impressed. "Bees or no bees, however, you'll have to make an appointment first. I'm not permitted to break the rules—not even for sisters."

This was so nearly what I might have said myself to an exasperating explorer at the end of the world that I almost laughed. "Rules are very important," I told her. "I love them; I swear I do. And I promise I'll make an appointment next time. I'll make fifty appointments if you'd like, but right now, we can't afford to wait. The doors at both ends of the world are broken, no one can travel in or out, both gatekeepers are missing, they might be in awful danger, and we think it's all been done on purpose, so unless you'd like to create even more of a crisis, you'd better let me see my brother immediately."

I must have sounded even more firm and important than I'd hoped, because JEANNE took a few steps back and stared at me. She didn't look at all bored anymore. "Are you serious?" she whispered.

"Utterly," I said.

She tried to smile blandly again, but it didn't quite work. "Please wait here, Miss Eberslee," she said. "I'll see what I can do."

JEANNE wasn't gone long. "Excuse me, Miss Eberslee?" she said, coming back to the information desk a little out of breath. "Your brother is here. He'll see you now—both of you. And those bees, I suppose." She pointed down one of the hallways, where Thomas stood waiting in a crisp gray suit and polished shoes.

I looked around for Rosemary, but she hadn't come back yet, and I didn't particularly want to go and find her. "If you see a girl with curly hair come out of the washroom," I asked JEANNE, "could you tell her where we've gone?"

JEANNE said she would, and we walked down the hall toward Thomas. He was shifting back and forth from one foot to the other, as though he were almost too busy to stand still, but he still managed to give me a smile and a quick hug.

"Hello, little Goose," he said. "It's good to see you. Is this a friend of yours?"

I nodded, even though I wasn't sure *friend* was quite the right word for it. "This is Arthur," I said.

"Nice to meet you," said Thomas. He sounded distracted, though; his shoulders were tense, and he barely even glanced at the bees. THE PLEASURE IS OURS, they said. I couldn't help wondering if they were being sarcastic.

"How are you?" I asked as we walked down the hall and up a few flights of stairs. Thomas was half a foot taller than me, and I had to hurry to keep up with him. "How are Mom and Dad? I haven't heard from them in a while. Letters get lost so easily at the end of the world, though; I can't really blame them. And I'm sure you've all been busy—"

"I'd love to catch up, Goose," said Thomas, "but right now we don't have the time. I told Mrs. Bracknell I'd bring you to her immediately."

"Mrs. Bracknell?" I grabbed at Thomas's elbow. "Do you mean *Governor* Bracknell? The *head of Interworld Travel* Governor Bracknell?"

"The very same," said Thomas.

"But we came to see you!"

"That's what Jeanne told me," said Thomas. "She also told me why you were here. Is it true that the worldgates are broken and both gatekeepers are missing?"

I nodded.

"Then Mrs. Bracknell is the person you need to talk to. If

52

what you said is true, something serious is happening at the ends of the world, and I'm not close to senior enough to deal with it." Thomas led us around a corner, squeaked to a stop in his polished shoes, and paused with his hand on the door in front of us. "It's a good thing you came to Interworld Travel, though. All you need to do is tell Mrs. Bracknell what's happened, just the way you were going to tell it to me. And don't look so frightened, Goose. She may be a governor, but I swear she's not going to eat you alive." He winked at me. "She's already full from lunch."

7

Clara Bracknell was a small, bright-eyed woman with brown hair turning unabashedly gray at the temples. I doubted anyone ever gazed over her head when she tried to talk to them: even with her sleeves rolled up, a pair of scissors sticking out of her pocket, and a pencil tucked behind her ear, she practically radiated importance. "Thank you, Mr. Eberslee," she said, standing up from her desk as Thomas led us in. "That *was* immediate." Then she turned to me and gave me a good long look. "This must be your sister," she said, putting a hand out for me to shake. "It's nice to meet you, Lucy. Thank you for all the work you do for us at the gatehouse."

"Oh!" I said. "You're welcome." No one had ever thanked me for that before, not even the Gatekeeper. It felt awfully nice to be noticed.

Then Mrs. Bracknell shifted her gaze to Arthur. "You're not

one of my employees. You look like an Easterner. Are you?"

I'd been hoping she wouldn't notice *that*. When I'd promised Arthur that no one at Interworld Travel would get him in trouble, I hadn't realized we'd be coming face-to-face with the woman who actually ran the place. I wasn't about to tell her I'd brought someone over from East illegally, but I couldn't just stand there and refuse to introduce him, either. "This is Arthur," I said hastily. "He's been traveling with me. He's . . . um . . ." I tried to think of something halfway believable that Arthur might be.

"A prince!" said Arthur.

"A prince?" Mrs. Bracknell cast a skeptical eye over the shirt Arthur had been wearing for days and the pants smudged with motor oil.

"Oh, yes," I said, inventing wildly. I'd been thinking of calling Arthur a foreign ambassador, or maybe a governor's assistant, but he'd gone and made himself royalty, of all things, and now we were stuck with it. "Arthur is an Eastern prince on a tour of the worlds, but he doesn't want anyone to know who he really is. That's why he's disguised as an ordinary person: he doesn't like all the fuss. He's sick to death of all his courtiers and golden robes and things."

"That's right," said Arthur. "Golden robes are awfully heavy. And you wouldn't believe how hot they get in the summertime."

"I'm sure I wouldn't," said Mrs. Bracknell carefully. Then she smiled and shook Arthur's hand, too. "It's a pleasure to meet you, Your Highness. You'll have to tell me all about your kingdom later on. I'm curious to hear more."

Once it was clear enough that no one was going to be arrested on the spot, Arthur and I sat down in the chairs Mrs. Bracknell pulled out for us. They weren't uncomfortable, exactly, but their backs were stiff enough to nudge your spine back into place if you even thought about slouching. We left a third chair open for Rosemary, who still hadn't come back from the washroom. The far wall of the office was paneled in glass, and the bees hovered near it, taking in the view of Centerbury, while Thomas stood by Mrs. Bracknell's door like a sentry.

Mrs. Bracknell herself leaned against the desk. "I don't have much time," she said, "and I suspect I'm about to have even less of it, depending on what you have to tell me, so let's get down to business. Thomas has given me a general idea of the situation, but I'd like to hear it directly from you, Lucy. What's going on at the ends of the world?"

I told her almost everything I could remember, from the morning of Maintenance Day all the way to our arrival in Centerbury. The only thing I left out was an explanation of exactly how Arthur had turned up in Southeast in the first place. Mrs. Bracknell listened to the whole story with her mouth pursed and her gaze pinned directly on me. She didn't take notes, but then again, she didn't seem like the sort of person who had to. When I finished by explaining how we'd noticed the lights on the world sculpture had gone out, she shook her head and sighed.

"That awful sculpture," she said. "We'd assumed it just needed repairs. A magician has to come over from South every three months to maintain the thing." She looked over at Thomas.

"That's no excuse, though. We should have known better."

"I'll have someone take a closer look at it," Thomas offered, "to make sure there aren't any more problems we've missed."

"Thank you." Mrs. Bracknell turned back to me. "Lucy, you said Florence's deputy came with you. Where is she now?"

"In the washroom." I turned around to stare at the door, willing Rosemary to walk through it. I was starting to worry she'd gotten lost somewhere in the depths of Interworld Travel. "She should be here soon."

"I hope so." Mrs. Bracknell looked worried, too. "Now, you told me the climate was exceptionally normal at the Southern end of the world. What was it like at the Eastern end after the worldgate was sealed?"

I tried to remember. It had only been a few days ago, but it already felt like months. "We had a hailstorm later that day, but it wasn't a very large one. And we didn't get quite as lost as we should have when we left the gatehouse."

"Remarkable," said Mrs. Bracknell. "I can't say I'm surprised, though. When the physical connection between two worlds is cut off, it's only natural that each world's influence on the other would weaken as well. Since you say the sense of normalcy was stronger at the Southern end of the world than at your own, I assume that worldgate was sealed first, perhaps a few days before yours."

Mrs. Bracknell spoke in long, brisk strides of language, and I couldn't run to keep up with her the way I could with Thomas. "You mean things are becoming more normal at my end of the world, too?"

"I'll have to send my officers over to investigate more thoroughly," said Mrs. Bracknell, "but yes, that's exactly what I expect. In a few days, if the worldgate can't be repaired, the area will be just like anywhere else: no more missing socks or hailstorms. At least, not any more than usual."

Arthur gave a nervous sort of cough.

"But it *can* be repaired," I told him. I looked at the others. "Can't it?"

Mrs. Bracknell and Thomas exchanged the sort of glance my parents used to give each other when they didn't want to talk about something unpleasant until I was safely in bed.

"I'm the Gatekeeper's deputy," I reminded them, "and the Gatekeeper is missing. I should know what's going on."

"Of course. You're right." Mrs. Bracknell stood up. She was quiet for a moment. "I'm not sure we'll be able to fix the worldgates," she said carefully, "because the problem we're facing is more than a matter of broken locks. Worldgates don't seal themselves, and gatekeepers don't abandon their posts and leave without a trace. It's clear to me, as I'm sure it's clear to you, that we are under attack. Someone is tampering with our world on purpose. I don't know who that someone is or what that purpose might be, but I'm hoping you'll be able to help us find out. I'd like you to think hard, Lucy: before the worldgate broke, did anyone unusual pass through the end of the world? Anyone suspicious? Even if you can remember who came through the door most recently, that would be a great help."

The person who'd passed through the door most recently

had been Arthur, of course, but I couldn't tell her that. "No one suspicious," I said. "Just some tourists and Interworld Travel employees—and the Gatekeeper, of course. Once she'd left, I wasn't allowed to let anyone in or out." At least that wasn't a lie.

Mrs. Bracknell didn't look satisfied. "Do you have the travelers' records with you?"

"They're back at the gatehouse. I'm sorry. I didn't realize I'd need them." I shifted in my chair, trying to get comfortable. "I thought you should know, though, that Henry Tallard was poking around the end of the world just after the door closed, and it wasn't the first time he'd done it."

Mrs. Bracknell's eyebrows went straight up. "Henry Tallard?" she said. "The same Henry Tallard who crossed the Uncrossable Desert? Who found the bottom of Bottomless Lake?"

"The same," I said. "I don't know what he's up to right now, but I'd bet it's not anything good. He wasn't being truthful with me at the gatehouse. And the bees don't like him."

THAT'S RIGHT, said the bees.

Mrs. Bracknell frowned at them. "Have a team bring Tallard in to speak with me," she told Thomas, who nodded and scribbled something on a pocket-sized notepad. "Tell him we're giving him an award. He'll enjoy that. If he knows anything about the worldgates, it shouldn't take me long to find out, and if he doesn't, we'll send him on his way with a plaque or something like that." She looked up toward the door. "What about Ophelia? Did she see Tallard at her end of the world, too?"

It took me a moment to realize this question was directed at me. "Ophelia?" I asked. I'd never met anyone named Ophelia.

"Ophelia Winston. Florence's deputy." Mrs. Bracknell frowned again, this time at me. "You said she was on her way. I can't imagine what's taking her so long. I'll send someone to look for her." She started across the room.

"Wait!" I said. "The girl we met at Florence's house said her name was Rosemary. My age, a little taller than me, with brown eyes and curls?"

Whatever Ophelia Winston looked like, I could tell it wasn't anything like that. Mrs. Bracknell was shaking her head, and Thomas had set down his notepad. Arthur didn't say anything, but he sat up even straighter than before, as though he'd been jabbed.

"Oh, worlds," I said quietly. "Rosemary doesn't work for Interworld Travel."

"No," Mrs. Bracknell agreed. "I've never heard of her."

"Then who is she?" asked Arthur. "What was she doing at Florence's house?"

The bees hummed smugly. LIAR, they said.

I shrank into my chair, feeling exactly as foolish as Rosemary had guessed I was. "She's probably gone out the washroom window by now," I said to the others. "Someone should check."

By the time a team of travel officers got into the lobby washroom, Rosemary was long gone. No one in the building had seen her pass by, and no one in the busy street outside had noticed a curly-haired girl slipping out of sight. "We'll keep an eye out for her," said the travel officer who'd come to deliver the news to Mrs. Bracknell and Thomas. "I don't like our odds, though. We don't have a photograph of the girl, and we can't haul every child in the city up here for questioning."

I'd been standing at the glass-paneled wall, looking down at the city below. Centerbury stretched out below me in a patchwork of buildings and fields, hemmed in here and there by a stream or a roadway. The day had kept itself busy by turning into a damp gray afternoon, but the markets were bustling, and so were the streets all around the House of Governors. If Rosemary was anywhere in that crowd, I couldn't pick her out from this distance. I'd lost her, and I'd lost the Gatekeeper, and I'd dragged Arthur across the world making everything even more disastrous than it had been to begin with. "I know what Rosemary looks like," I said, turning back to the others. "Send me out with the travel officers. Let me search for her."

Thomas tugged at the sleeves of his suit jacket. "I'm not sure that's a good idea, Goose," he said. "It might not be safe, and you're not trained—"

"I'll be fine," I told him. "If Rosemary knows something about what's happening to the worldgates, we've got to find her fast, and I can help. I *want* to help."

"I can help, too," said Arthur. "I'll go with Lucy."

But Mrs. Bracknell was shaking her head. "I'm sorry," she said. "I agree with Thomas. I appreciate your enthusiasm, but this is a job for professionals. You did the right thing coming to us. We can take care of the problem with the worldgates from here." She turned back to the travel officer.

Arthur nudged me. "What do we do now?"

I had no idea. Arthur couldn't go home to East, and I wasn't about to go back to the empty gatehouse and sit by myself behind the desk, next to the fern, waiting for travelers who never came. "Please, Mrs. Bracknell," I said. "Let us do something."

She gave me another of her long looks.

"All right," she said at last. "I don't want you chasing down interworld criminals in the streets; it's too dangerous. But the two of you can stay here for a few days and work in the archives. If Rosemary is a Southeasterner with a passport, her information will be filed somewhere, and we'll need someone to dig through the archives and find it. Do you think you can do that for us?"

I ignored the face Arthur was pulling and nodded. "We'd be happy to."

"Good." Mrs. Bracknell gave me an approving sort of nod. "I appreciate your help, Lucy. I'm glad your brother convinced us to make an exception for you."

Before I could ask what *that* meant, Mrs. Bracknell was sweeping us out of her office and into the hallway. "Thomas can show you around the building," she told us. "If you find anything important in the archives, come straight to him or to me, but please don't do anything more without our approval. The last thing we need is another disaster."

8

Thomas led us up the spiral staircase at the center of the Interworld Travel building, giving us a hasty tour as we went. "The Center for Otherworld Linguistic Studies is down that hall," he said, waving an arm vaguely as we passed the fifth-floor landing, "and the universal armory is the third door on the left, though you won't be able to get in there without top-level credentials. We don't want people helping themselves to Western double-edged defense rays or Northern boatsinkers."

I hadn't realized the Interworld Travel Commission had any need for weapons. "Do *you* use those things?" I asked.

Thomas laughed. "Don't worry, Goose; they're just for our researchers to study. It's important to learn about otherworld technologies. On the sixth floor, we've got the botany lab and the map room. The Explorers' Museum is down on the second floor, if you want to look around, and so is the staff café. That's where you'll be having meals while you're here. Let me say in advance that I'm very sorry."

"Sorry for what?" asked Arthur.

"You'll know it when you taste it." Thomas made a face. "Most of the building is open for you to explore as you'd like, but don't barge into anyone's private offices without knocking, and don't try going up to the eighth floor. You won't get very far." We'd reached the seventh-floor landing now, and while the staircase continued up, we didn't. The stairs to the eighth floor were barricaded with plywood and bright yellow tape. "We're doing some construction work up there at the moment," Thomas explained. "It's not safe for visitors."

Our rooms were on the seventh floor in a part of the building called the Travelers' Wing. "It's for visiting otherworld diplomats, mostly, if they don't have a place to stay in the city while they're here on government business," Thomas told us. "Luckily for you, though, it's almost empty right now. We've got a trade official from West who's come to talk to the House of Governors about some problems they're having with interworld smugglers, and a farmer from Northeast who's asked to meet with Mrs. Bracknell about his cows, though I have no idea why he thinks they're any of her business." He looked over his shoulder at Arthur. "You should find the guest rooms very comfortable, Your Highness."

"Oh!" said Arthur. "Er. Thank you. I'm sure I will."

My room in the Travelers' Wing was twice the size of my bedroom back at the gatehouse, with its own washroom, a bed

64

piled high with pillows, a long sofa, and a closet that connected to Arthur's room on the other side. The bees buzzed back and forth curiously as I put down my rucksack and unpacked the few things I'd brought: a jumble of shirts and pants, a sweater, a book I'd forgotten I'd stashed in one of the outer pockets. I'd been feeling unsettled ever since I'd left the Gatekeeper's house with all my things squashed into a bag, and it felt good to organize them on shelves and in drawers, to put them back in the places where they belonged.

"Will you be all right in here, Goose?" Thomas poked his head into the room. "Do you have enough blankets? Towels?"

"Yes, thanks. I'll be fine. Except—" I lowered my voice, hoping Arthur and the bees wouldn't wander in unannounced. "I've been wondering what Mrs. Bracknell meant when she said you'd convinced her to make an exception for me. What sort of exception did she make?"

Thomas didn't look away from me, exactly, but his gaze landed somewhere near my shoes. "I'm not sure what she was talking about, Goose, but I wouldn't worry about it if I were you. I'm sure it wasn't important." He shifted back and forth from one foot to the other again; before, I'd thought he was busy, but now I wondered if he was nervous. "When you're done unpacking, let me know, and I'll show you down to the archives."

The archives were stored in the basement, in a dim, wood-paneled room with rows of shelves that must have stretched halfway across the building. Each shelf was loaded with dusty books and boxes, and each box had a different label: Maintenance Logs East, Known Criminals A–G, Reports of Unusual Weather, Historical Documents #5. Someone had shoved a battered old desk and two folding chairs into one corner of the room, where a lamp flickered unconvincingly.

"Here we are," said Thomas. "Every document the Southeastern Interworld Travel Commission has ever produced is somewhere in this room. It's all in alphabetical order, or at least it's supposed to be. Things can get a little confusing down here."

"Your records aren't digital?" Arthur poked at one of the boxes, leaving a fingerprint smudge in the dust. "Or, I don't know, magical?"

"I'm sorry." At least Thomas sounded as if he meant it. "But Rosemary's file must be here somewhere. If I were you, I'd start with the most recent box of passport records and work backward from there. If you need me, I'll be in my office; that's on the third floor, down the hall from Mrs. Bracknell's. And, Goose?" Thomas bent down to look me in the eye. "Don't leave the building alone, all right? Considering what's happened to the other gatekeepers, you shouldn't be wandering across Centerbury by yourself."

This seemed deeply unfair, but Thomas was right, as usual: I was at Interworld Travel to help find Rosemary and rescue the Gatekeeper, not to make more trouble. It was best to be cautious. "All right," I said. "I'll let you know."

Thomas smiled at us on his way out the door. "Good luck, Goose. Good luck, Your Highness."

"Your *Highness?*" I hissed at Arthur once we were alone. The bees had flown deeper into the archive to search for boxes of passport applications, and Arthur was looking at the spines of old books on a shelf. I flopped down in one of the folding chairs. Its legs wobbled under me, as if it were on the verge of giving up. "What were you *thinking?*"

Arthur grimaced. "Should I not be a prince? Sorry about that. I didn't know what else to say, and Mrs. Bracknell was making me nervous."

"It's all right," I told him. "You'll just have to remember to act princely." I hoped Arthur had a better idea than I did of exactly what that meant. "Princes probably have lots of servants to do things for them," I said, thinking about it, "so don't mention that you drive your own car or make your own sandwiches or anything like that."

"A prince can make sandwiches!" Arthur said indignantly.

We were interrupted by the bees, who'd found the passport files. They weren't far away, but the shelves were stacked higher than I could reach, and the rows of boxes marked Passport Applications went on forever. At least they were numbered and more or less in order. After a few minutes of searching, I found the least dusty box—Passport Applications #8442-8570—and hauled it back to the desk in the corner of the room. The papers inside couldn't have been stored for long; they were still crisp and white, and the first three files I pulled out had all been completed in the last few months. Each form had a picture of the applicant clipped to the top, so it was easy to tell at a glance that none of them belonged to Rosemary. I hauled an armload of papers out of the box and started flipping through them. Every so often, footsteps would pound on the lobby floor above our heads and I'd wonder whether Mrs. Bracknell's travel officers had already found Rosemary in the time it had taken me to glance at half a dozen files. Sitting behind a desk and organizing papers into stacks wasn't particularly exciting, but I guessed someone had to do it, and at least I had experience.

Arthur, who was supposed to be searching through files of his own, was still wandering the aisles, peering into boxes and chatting with the bees about what he'd found inside. At one point he wandered back to the desk carrying a tall stack of books. He dumped them on the floor in front of me, sending up a dust cloud that made both of us sneeze.

"All these books," Arthur announced, "are about Henry Tallard. And these are just the ones I could carry." He held up a yellowing copy of Tallard's autobiography, *Great Explorations*. "Maybe there's something in here that will tell us more about what he's been doing at the ends of the world."

"The travel officers will interview him soon enough," I said. "We're supposed to be looking for Rosemary."

"I know." Arthur frowned down at the picture of Tallard on the book's back cover. "He really does look like he's up to something, though, doesn't he? Like he knows something the rest of us don't? I can't believe I told him all about our troubles." He set down *Great Explorations* and picked up another book from the pile on the floor, a thick hardcover with a purple dust jacket and the words *Tallard: A Life* printed in yellow. I recognized it right away: I'd read it in school, and so had every other person in Southeast.

"That one's about Arabella Tallard," I said. "She was Henry's great-great-aunt or something like that."

"And she was a famous explorer, too?"

"Better than that." I liked Arabella Tallard, or at least I liked all the stories I'd heard about her, and growing up in a family of diplomats and governors, I'd heard a lot. "She created the worldgates."

Arthur sat down in the other folding chair. "What do you mean?"

"Well, our worlds haven't always been connected." I set down my work. "They've always been right alongside each other, but for the longest time, none of the eight worlds knew the other seven existed, and you couldn't travel from one to another. Sometimes, in the places where the fabric between the worlds was especially thin, people would hear things—a phrase of otherworld music, maybe, or the first few words of a story. If you were standing in just the right place at just the right time, you might have seen a shadow you couldn't explain or felt a warm breeze come from out of nowhere. Those were the only things that could pass between the worlds back then: sounds and winds and light."

Arthur's chair squeaked as he leaned forward. "How long ago was that?"

"Not so long. A few hundred years. Southeast was a different kind of place back then. We couldn't get crops from Northeast, or electric light from East, or magic from South. The whole world was very poor, and most of the other worlds weren't much better off."

"Until Henry Tallard's great-great-aunt came along?"

I nodded. "Arabella Tallard wasn't an explorer at first; she was an inventor. Her mother was a seamstress in South, and she was always complaining about the dull fabric shears she had to use to cut her patterns, so Arabella decided to invent a magical pair that would never lose their sharpness. She never told anyone exactly how she did it, but after a few years of experimenting, she'd created a new kind of metal that could be sharpened down to the thinnest blade and could cut through any fabric. She used it to make one pair of scissors and took them back for her mother to test. But women's fashions weren't very practical back then, particularly in South, and Arabella's shoe got caught in the cobblestones outside her mother's shop. When she reached out with her scissors to stop herself from falling, she sliced a hole right through the fabric of time and space and toppled into Southwest."

"She fell out of her own world accidentally?" Arthur looked delighted. "Then I'm not the only one!"

I'd always been curious about that detail myself. It made for a good story, but Arabella Tallard had been a genius, and I thought she might have known exactly what she was doing when she'd reached out and snipped her way into another world. "Once that first worldgate was open," I said, "Arabella became an otherworld explorer. She and her friends traveled all through the worlds, finding the places where the fabric of time and space was thinnest and using the gatecutters—the scissors she'd invented—to snip new worldgates open. They were just ragged holes at first, but those first explorers trimmed the edges and built sturdy doorways around them to keep them from unraveling. The worlds started communicating with one another, and then they started visiting and trading. The Interworld Travel Commissions were formed to keep track of it all. More people became explorers, but Arabella was the only one with gatecutters, and once she'd opened doorways to connect all the worlds, she never used them again."

Arthur had cracked open *Tallard: A Life* and was studying an illustration of Arabella in the practical explorer's uniform she'd designed herself, complete with flat-soled shoes that would never get caught between cobblestones. "Where are the gatecutters now?" he asked. "Do you think someone could use them to open the worldgates that are sealed?"

"I think they're in a museum in another world somewhere. I've got no idea if they still work. They're hundreds of years old, so they're probably rusted shut anyway." I shrugged. "It's a good idea, though. We should ask Mrs. Bracknell about it."

By the time we'd looked through two full boxes of passport applications, it was past sunset. While I'd managed to lose my favorite pen somewhere in the archives, I still hadn't found any more information about Rosemary. We lugged the boxes back to their shelves and went upstairs to see if the café was still serving dinner. Arthur chatted with the bees as we walked, but I didn't feel like joining in; all that afternoon, I'd been thinking about Arabella Tallard and about how poor and isolated Southeast had been before she'd opened the worldgates. Now that we were shut off from all the other worlds again, what would happen to us? Would our lives start to change? Would that change take years, or months, or days? Maybe a crew of travel officers had already made it to the gatehouses, I told myself; maybe they were already working on ways to fix the doors at the ends of the world. It was just like Mrs. Bracknell had said: they were professionals. There was no reason to panic.

As we passed the lobby, Arthur stopped walking. A crowd of people had gathered in the center of the marble floor, and everyone was staring up at the sculpture of the eight glass spheres. We stared, too. The lines of light that should have connected Southeast to East and to South still hadn't returned, and now the light connecting East to Northeast was flickering wildly, like a trapped firebug. As we watched, there was a fizzing noise in the air, followed by a tiny pop, and the light went out completely.

I spotted Thomas in the crowd and pushed my way through to him. "We've lost another worldgate, haven't we?"

"It looks that way." Thomas sounded exhausted.

"Do you think the same people who closed the other two worldgates closed that one?"

"I don't know, Goose. I'm a travel officer, not an all-seeing magician. I've got no more idea what's going on than you do."

"Look!" shouted someone in the crowd, and we all looked up again. The light between Northeast and North was flickering now, too.

"Oh, worlds," said Thomas. "That can't be good."

I nodded. It didn't take an all-seeing magician to realize *that*.

9

News about the sealed worldgates traveled fast. We hadn't been in the city for more than few days before all of Centerbury was humming with alarm. Diplomats, explorers, and traders were gathered around the information desk in the lobby, asking if it was true that they were stranded in our world and demanding to know what Mrs. Bracknell planned to do about it. Mrs. Bracknell herself was meeting with a steady stream of government officials, each one more panic-stricken than the last. Her travel officers reported that at both ends of the world the weather was mild and partly cloudy, and all the morning newspapers had been properly delivered. No one nearby had misplaced their glasses, their house keys, the books they'd been reading, or anything else, for that matter. And no one could figure out how to reopen the doors.

I spent each day squirreled away in the archives, reading

through thirteen years of passport applications as fast as I could. I'd found plenty of girls and women named Rosemary, but most of them looked nothing like the girl I'd met, and almost none of them were the right age. There were only three exceptions: Rosemary Weber, whose passport photo had gotten lost; Rosemary Silos, who'd been photographed when she was only a baby; and Rosemary Baker, who had a tumble of brown curls but had moved to Northwest with her family five years earlier.

Each time I found a potential Rosemary, I ran upstairs to show Thomas, but each time, he took a quick glance at my papers and sent me away. "I'm sorry, Goose," he said the third time, handing Rosemary Baker's passport file back to me, "but even if this is the right Rosemary, I'm not sure how we'd find her. She doesn't even live in this world anymore. And we don't have any proof that this girl is the one we're looking for."

"That's what you said the last two times!"

"That's because it's true." Thomas sighed loudly and sat back down behind his desk. It was only nine in the morning, but he'd obviously been working through the night; his office was scattered with blueprints, memos, and cardboard coffee cups, and the tie I'd seen him wearing the day before was still draped around his neck.

"I'll find proof," I offered. "I'll go to Rosemary Baker's old address and ask if anyone's seen her, or if they remember her mentioning the worldgates. I'll visit the other two girls, too. I'll find another travel officer to come with me, Thomas; I know you're busy—"

75

"Very busy." Thomas took a sip from one of his coffee cups and grimaced. "Honestly, Goose, none of us have time to worry about any of these girls. Our travel officers found Henry Tallard sneaking through the woods outside Florence's gatehouse a few days ago, and he took off running. Now we've had to send more officers into the field to track him down, and the rest of us are working overtime. Five more lights are out on the sculpture, we're trying to work out exactly how many otherworlders are stranded here, and the Northern ambassador is threatening to force our worldgates open by blasting them with cannonballs. This Rosemary business will have to wait."

"All right," I said quietly. "I'm sorry to bother you."

"You're not a bother," Thomas said automatically, but he'd already turned back to his work, and he didn't look up when I went out the door.

Arthur was down in the archives when I got back, talking to a tall, broad-shouldered man I didn't recognize. "This is a huge honor," the man was saying. "I've never met a prince before!"

"Well, I've never met someone who owns quite so much livestock." Arthur sounded genuinely impressed. "The honor's mine, Huggins."

Both of them looked over at me as I tossed Rosemary Baker's file back on the desk. "Lucy!" said Arthur. "Meet Huggins! He took a wrong turn on his way to breakfast."

I introduced myself and shook Huggins's hand. "You're the farmer from Northeast, aren't you? The one who's here to see

Mrs. Bracknell about some cows?"

"That's right," said Huggins. "It's a bad situation, Miss Eberslee. My girls won't go into their normal grazing pastures, won't even walk across the field. Mrs. Bracknell needs to know about it, but she's been so busy, she hasn't had a chance to meet with me. If either of you happen to see her, would you pass the news along?"

I couldn't imagine why Mrs. Bracknell would need to know about some stubborn Northeastern cows, but I promised I'd let her know. Then Arthur left to show Huggins the way to the café, and I got to work, digging some masking tape out of a desk drawer and sticking each of the three Rosemarys' passport applications to the wall. I stared at them. If Thomas wanted proof that one of these people was the girl I'd met at Florence's, then proof was what I'd give him.

But I didn't know where to start. I was still staring at the pages on the wall when Arthur came back ten minutes later. "Do any of these girls look suspicious to you?" I asked him. "Like the sort of person who might lurk around a sealed-up worldgate?"

"I think it's the baby. She looks too smart for her own good." Arthur tossed me a pear he must have snagged from the café. I bit into it gratefully; I'd skipped breakfast that morning so I could come straight down to the archives, and I was already regretting it. "Didn't Thomas want to hear more about your latest Rosemary?" Arthur asked.

"He didn't even seem interested. And I don't think

Mrs. Bracknell cares, either. I ran into her this morning and asked her if she knew where Arabella Tallard's gatecutters were, but she just stared at me and said she had no idea." She'd been in a rush, to be fair, hurrying down the stairs from the eighth-floor construction zone, and she hadn't even stopped long enough for me to tell her about all the work I'd been doing. "I don't understand it," I said. "The worldgates are closing faster now. Most of the lights on the sculpture are out, everyone in the world is panicking, and Mrs. Bracknell has a whole team of officers running after Henry Tallard. You'd think they'd want to track Rosemary down, too. For all we know, she's the criminal behind it all!"

Arthur looked up at me. "Hold on," he said. "You've given me an idea." And he vanished into the archives.

When he didn't come back after five minutes, I went after him myself. "Arthur?" I called as I walked. "Are you still in here?" The room was so huge and dim that it would have been easy for someone to get lost in the maze of shelves, maybe even for good. I wondered what would happen if I *did* get lost down here. Would Thomas send a search party? Would Mrs. Bracknell click efficiently down the aisles until she'd found me? How long would it be until either of them noticed I was missing? I shuddered. "Arthur?" I called again.

Then I realized where I was standing. I'd wandered to one of the far corners of the archives, where all the boxes around me were labeled with dates and the same two words: Employee Records. And I had an idea of my own.

I ran my fingers over the boxes until I found the most recent one, full of information about all the people Interworld Travel had hired in the past two years. I looked around. Arthur still wasn't in sight, and no one else was around to tell me I was being foolish. I lifted the lid off the box and dug through it until my fingers hit on the file I was looking for: a thin brown folder marked Eberslee, L. There was only one slim packet of papers inside.

The air started to hum. When I looked up, the bees were swarming down the aisle toward me. I stuffed the papers in the back pocket of my pants and pushed the box of records away so fast I almost knocked it off the shelf. If the bees noticed, at least they didn't mention it. LUCY! they said instead. COME!

I ran through the aisles after them. "Is it Arthur?" I asked them. "Is he all right?"

"I'm fine," said Arthur, hurrying toward us with a bundle of pages tucked under his arm. "I heard all the buzzing. What's happening?"

The bees hovered impatiently above us. HENRY TAL-LARD, they said. HE'S HERE.

10

When we reached the lobby of Interworld Travel, we found Henry Tallard standing at the information desk. His pants were mud-crusted and torn, his checked explorer's shirt looked as if it had been singed, and he was speaking so loudly that I wondered if everyone across all eight worlds could hear him.

"Clara Bracknell!" he shouted at JEANNE. "Where is she? I need to speak with her immediately."

JEANNE's eyes were wide. "Calm down, please, Mr. Tallard," she said. "You're alarming the other patrons." All around the lobby, tourists and diplomats and businesspeople in suits were clustered together, looking nervously at the most famous explorer in all the worlds. Someone even started snapping photographs.

"They *should* be alarmed!" said Tallard. "Aren't you?" He waved his hand above his head, where the last remaining light on the sculpture of the worlds was flickering. "Now, tell me: Where is Clara Bracknell?"

He tried to walk past the information desk, but JEANNE stepped in front of him. "I'm sorry, Mr. Tallard," she said, "but I can't let you do that. Do you have an appointment?"

"An appointment?" He was practically hollering now. "I've been chased through a field of poisonweed! Across five different rivers! Through the Great Southeastern Swamp and the fire pits of Pitfire! Well, I've had enough. If Mrs. Bracknell wants to talk to me, she can come down here and do it. I've got plenty of questions I'd like to ask her, too."

"He *wants* to see Mrs. Bracknell?" Arthur whispered. "What's he thinking?" We were standing on the staircase just past the information desk, not as far out of Tallard's line of sight as I would have liked. In his tattered clothes, all bruised and scraped, with his fists waving at JEANNE, he didn't look much like the explorer whose portrait had hung on my schoolroom wall, or even like the man we'd met back at the gatehouse. He looked dangerous.

"I've got no idea," I whispered back. "Maybe that poisonweed he ran through sent him out of his mind."

"Why are people just letting him stand there? Is he going to hurt anyone? Should we hide?" Arthur inched backward. "Maybe we should hide."

Before we had a chance to do anything, though, a pack of travel officers in white uniforms and visored helmets burst through the revolving doors. Henry Tallard rolled his eyes as two of the officers seized his arms. "Well done," he said to them. "You've tracked me down at last. You know, if you'd just waited here at Interworld Travel, you wouldn't have had to waste all that energy running after me from one end of the world to the other." He smirked. "Probably best not to think about it."

One of the travel officers pushed up her visor and looked around at the gathered crowd. "The suspect is secured," she announced. "We'll be taking him across the bridge to the House of Governors directly. For your safety, please don't approach the suspect or the Interworld Travel operations team."

"Stand back," I told Arthur under my breath. The travel officers were marching Henry Tallard toward the staircase—and right toward us. We pressed ourselves against the wall. Even the bees had gone silent. Tallard's gaze skimmed over the top of my head, and for the first time in my life, I was relieved to be unnoticed.

Then he spotted Arthur.

"I've met you before." Tallard stumbled to a stop and jutted his chin in Arthur's direction. "You were at the end of the world."

"Me?" Arthur looked around wildly, as though he hoped Tallard might be staring at someone else. I moved in front of him, not that it helped; he was at least a head taller than I was. But the bees moved, too. They rose up around us in a thick, buzzing cloud.

If Tallard was afraid of them, he didn't show it. "Let them sting me if you'd like," he said. His eyes were still locked on

Arthur's. "I've been through worse, and it won't get me off your trail. I know what you're up to. You're not from this world, are you? Did *she* let you in?" He looked down at me as though I were something sticky he'd just found on the bottom of his shoe. "She thinks she's got everyone fooled, but she doesn't fool me."

I froze. The swarm of bees around me grew louder, or maybe the buzzing was inside my own head now; either way, I could hardly hear myself think. Did Tallard know about my accident with Arthur? Was he here to tell Interworld Travel all about it? And why did it make him so furious? I wasn't sure what was happening, but I knew I wanted to be anywhere else than on the receiving end of Henry Tallard's stare. "I don't have anyone fooled," I said firmly. "I don't know what you're talking about. Leave us alone."

The travel officers had finally muscled Tallard forward, but even they couldn't keep him quiet. "What I'd really like to know," he shouted back to Arthur as they dragged him away, "is how you smuggled in those gatecutters. I hope you don't mind my saying so, but you don't seem brave enough for the job!"

"That's enough," snapped the travel officer in charge as she led him away around the curve of the staircase. There was a brilliant flash in the air above us, and the final light in the sculpture went dark.

It took Arthur a long time to unpeel himself from the wall.

"What was that all about?" he asked, sitting down on the stairs. He stared up at me, looking just as worried as he had when he'd fallen through the door at the end of the world and landed at my feet.

I sat down next to him. "I wish I knew."

"Did Tallard say something about gatecutters?"

"I think so. It didn't make much sense. *Nothing* he said made sense." The bees had settled down, but the buzzing sensation I'd felt still hadn't quite faded away. Was everyone staring at us? No, of course they weren't. I shook my head and tried to calm my nerves. "Anyway, Interworld Travel's got Tallard now. We don't have to worry about him."

"And I guess we won't be needing these anymore." Arthur patted the papers he'd carried out from the archives. He'd been clutching them the whole time Henry Tallard had been shouting, and the pages were wrinkled and damp. From the top sheet on the stack, a man's face leered up at us.

"Who's that?" I asked.

"Someone called . . . Crowbill Packard?" Arthur squinted at the name below the photograph. "He's a criminal, I guess. They all are." He fanned out the rest of the papers, revealing a whole prison's worth of frightening faces. "I'd gotten as far as *P* when I heard the bees. I haven't looked at the rest of these yet."

He held out the papers to me, and I shuffled through them. "You were looking for Rosemary?"

"That was the idea. When you said she was a criminal, I realized we might be looking in the wrong place. Anyone can apply for a passport, right? But not just anyone has a file in a box marked Known Criminals." Arthur shrugged. "I didn't find

Rosemary, though, and if Interworld Travel has Henry Tallard to talk to anyway, I guess we can stop looking for her."

The known criminals scowled up at me. I scowled right back. "No," I said. "We can't stop yet. What if Tallard's innocent?"

"Did he seem innocent to you just now? When he was shouting at us about the end of the world?" Arthur shook his head. "He's got to be the one who's been breaking the worldgates."

"But the last gate broke just now, while he was standing right in front of us!"

"Then he's . . . um . . . he's got accomplices."

"Exactly!" I said. "And Rosemary might be one of them. She lied to us, Arthur. She climbed out a window to escape from Interworld Travel. She's definitely guilty of *something*." When I reached the end of the pile of criminals without spotting Rosemary's face, I turned back to Crowbill Packard and started looking through them again. "I told Mrs. Bracknell I'd find her. I promised I'd help."

Arthur was quiet—the sort of quiet that lasts so long it fills the room. "You know, Lucy," he said at last, "I'm not sure anyone actually *wants* our help."

"What?" I said. "That's ridiculous. Why wouldn't they want it?"

Arthur shrugged. "I have seven older brothers and a father who hasn't got time for any of us. I'm used to being inconvenient. It feels a lot like this." He waved his arms, almost whacking a travel officer who was pushing her way past us up the stairs. "Mrs. Bracknell hasn't been down to the archives to see us once, and Thomas keeps sending you away—"

"Because they're *busy*. That's why they need us!" I was flipping through the photographs so quickly now that the pages sighed under my fingers, each one sounding a little more disappointed than the last. "Anyway, it's my job to help Interworld Travel. You're welcome to leave if you'd like, but I'm going to stay right here and . . . Oh!"

I blinked at the criminal's face on the page in front of me. For a second, I'd thought it was Rosemary. It wasn't, of course; the person in the photograph was a man old enough to be my father. But he had wild, curly hair, and instead of scowling at the camera, he wore a mischievous grin. "Leon Silos," I read. "Smuggler of otherworld goods, currently in prison."

"Silos?" Arthur took the paper, first holding it at arm's length, then bringing it right up to his nose. "Didn't you find a Rosemary Silos?"

I nodded. "She's the one who got her passport when she was just a baby. She'd be thirteen years old now."

"And you think she's the one we're looking for?"

"I think she could be." I got to my feet and took a few steps up the staircase, toward Thomas's office. Then I stopped. All the travel officers would be busy with Henry Tallard; if we barged in, it really *would* be inconvenient. "Come on," I said to Arthur, turning around. "We're going to show Interworld Travel just how helpful we can be."

11

"Are you sure we should be doing this?" Arthur asked as we stepped out of the revolving doors. "Didn't Thomas tell you not to leave the building?"

"He told me not to leave *alone*," I said, "and I'm not alone! Besides, we're not going far." According to her passport application, Rosemary Silos lived in Centerbury, only a short walk from the Interworld Travel building. "We'll be back before anyone notices we're not up to our elbows in archive files."

"What if Rosemary's moved?" asked Arthur. "Or—oh no— what if she *hasn't* moved, and she's not alone, and the house is full of criminals?"

I hadn't exactly thought of this. "We'll be careful," I promised him. "We won't go inside unless we're sure it's safe. We don't even have to talk to Rosemary; we only need to know if we've found the right girl. And we've got the bees for protection." At that particular moment, they were so happy to be out in the fresh air that they might have hummed past a whole band of smugglers without a second thought, but the Gatekeeper had always trusted them, so I did, too.

We walked along the main road past the House of Governors, the wide brick library, and the city's green promenade. Then the road turned a corner and deposited us in a shadowy, cramped neighborhood where skinny houses were packed together like teeth. The streets here were all knotted in tangles of pavement, turning back on themselves, looping in endless circles, and coming to sudden halts in front of dim alleys or high stone walls. I'd thought I'd known where I was going, but after six wrong turns in a row, I'd lost sight of the Interworld Travel building behind me, and I could hardly tell which way was up. Even the bees sounded agitated. "Can you figure out the way to Rosemary's?" I asked them. "Or at least the way back to the city center?"

SORRY, they said, moving uncertainly. LOST.

Arthur groaned. "I thought magical bees didn't have those kinds of problems."

As we turned onto a narrow street, the sun slipped behind a cloud and the wind picked up, blowing along my spine and making me shiver. I wished I'd thought to wear something warmer. "For worlds' sake, Rosemary," I said, "where *are* you?"

I hadn't noticed the man sweeping his front path, but as soon as I spoke, he noticed me. He raised his head from his work and peered at us. "Are you looking for my Rosie?" he called out.

Arthur and I stopped in our tracks.

"You must be." The man put his broom over his shoulder and started walking toward us. He had wild, curly hair and a mischievous grin. "Nonsensical girl. She never told me she had friends! I'm Mr. Silos, Rosie's pa."

"Smuggler of otherworld goods," Arthur whispered to me. "Currently *not* in prison."

"What's that?" Mr. Silos tilted his head. Then, before I knew quite what was happening, he was laughing and shaking hands with us both. "Come in and see Rosie before it starts to rain. And bring those bees with you. I hate to get on the wrong side of any animal with a stinger and an opinion."

Mr. Silos didn't give us much of a choice. He showed us up the stairs of a gray-painted house and into a narrow hallway. A chandelier flickered uncertainly above us; ahead of us was a closed door. Mr. Silos walked down the hall and gave the door a few good hard knocks. "Rosie?" he called.

"Should we leave?" Arthur whispered to me. "Right away, while his back is turned?"

I shook my head. Where would we go? Even if we could find our way back to Interworld Travel, I'd have to drag myself up to Thomas's office and tell him I hadn't been able to find Rosemary. If she was on the other side of that door, I wanted to know about it. "We'll be fine," I told Arthur.

"Even though Mr. Silos has a gun in his back pocket?"

I hadn't noticed that. It was an otherworld model, small and sleek, and it made my stomach turn cartwheels. I started inching backward down the hall.

Then Rosemary stuck her head out the door.

"I still haven't found the powdered lightning, Pa, if that's what you're wondering," she said. "I think the jar might have rolled behind those Rembrandts I brought back from East, but—Oh, *worlds!*" Rosemary stared at me, Arthur, and the bees. Then she slammed the door. Even from halfway down the hall, I could hear a series of locks clicking into place.

"She's been a little difficult lately," Mr. Silos said to us. Then he raised his voice and called through the door. "You can stop working, Rosie. Your friends are here to see you."

"They're not *friends*, Pa." Rosemary's voice was muffled but furious. "They're from Interworld Travel."

Mr. Silos turned back to look at me and Arthur, studying us as if we were exhibits behind glass at a museum. His right hand crept toward his gun. "They're children."

"They're the ones I told you about, don't you remember? Lucy and Arthur. The ones who are useless."

"Ah, you're right; that sounds familiar. Well, they've managed to get themselves here, so maybe they're not as useless as you thought." There was still a laugh in Mr. Silos's voice, but it wasn't quite so kind anymore. "You're travel officers, then?" he asked us.

"No," I said. "I work at the end of the world, and Arthur's a friend of mine. An Easterner."

"A prince!" said Arthur.

Behind the door, Rosemary snorted.

"And you're a smuggler," I called to her, "aren't you?"

Rosemary didn't answer. The fingers on Mr. Silos's right hand twitched.

"We're not dangerous," Arthur said quickly. "We just have some questions about the worldgates."

"The ones that have closed?" Mr. Silos raised an eyebrow.

"They've all closed," I told him.

His other eyebrow went up, too. "And you want Rosie to tell you all about it."

"I'm not talking to you!" Rosemary called. "You're wasting your time!"

"Hmm," said Mr. Silos. "Why don't we make a deal? Rosie will tell you what she knows about the worldgates—"

"Oh, *Pa*!"

"—if you'll answer a few of our questions in return. What do you think?"

I looked sideways at Arthur. He nodded.

"All right," I said, "but the bees stay with us."

A grin slid back across Mr. Silos's face. "Fair enough."

When Rosemary finally opened the locks on the door, Mr. Silos led us through it into a windowless sitting room hung with lanterns. The room smelled of smoke and spices, and it was filled with what could only be described as *stuff*. Wooden crates of all sizes lined the walls, hulked in corners, and surrounded a squat old sofa. They overflowed with otherworld goods: tins of preserved fish from North, tubes of repair-all glue from South, packets of bitter Northwestern karoa beans, and jars of fine-grained Southwestern sand. Books were piled everywhere, some titled in alphabets I'd never seen before. There were other objects, too: carved stone figurines of humans and animals, bolts of colorful fabric, jugs and bottles and beakers and tins. Even the bees hummed in wonder.

"Look at all this stuff, Lucy!" Arthur rapped his knuckles on one of the crates. According to the words stamped on its lid, it was full of something called Florida grapefruit.

"Don't touch that," I whispered. "It might be poisonous."

Mr. Silos cleared off two straight-backed chairs and steered us into them. "Sorry about the mess," he said. "If we'd known Interworld Travel would be making a visit, we would have cleared this room out days ago."

Rosemary sat in the center of the sofa. "You can't tell anyone what you've seen here," she said, "or I'll feed you both to a thistle-backed thrunt."

"What's that?" said Arthur.

Rosemary glowered at us. "You don't want to find out."

I didn't trust Rosemary much, but I believed her about that. "Did your pa smuggle all these goods into Southeast, then?"

"Oh, I don't smuggle anything at all." Mr. Silos settled down on the sofa next to Rosemary. "It's true I was a smuggler once, but that old Eastern gatekeeper caught me at it years ago. I went to prison, learned the error of my ways, handed over my passport—all the usual acts of contrition. I'm a model citizen."

"But all this stuff . . ."

"My three daughters love to travel. They bring home oth-erworld souvenirs from time to time, and I try to find good homes for their knickknacks. It's our family business. Silos and Daughters: purveyors of premium otherworld artifacts." Mr. Silos gestured around the room. "As you can see, we're very good at our work."

They must have been. All the gatekeepers were supposed to search travelers' bags before letting them pass through the worldgates. My Gatekeeper had always been particularly dili-gent about this part of her job. She liked to boast that she had a nose for smuggled goods, and she'd certainly found a lot of them: Every month, I handed off a heavy sack of contraband to the courier who came by from Interworld Travel. But we'd never caught Rosemary or her sisters bringing any otherworld goods into Southeast illegally. I didn't even remember meeting them at all. "How do you manage it?" I asked.

Mr. Silos laughed. "That's a family secret." He tousled Rosemary's curls. "I keep telling Rosie to stay home and out of trouble—she's my youngest—but she's stubborn. Aren't you, Rosie?"

Rosemary swatted his hand away and put her feet up on a crate. She was wearing real Northern military boots with gleam-ing steel toes; even if they were stolen, I couldn't help admiring them. "You might as well get to the point," she said, looking at me. "What do you want to know?"

"What were you doing at the end of the world?" I asked. "You're not Florence's deputy."

"No," Rosemary agreed. "I never said I was."

"You did! I'm sure of it!" I looked over at Arthur. "Didn't she?"

Rosemary sighed. "I didn't say anything. When we met, Lucy, you assumed I must be the gatekeeper's deputy, and I decided not to correct you. I figured you'd trust someone who worked for Interworld Travel."

I sank back into my seat. Was that how the conversation had gone? No wonder Rosemary had thought I was foolish. "Never mind that," I said. "You still haven't answered my question. What were you doing at Florence's house? Were you sealing the worldgate?"

"Of course not." Rosemary started pulling off her boots. "Why would I want to do that?"

I waited. The bees rumbled like far-off thunder.

"Fine," said Rosemary at last. "If you really want to know, I was supposed to go to South that day to pick up a shipment of flying carpets. People go wild for those things, especially in the worlds where they don't have much other transportation, and I'd been in touch with a woman who said she could find me a few. When I got to the end of the world, though, the gatehouse was a mess, and Florence was gone. Her deputy was, too. I didn't know what to do about it. I tried the door myself, but it wouldn't budge. Then after a while, you showed up, so I caught a ride with you back to Centerbury and made my way home."

"You climbed through a washroom window!"

"I'm a smuggler!" Rosemary said. "Just being in the lobby of

Interworld Travel makes me itch. I had to get out of there." She set her boots on the floor and pulled her knees up to her chest. "You probably think I'm awful, but I swear I'd never do anything to break the worldgates. We smugglers need them most of all! If they aren't opened soon, Silos and Daughters will go out of business."

Mr. Silos nodded. "My oldest girl, Sarah, is trapped in North, and Tillie is stranded somewhere in East. As long as those doors stay shut, they can't make it home. We've all been passing messages through the smugglers' channels, but no one in any of the worlds knows what's going on or who might be behind it all. That's why I'm keen to talk to you." He picked up a ball of something green and fuzzy from the floor—a fruit, maybe? an animal?—and tossed it into a crate behind him. "What's the news from Interworld Travel? What's Governor Bracknell doing to fix all this?"

"I'm not sure." I knew I'd promised to answer Mr. Silos's questions, but that didn't mean I was eager to do it. "Like I told you, we're not travel officers."

"You must know *something*. You've been there for days." Rosemary sounded impatient. "Or has Mrs. Bracknell just stuck you in a basement and forgotten about you?"

Arthur glanced at me. "As a matter of fact—"

"We're working in the archives," I said firmly. "The last worldgate just closed. That's the one between Southeast and South. All the worlds are cut off from one another now. The travel officers think Henry Tallard might be responsible."

"The otherworld explorer?" Rosemary shook her head. "That doesn't make sense."

"Lucy thought you might be his accomplice," Arthur put in.

This made Rosemary laugh. "Henry Tallard won't even speak to smugglers. He cares too much about his reputation. I can't believe he'd do anything to harm the worldgates."

"You should have seen him this morning, then," said Arthur. "He ran into the lobby and started shouting at everyone. The travel officers dragged him off to the House of Governors."

At this, Mr. Silos raised his eyebrows again. "I'd like to hear more about that."

With occasional contributions from the bees, Arthur and I told Mr. Silos and Rosemary what we could remember. The more we talked, the more confused they looked.

"And you're sure he said gatecutters?" Mr. Silos asked. "He thought you had Arabella Tallard's gatecutters here in East?"

Arthur nodded. "I can't understand it, either. Lucy told me they're locked up in a museum somewhere."

"They *were* in a museum," said Mr. Silos. "The Southern Museum of Magic and Industry. My parents took me on a trip to South when I was a boy, and I saw them myself."

"But they're not there anymore?"

"They were stolen." Mr. Silos gave me a curious look. "Half a year ago. No one at Interworld Travel told you?"

They hadn't, of course. Maybe the Gatekeeper had been alerted, but she hadn't passed the news along to me. "It never came up," I said.

"Then they kept the news quiet. I'm not surprised. None of the Interworld Travel commissions would want people to panic. The whole story blazed through the smugglers' channels, of course. We've had people searching for the gatecutters for months, but no luck yet."

Rosemary looked up at her father. "Do you think the person who took them is the same person who closed the worldgates?"

Mr. Silos hesitated. "It could be. If I wanted to separate all the worlds from one another, the first thing I'd do would be to steal the gatecutters. I wouldn't want anyone else undoing my hard work." He shrugged and put an arm around Rosemary. "All I know for sure is that if we don't get those doors open again soon, I'll go out of business, Sarah and Tillie won't be able to get home, and we'll all be in for eight worlds' worth of trouble."

12

Rosemary walked us as far as the main road. When we reached the intersection, she crossed her arms and stood there waiting, like she expected us to say something. I didn't know what it could be.

"Um," tried Arthur. "Thank you?"

"Don't come back to my pa's house," Rosemary said. "Leave us alone, and we'll do the same for you. Get us in a jam, and . . . well, you heard what I said about the thistle-backed thrunt." She pointed down the road. "Interworld Travel is that way. Don't get lost."

"I'm sorry about your sisters," I said, but Rosemary had already turned away.

The rain had stopped, but the air was unusually cold and the clouds still hung low. As we walked back into Centerbury, it felt to me as if the city was holding its breath, as if someone had shoved a breakable vase too close to a table's edge and everyone was waiting to see if it would topple and crash. People were gathered on the sidewalk to talk in low voices about the bakery that had run out of Northeastern flour, or about the medicines they badly needed from West, or about the eight Centerbury boys on a camping trip in Northwest whose parents were frantic with worry. A woman outside the library was asking for money to help her travel to both gatehouses and break the doors down herself. All the trains coming into the city were packed with people from the countryside who'd heard the ends of the world had been attacked and worried their villages might be in danger. They huddled together outside the train station, making clouds with their breath as they murmured the latest news: all eight worldgates closed, Henry Tallard taken away by travel officers, and no word from the House of Governors about what might happen next. As we passed the greenmarket, it began to snow. "The weather's all flummoxed," I heard one grocer call to another. "Clear skies at the ends of the world and spring snow in Centerbury! I don't like it. The world-fabric's not meant to be tampered with."

We'd been gone a lot longer than I'd hoped, but back at the Interworld Travel building, it seemed that no one had missed us. None of the travel officers even gave us a second look as we trudged up to the café for lunch and then back down to the basement. "What now?" said Arthur, closing the door to the archives behind us. "Do we go to Mrs. Bracknell and Thomas? Tell them we've found Rosemary?"

"I don't know," I admitted. I was reluctant to take a smuggler's word as fact, but Rosemary had made a good point: She had no reason to want the worldgates closed, and every reason to want them open. "I think she told us the truth," I said to Arthur, "or most of it, but it's hard to trust someone who says she wants to feed you to a . . . a spiky-bottomed . . . what was it?"

"A thistle-backed thrunt! I've been wondering about that, too." Arthur wandered down the archive shelves and came back carrying a thick book. "*Carnivorous Beasts Around the Worlds*," Arthur said, setting it down on the desk. "It was next to all those books about Henry Tallard."

I picked up the book and thumbed through it. The entry about thistle-backed thrunts was toward the end. "Found only in its native Western habitat," I read, "this common pest can chew through almost any substance and travel as fast as an automobile. It has four rows of teeth, a powerful jaw, and an insatiable appetite. A double-edged Western defense ray can destroy a thistle-backed thrunt, and most Westerners carry one at all times for this very purpose. If an unprepared traveler stumbles across a thrunt, however, he will certainly be devoured." I glanced at the illustration at the top of the page. "Honestly, Arthur, it looks kind of cute."

"Like a ball of fuzz with teeth?" Arthur asked. "And two beady eyes, and lots of spikes?"

"Yes," I said, "exactly."

"That's too bad," said Arthur, "because I think one is about to eat us."

The thrunt wasn't any bigger than my fist, but it was hungry, and it was fast. It rolled across the floor of the archives, blocking our path to the door. I clambered onto the desk. "This isn't West!" I said. "What's that thing doing here?"

The thrunt seemed to hear me. It paused for a moment. It munched the floorboards, making a noise like a chorus of saws. It blinked its small black eyes. Then it zoomed forward in a cloud of sawdust, heading straight for us.

Arthur climbed onto the desk, too, and I stepped aside as well as I could to make room for him. "Speaking of double-edged Western defense rays," he called over the din, "do you happen to have one?"

"Of course not!" I shouted. The thrunt had sunk its teeth into the bottom of the desk and was starting to gnaw through the solid oak. At the rate it was going, we'd be dumped straight into its path in a matter of minutes. We couldn't even send the bees for help; they'd flown up to the Travelers' Wing to thaw out after the snowstorm. "What are we going to do?"

"Maybe we can leap over the thrunt," said Arthur uncertainly, "and get to the door before it notices we're gone." He bent his knees, ready to jump.

"Wait!" I said. "We'll try this first and see what happens." I picked up *Carnivorous Beasts Around the Worlds*, held it in both hands, and heaved it toward the door.

The book hit the floor with a thud. The thrunt looked around, surprised. In less than a second, it had rolled over to the book. In five seconds more, it was gnawing on the desk again, and the book was nothing but pulp.

"Uh-oh," said Arthur.

The thrunt burped.

The desk began rocking under our feet. Arthur wobbled, and I grabbed his arm. "Help!" we shouted over and over, but no one came. I threw a folding chair at the thrunt, but the chair only bounced off its spikes. When Arthur dropped a box of passport files on top of it, it shredded the papers and the box into confetti.

"We're doomed," Arthur called to me. "That thing's indestructible!"

The battered old desk was tilting dangerously to one side now, and I had to brace my knees to keep from sliding to the floor. Arthur lay down on his stomach, grabbing the edge of the desk so tightly his knuckles went pale. One of his feet dangled a few inches above the thrunt's mouth. There was no point in trying to escape; I couldn't sprint half as quickly as the thrunt could move. What would it feel like, I thought in a panic, to be eaten from the toes up?

The door to the archives flew open, and someone cursed. Then a beam of golden light shot out from the doorway, there was a loud sizzling noise, and the thistle-backed thrunt split neatly in two.

I stared down at the halves of the thrunt. They lay steaming on the floor, filled with a thick orange sludge that had splattered everywhere. Arthur lifted his head and wiped the sludge from his glasses. "What just happened?" he said. "Is it dead? Am *I* dead?"

"Not a bad shot, right?" said Rosemary from the doorway. She was dressed all in black, with her gleaming military boots on her feet and a bag slung across her chest. "You're welcome, by the way."

I jumped off the wreckage of the desk. "What are you doing here?"

"Saving your lives, apparently." Rosemary walked into the room, picked up the pieces of thrunt, and wrapped them gingerly in cloth. "You two were about ten seconds away from being lunch. Which, coincidentally, is what *this* will be tomorrow." She tucked the cloth bundle into her bag. "Pa's going to love it. He makes a really excellent thrunt soup."

"How did you kill it?" I asked.

"Double-edged Western defense ray." Rosemary dug a coin-sized metal disc out of her pocket and held it up for me to see. "If you're going to spend any more time around thistle-backed thrunts, you should probably get one yourself."

"I'm not exactly planning on it," I said, "but thanks. For saving us, I mean."

Rosemary shrugged and looked away. "It wasn't any trouble."

"I'm confused," said Arthur, sliding off the desk. "I thought you were the one who let the thrunt loose in here in the first place."

"Me?" Rosemary shook her head and started walking around

the archive. "I said I'd have you eaten *if* you got me in a jam, and you haven't. Have you?"

Arthur and I both swore we hadn't.

"Then I don't want you dead," said Rosemary. "But I guess someone else feels differently. Or do you generally have thrunt infestations in this building?"

"I don't think so." I tried to clean the sludge from my arms but only ended up spreading it further. "The thrunt must have gotten here from West somehow. Could it have chewed its way between the worlds?"

"The fabric of time and space," said Rosemary, "is one of the few things a thrunt can't eat through, luckily enough. Otherwise, it would all look like Swiss cheese by now."

"Like what?"

"It's an Eastern thing," Arthur murmured to me. "Lots of holes."

"My point," said Rosemary, "is that the thrunt didn't end up here by itself. Someone put it here. It's a good thing I got here when I did. I would have showed up sooner, but I got turned around on the stairs somehow and ended up in a room with lots of fish tanks." She picked up a box from the shelves and peered into it.

"Wait a minute." I took the box out of her hands. "You still haven't told us why you came to Interworld Travel in the first place. Don't you hate this place? Doesn't it make you itch?"

"Like crazy," said Rosemary. "But I came to ask you a question. Are you sure the travel officers took Henry Tallard to the House of Governors this morning?"

"Sure enough," I said. As far as I knew, they'd marched him across the footbridge and down to the cells in the basement of the building. "That's where the woman in charge said he was going."

"That's strange," said Rosemary, "because after you left our house, I went by the House of Governors myself. I've got a friend who works in maintenance there, and I thought she might get me in to see Tallard. If he really knows what's happening to the worldgates, Pa and I want to hear about it. But when my friend went to look for Tallard, she said she couldn't find him. He wasn't in any of the cells, or anywhere else in the building." Rosemary looked grim. "So I wanted to know: are you wrong, or are you lying?"

Before I could think of anything to say to that, the door to the archives opened again, and Mrs. Bracknell came through it.

"Lucy?" she called. "Prince Arthur? I just wanted to see how you were getting along, and . . ." Her voice trailed off. She took in the half-eaten desk, the confetti of paperwork, and the explosion of orange sludge. Then she turned and saw Arthur, Rosemary, and me. The muscles of her jaw were tight.

"Lucy Eberslee," she said, measuring out each word precisely, "what in all the worlds is going on?"

13

Mrs. Bracknell wasn't the sort of person who wasted time. We'd hardly finished telling her about the thistle-backed thrunt before she'd called for a small army of travel officers to join us in the archives. They spread out through the aisles with weapons and searchlights, looking for stray otherworld creatures under shelves and in boxes. "And who are you?" Mrs. Bracknell asked Rosemary. Then she held up a hand. "Wait. I've got it. Brown eyes, curls, a few years younger than you'd like to be: you must be the girl who pretended to work for Florence."

Rosemary took a step backward. I could see her eyeing the doorway, as if she were calculating how fast she could run through it, and her hands were clenched into fists. I wondered if she was nervous. She didn't look half as brave as she had after slicing up the thrunt.

"I was wrong, Mrs. Bracknell. About Rosemary, I mean." I

hadn't meant to say it loudly, but my voice echoed through the archives, and half of the travel officers in the room turned to stare at me. Mrs. Bracknell's eyes were brighter than ever and fixed on mine. Being eaten from the toes up would have been excruciating, I knew, but it couldn't have been much worse than this. "I made a mistake."

"A mistake?" Mrs. Bracknell repeated the words carefully.

I nodded. At least Rosemary's fists had unclenched. "She didn't have anything to do with sealing the worldgates. She's not dangerous. And she saved our lives just now."

Mrs. Bracknell gave Rosemary a thoughtful look. "All right," she said, "but I'd like to talk to her just the same. If she was near the Southern worldgate when it closed, her observations could be helpful to us." She turned and strode toward the door. "For now, all three of you can come with me. Quickly, please, before anyone gets eaten."

With two travel officers close behind us to keep us in check, Mrs. Bracknell marched us up the stairs to the seventh floor. "This is my fault, really," she said, shepherding us all into my bedroom. "I thought you'd be out of harm's way at Interworld Travel, but it's clear I was wrong about that. With otherworld creatures roaming the halls and explorers storming the lobby, who knows what might happen! You aren't trained travel officers, and I'm responsible for your protection." She looked over our heads at the officers who'd come with us, a tall, wiry woman and a short, stocky man wearing identical suits and solemn expressions. "Celeste, Kip, I'd like you two to stay with our guests until the situation with the worldgates is resolved. Don't let them leave the Travelers' Wing, and don't let any unauthorized visitors into their rooms without my permission. I'll have the café bring their meals up to them."

"Excuse me?" Arthur looked as dismayed as I felt. "You mean we're stuck here?"

"A thrunt didn't try to eat *me*," Rosemary pointed out. "Can't I go home? My pa will be wondering where I am."

"I'm sorry," said Mrs. Bracknell, "but I can't allow it. All the worlds are in crisis. The safest place for all of you is right here in this room."

"But we can still be helpful!" I said. "There's got to be something more we can do. With the worldgates closed, and the crowds in the lobby to deal with, and—"

Mrs. Bracknell sighed. There were dark circles under her eyes, and I wondered how long it had been since she'd had any sleep. "The most helpful thing you can do now, Lucy, is to follow my instructions. As soon as I'm sure there's no threat to you or to your friends, you'll be free to leave. Meanwhile, you'll be perfectly safe with Kip and Celeste. They've worked in the most unstable corners of the worlds and lived to tell the tale."

"We'll be safe, all right," Rosemary said to me as Mrs. Bracknell left the room. "So safe it hurts."

Kip and Celeste stood guard outside our rooms: one in the hallway between my door and Arthur's, and one just outside the Travelers' Wing. Every so often they'd switch positions, but they didn't have much to say to us, and they never once cracked a smile.

To be fair, there wasn't much to smile about. Rosemary stomped between my room and Arthur's, shouting about being kidnapped and imprisoned against her will. Arthur chased after her, urging her not to slice up the furniture with her double-edged defense ray. The bees flew listlessly around a vase of flowers someone had left on the table beside my bed. Rain splattered the windowpanes. And I sat hunched on the sofa, trying to think of something I could say to Mrs. Bracknell to convince her I wasn't most useful when I was locked up out of sight.

"I could go get the travel records from the gatehouse!" I said. "The ones from the past few days before the door closed. Mrs. Bracknell wanted to see them earlier."

Arthur shook his head. "She's probably had her officers bring them back here by now."

"Fine. Then I'll visit the families of people who are trapped in other words. Or I'll help to calm down the diplomats. I'll tell them everything will be all right."

"What makes you think it will be all right?" Rosemary snapped. "We're trapped in this place that's practically making me break out in hives. Southeast is totally cut off, no one in this entire city seems to be able to do anything about it, Henry Tallard has gone missing somehow, someone is probably trying to kill you, Mrs. Bracknell wants to interrogate me later, I'm going to be in buckets of trouble with Pa, I might never see my sisters again, I've got a perfectly good thrunt going to waste in my bag, and I've lost my house keys!" She flopped down next to me on the sofa. "Please, Lucy, go ahead. Tell me everything will be fine."

I moved to make room for Rosemary, and something in my back pocket crinkled. I pulled it out: it was the folded-up packet of papers I'd snuck from my own file in the archives that morning. "Oh, worlds," I said. I'd forgotten all about it.

I unfolded the papers and pulled my knees up to my chest. There was my own handwriting in careful blue ink: my application to work at the end of the world. Bits of it had been underlined and circled in red pen, as if it were a school assignment, and there was an extra page clipped to the back. *Candidate assessment*, it read in Thomas's familiar scrawl:

CANDIDATE DOES NOT MEET MINIMUM REQUIREMENTS FOR EMPLOYMENT (EXPERIENCE, EXPERTISE, TALENT, ETC.). UNDER NORMAL CIRCUMSTANCES, CANDIDATE WOULD NOT BE ELIGIBLE FOR A GATEHOUSE POSITION. HOWEVER, RETIRED GOVERNOR W. EBERSLEE, GOVERNMENT OFFICIAL G. EBERSLEE, AND THIS TRAVEL OFFICER ALL RECOMMEND AN EXCEPTION BE MADE IN THIS CASE. OTHER APPLICATIONS HAVE BEEN UNREMARKABLE, AND GATEKEEPER STATES THAT THE DEPUTY POSITION IS NOT CRUCIAL AT THE EASTERN END OF THE WORLD. CANDIDATE WILL RECEIVE NECESSARY TRAINING AND IS UNLIKELY TO GIVE US TROUBLE. —T.E.

Underneath that, there was a single line added in someone else's writing:

EXCEPTION GRANTED. SHE CAN START NEXT WEEK. DON'T MAKE ME REGRET IT. —C.B.

My cheeks stung, and my whole face felt as hot as if I'd stuck it into an oven. I'd always guessed I couldn't have gotten my job on my own, but to know it for sure—well, I almost wished they'd never hired me in the first place. Had my parents been so worried about my future that they'd marched into Mrs. Bracknell's office and demanded that she find a place for me at Interworld Travel? Was Mrs. Bracknell already regretting her decision to bring me on? It was too embarrassing to think about.

Arthur sat down on the other side of me. "What's that?" he asked, craning his neck to look at the papers.

"Nothing." I crumpled up the whole packet, shoved it deep in the crevice between the sofa cushions, and walked over to the window. "It's not important."

It was raining harder now, and the wind had picked up. The sky was low and greenish. Toward the ends of the world, over the patchwork fields and the mountains, I could see hints of sunlight, but here in Centerbury, trees were bending, umbrellas were gusting inside out, and it looked like there was worse weather to come.

Back on the sofa, Arthur had dug out my Interworld Travel application. I wished I'd torn it into pieces. "Oh, Lucy," he said, reading it. "I'm sorry."

"Did something terrible happen?" Rosemary leaned over eagerly.

"Listen," said Arthur, "I know you must feel awful, but it's not the end of the world."

I blinked at him. Then I sat right down on the floor where I'd been standing. The bees hummed around my head. "It's not the end of the world," I murmured. But Rosemary had lost her house keys. Everyone at Interworld Travel kept getting turned around on the stairs and in the hallways; even Huggins had tried to go to breakfast and ended up in the archives somehow. Arthur and I had gotten hopelessly lost on our way to Rosemary's, it was awfully late in the season for snow, and the storm gathering over us now was getting stronger by the minute. I wondered exactly how much of the Interworld Travel Commission's mail had been sent to the wrong address recently.

"Lucy?" Arthur looked worried. "Are you all right?"

I couldn't believe I hadn't realized it sooner. "What if this *is* the end of the world?"

14

Arthur and Rosemary looked blank.

"Think about it," I said. I kept my voice low so Kip and Celeste wouldn't overhear me. "Have you lost anything lately? Other than the house keys?"

Arthur frowned. "My bath towels keep going missing," he said. "I've had to ask the information desk for more three times so far."

"And I never found that jar of powdered lightning," said Rosemary. "But you can't actually mean . . ." Thunder rumbled overhead, and Rosemary trailed off. She twisted a curl around her finger. "When I ended up in that room with all the fish tanks," she said quietly, "I couldn't figure out how I'd gotten so turned around."

"I couldn't find the Travelers' Wing yesterday," said Arthur. "I thought I was going in the right direction, but somehow I wound up in a room full of typewriters on the fifth floor instead. I was too embarrassed to mention it."

"And I made three wrong turns before I found Thomas's office this morning," I said. "Either we're all having the worst luck possible, or someone has opened a door into another world nearby."

"How?" Arthur wanted to know. "With the gatecutters?"

"Never mind how," said Rosemary. "I'd like to know *who*."

They both looked at me. It took me a few seconds to realize they were expecting me to answer their questions.

"I've got no idea!" I said. "I'm as confused as you are."

Arthur stood up and started pacing the room. "First all the worldgates were closing," he said, "and no one knew why. Now it's possible that new worldgates are opening, and still no one knows why."

"Well, *someone* knows why," said Rosemary. "The person who's doing it ought to know pretty well."

"It might not be the same person," I pointed out. "Anyway, we don't know for sure that we're right. Should we tell Interworld Travel what we think? If there really is a new worldgate that's opened up, maybe we can help them find it."

"We are *not* telling Interworld Travel," Rosemary snapped.

"The travel officers probably won't even pay attention to us," said Arthur, "and even if they do, they'll only tell us to let the professionals take care of it."

"All right," I said. "Then we'll find the worldgate ourselves."

"Good." For the first time since we'd met, Rosemary smiled at me. "Let's do it."

114

Kip and Celeste couldn't stay awake all night to guard us, they explained, so they were taking the overnight hours in shifts. This suited our plan perfectly. As soon as Celeste had trudged off to get some sleep, Rosemary dug through her bag and pulled out a wad of plastic the size of a pencil eraser. At least, that's how big it was at first. As she peeled away the plastic layers, though, the bundle grew and grew. "Shrink wrap," I told Arthur, who was staring at Rosemary as if she were some kind of magician. The stuff was so expensive that almost no one in any of the worlds could afford it, but if Silos and Daughters had access to a stash of Southern shrink wrap, at least I knew how they were able to sneak so many smuggled goods through the worldgates. Wherever she was, the Gatekeeper would want to know about this.

When the last layer of shrink wrap fell away, Rosemary lifted the lid of the box that had been wrapped inside it and pulled out two thin silver cards a little bigger than my palm. The bottom half of each card was engraved with letters from the most common interworld alphabets, and the top half was a smooth piece of metal. I'd never seen anything like it. "What are they?" I asked as Rosemary fiddled with the silver cards, pressing buttons I couldn't see.

"Smugglers' tools." Rosemary didn't look up. "They're called InterComs—interworld communications devices. Western technology, not magic. They can send messages to other Inter-Coms anywhere else in the worlds. Don't ask me how it all works. It *does* work, though, and that's the important thing."

I'd wondered how Mr. Silos had been communicating with his friends in other worlds since the doors had closed. "Are these the smugglers' channels your pa was talking about?"

Rosemary looked annoyed. "You can't tell anyone, or—"

"You'll have me eaten?"

"I was going to say my pa will kill me, but all right." Rosemary handed one of the cards to me and the other to Arthur. "Here. I've set these up so we can all send messages to one another. I've got my own InterCom in my bag."

I flipped the card over and back again, admiring it. "What else do you have in your bag?"

"Things to sell. Things to trade." Rosemary gave me a squirrelly sort of look, buckled up the bag, and shoved it aside. "I'm supposed to be bringing those InterComs to a customer in Northwest, by the way. You'd better not lose them, or Pa will sell your ears on the black market to make up for it."

Arthur poked at his InterCom. "Please tell me you're joking about that."

"Of course." Rosemary grinned at him. "Your ears aren't even worth half the cost."

I hadn't considered the exact price of Arthur's ears before, but his lungs, at least, turned out to be extremely valuable. Just before midnight, we all said good night to Kip, Arthur and I crawled into our beds, Rosemary curled up on my sofa, and we switched off the lamps.

A few minutes later, in the stillness of the Travelers' Wing, Arthur let out a shout.

"Help!" he called. It was loud enough to make me sit straight up in bed, even though I'd been expecting it. "I need help right away!"

I rolled out of my blankets and listened: there were Kip's footsteps as he hurried down the hall, there was Arthur's door swinging open on its squeaking hinges, there was the slam as someone closed it again.

"That's our cue," said Rosemary in the darkness.

Soon I could hear Arthur's voice again, quieter this time. "I thought there might be someone hiding in my bedroom," he was saying earnestly. "At home—in my palace, because that's where princes live, you know—I have servants who sweep all the spies and assassins out from behind the curtains every night. I'm just not used to doing it myself. Would it be too inconvenient for you to take a look?"

I didn't know how long Kip would be willing to put up with His Royal Highness's demands, but I guessed time wasn't on our side. Rosemary and I hurried out of the bedroom as silently as we could. The Travelers' Wing was empty, thank the worlds, and so were the hallways beyond it. Somewhere below us, Thomas and the rest of Mrs. Bracknell's team were probably working late into the night, but up on the seventh floor, every-thing was dark and quiet.

Rosemary took out her InterCom. As she tapped away on her own card, a message in glowing white light appeared on the plain silver surface of mine: *Everyone ready?*

Yes, I wrote back. The message popped up at the top of

my device, and on Rosemary's, too, but these letters were blue instead of white. The way they flickered on the surface reminded me a little of the bees, who were back in the Travelers' Wing with Arthur. I hoped they were doing their best to keep him out of trouble.

After a few seconds, my message vanished, and new letters took their place. This time, they were green. *Hello!* said Arthur. *Have sent Kip into washroom to look for assassins. Princes are very demanding.*

Rosemary snickered a little at this. *Where first, Lucy?*

It didn't take me long to type out the answer: *Sculpture.*

We wound down the seven flights of stairs, keeping our eyes open for worldgates and our ears open for travel officers. The lights in the lobby were off, and all the worried people who'd been waiting there had been led away to worry somewhere else. No one stood behind the information desk. On the other side of the tall glass wall, a few streetlamps flickered, casting just enough light for us to make our way to the sculpture.

At first I thought the space between the glass globes was completely dark, just the way it had looked in the daylight. Then Rosemary nudged me with her elbow, and I looked where she was pointing. The Southeast globe was glowing, not at either end of the world but at a spot near the middle. The glow was so faint that if the room had been any brighter, I wouldn't have noticed it. Even in the darkness, I had to squint to make it out. The longer I looked, though, the more sure of it I was: thin, tentative lines of light radiated across the fabric of time and space, each connecting Southeast to one of the other worlds. There had to be at least four of them.

I heard Rosemary draw in her breath.

Many worldgates? I asked her.

I think so, she wrote back. *But where?*

We made our way around the lobby, opening all the doors we could find. Some of them led to washrooms or coatrooms, but none of them led to another world. On the second floor, we searched through the café without any luck and headed toward the Explorers' Museum. *Found that other world yet?* Arthur asked as we walked. *I'm telling Kip about my greatest fears. Death. Ghosts. Cats.*

"Cats?" I whispered to Rosemary.

She shrugged. "People from East are strange."

Anyway, said Arthur, *I think he's getting bored. And maybe a little angry.*

We're going as fast as we can, I typed. *But we can't possibly open every door in this building.* And what if the door to another world was just *outside* Interworld Travel? What if it was across the street, in the House of Governors, or tucked away in a back alley behind some trash bins? *We need more time,* I told Arthur.

All right. The green letters flickered skeptically. *I'll try.*

There wasn't another world behind the museum door, or in any of the dusty exhibits. We gave up on the second floor and headed back to the spiral staircase.

Halfway up the flight of stairs, I froze. The lights were on in the third-floor hallway—the hall where Mrs. Bracknell and her

119

travel officers worked. We'd run past the landing on our way downstairs, hoping no one would see us, but this time I could hear voices nearby. Somewhere very close to us, two travel officers were laughing.

"Wait," I whispered to Rosemary. We crouched in the shadows.

The travel officers were complaining about their job assignments. One of them, with a voice that rasped like a pepper grinder, had just gotten back from chasing Henry Tallard, and her boots had been ruined in the Great Southeastern Swamp. "How's it been here?" she asked. "Any progress on the eighth floor?"

"Not as much as Mrs. B would like," the other officer said. "We've been quilting all week, but someone's got to have wondered about that snowstorm. We'll need to do more. And we still haven't shored up the fabric on the other side of the doorways; I'm not sure it's safe. . . ."

Rosemary elbowed me hard, and I yelped.

I clapped a hand over my mouth, but it was too late. The travel officers paused. "Did you hear something?" the one with the pepper-grinder voice asked. "Out in the hall?"

A prickle of panic spread over my skin. I tried hard not to breathe. Rosemary buried her head in her hands.

"Probably that otherworld farmer again," the other officer said. "He's always coming in and out at strange hours. Says he can't get any rest in this building."

"I know what he means." Both officers laughed again. Their voices faded away as they moved down the hall, away from us.

"What was that about?" I hissed.

"I was getting your attention!" Rosemary whispered. "The eighth floor! Did you hear what they said?"

"Of course I heard it." I blazed up the stairs ahead of her. "And I didn't need any help from your elbow."

The way up to the eighth floor was still blocked off with plywood and tape, but we made a gap in the barricade and squeezed through it. The stairs beyond were covered in dust. Someone—or several someones, it was hard to tell—had made footprints up and down them. "I ran into Mrs. Bracknell coming down these stairs," I whispered to Rosemary. "She said she'd been checking on the renovations."

The eighth floor really did seem to be under construction. It looked like a skeletal version of all the floors below it, as though someone had pulled away all the paint and plaster to reveal the truth of the building's bones: wood and metal, boards and nails. Some of the walls were hung with huge quilts of shimmering fabric. A few more unfinished quilts were strewn across the floor, leaking their cotton batting. There were skylights in the ceiling, and through them we could see the stars.

Rosemary pulled a flashlight out of her bag and cast the beam around the space. There didn't seem to be much of anything in front of us, but on the floor, a trail of footprints in the dust led to the left. "This way," I whispered, pointing.

Are you there? said Arthur. *Are you talking without me? You promised you wouldn't talk without me.*

We followed the footprints and found ourselves in a long,

121

empty corridor. Dust motes swirled like fireflies in Rosemary's flashlight beam as she cast it from one end of the passageway to the other. We both sucked in our breath, and I forgot all about replying to Arthur: one whole side of the corridor was lined with doors.

They weren't regular wooden doors, either—not all of them, at least. It looked as though a carpenter had run out of materials and started scavenging doors from other people's buildings. One was white, flanked by marble columns; one was black and perfectly smooth; one was painted a glossy red, with a brass knocker. As Rosemary passed the flashlight beam over each of them, I counted: there were seven doors in all. Two were blocked off with yellow construction tape. All seven were hung with padlocks.

Hello? It was Arthur again. *Lucy? Rosemary? Are you there? Are you safe? Where are you? What's happening? Are you in danger? Do you need help? Do you need sandwiches?*

Hush! said Rosemary. *We found something. Not sure what it is.*

I started walking down the corridor. I wasn't sure what was down there, either, but I was determined to find out.

15

The first door I came to was built of unfinished boards and tacked together with shiny nail heads. It looked as though it belonged on the side of a barn. When I got up close, I could see that the padlock had three little numbered discs on its side: you needed a combination to open it.

Or at least most people would have needed a combination. Rosemary, however, didn't seem to think this was necessary. She pulled out her double-edged Western defense ray, aimed its golden light at the padlock, and—

"Stop!" I grabbed her wrist. "Don't do that!"

"For worlds' sake!" Rosemary fumbled the defense ray, nearly taking off her own fingertips in the process. "Watch out, Lucy! Do you want me to slice myself into pieces?"

"Sorry," I whispered. "I just thought that . . . well, if you cut off the lock, whoever put it there in the first place will notice.

They'll know someone's been sneaking around."

"All right," said Rosemary, "but if I *don't* cut it off, we won't be able to open the door."

"Not necessarily." I took the lock in my own hands. "Let me try."

I couldn't see Rosemary rolling her eyes, but I felt sure that's what she was doing. "We're going to be here for hours," she said under her breath. "Kip is finally going to run out of places to search for assassins, and Arthur will show up here with a tray of sandwiches, and—"

The lock popped open in my hands. I grinned and handed it to Rosemary.

"Lucy Eberslee." She stared down at the lock, keeping it cupped in her palms like a jewel. "How in all the worlds did you do that?"

While Rosemary had been complaining, I'd turned the dials on the lock until the combination matched the one I'd used back at the gatehouse to put important papers in the Gatekeeper's special safe. It seemed like a great trick, but it wasn't, really; practically anyone else in the building would have been able to do the same. "I'm an Interworld Travel employee," I reminded Rosemary, "and Interworld Travel uses the same passcode for everything."

"They do?" Rosemary couldn't help sounding curious. I felt sure this particular piece of information was going to make its way through the smugglers' channels in no time at all. She looked down at the lock, but I'd learned a thing or two from the

Gatekeeper, and I'd already turned all the dials back to zero. "What's the passcode?"

"I know you think I'm foolish," I said, "but I'm not *that* foolish."

Rosemary groaned and handed the lock back to me. "Honestly, Lucy, are you still upset about that? I've already apologized for saying it."

I frowned at her. "You haven't, actually."

"I saved you from the thistle-backed thrunt!"

"Keeping someone from getting eaten," I said, "is not the same as apologizing to them."

"It isn't?" Rosemary looked genuinely baffled. "Well, then, I'm sorry." She hesitated. "And thanks for vouching for me with Mrs. Bracknell. I'd have been in bad trouble if you hadn't."

"You're welcome." I tugged at the handle of the barn door.

Rosemary wrinkled her nose. "What's that smell?"

I'd noticed it, too. As soon as I'd started to open the door, the air on the eighth floor had filled with the scent of fresh-cut grass, damp earth, and something more pungent, more fertile, something that could only be described as . . .

"Cows," said Rosemary.

We stared through the doorway. The cows stared back at us.

The barn door had opened into a wide green meadow under a sunny sky. The land was flat and it stretched for miles, but I could see forests in the distance, and beyond that, the hazy blue shadows of mountains. Here and there, buttercups sprang up. A cricket creaked in the grass nearby. Overall, it seemed like

125

a pretty nice place to be a cow. There were at least twenty of them grazing in the meadow, and they didn't look particularly happy to see us.

Rosemary didn't look happy, either. "Northeast," she said, making a face. "Of all the worlds to find behind a secret door. It figures." She shrugged and stepped through the doorway.

Watching her go was like staring at an optical illusion: she was still so close I could have touched her, but she was walking into another world. I'd never been allowed to stand near the worldgate while the Gatekeeper helped travelers through it, but I'd always imagined the process to be a little more dramatic than walking into the next room. Even Arthur had made a grand entrance, more or less.

"Are you coming?" Rosemary called back to me. She was standing in the grass on the other side of the door now. "I know it's only Northeast, but it's not the worst place in the worlds."

"All right." I tried to ignore the twinge of guilt in my stomach. I hadn't thought to bring my passport with me, and even if I'd been able to file all the necessary paperwork beforehand, it wouldn't have changed the fact that I was sneaking through an unauthorized worldgate in the dead of night. Still, when a door between the worlds opens up in front of you, you'd have to be crazy not to pass through it.

Folds of shimmering material rustled under my feet as I walked through the doorway. Someone had tugged at the fabric of time and space, gathering it together and bundling it up to shorten the distance between the two worlds. Around the edges of the doorway, where the fabric had been cut, it was starting to fray; if the Gatekeeper had been there to see it, she would have taken out her maintenance kit on the spot. "Shoddy workmanship," she would have said. "If we don't take care of the fabric of time and space, it'll be unraveling around our ears." I stepped carefully, trying not to do any more damage.

Then I came out into the sunlight and blinked.

Now that I'd reached the other side of the worldgate, I realized why the cows looked so dubious. I'd expected the barn door to be attached to an actual barn, but when I turned around to look at the doorway I'd just passed through, all I saw was a dark rectangle, a gaping hole in the fabric between the worlds. If I shaded the sun from my eyes, I could still make out the dusty floor of the Interworld Travel hallway. I reached back to pull the door shut behind me, wondering what it would look like—a door standing all by itself in the middle of the meadow?—but Rosemary stuck out her foot to stop me. "Leave it open," she said, "at least a little bit. We don't want to get stuck here."

She had a point. The meadow was beautiful, a hundred times nicer than the bustle of Centerbury, but it was a strange place to build a door between the worlds. The only signs of human life were a big whitewashed farmhouse and a few outbuildings. I hoped they wouldn't be wrecked by all the whirlwinds and hailstorms that were sure to be passing through.

"Are you sure we're in Northeast?" I asked Rosemary. "There are farms all over the worlds."

"Only three worlds have cattle, though. The cows in East and Southeast aren't exactly geniuses, but *these* cows—they know things." Rosemary bent over to look them in their deep brown eyes. "We're in Northeast, aren't we?" she asked.

Some of the cows nodded. The others couldn't be bothered.

"I wonder," I said, "if these cows know Huggins."

A few cows nodded again, as if they might.

"That worldgate in the middle of your pasture. Has it been here long?"

All the cows shook their heads vigorously. A few even mooed.

"Do you know Mrs. Bracknell?" I asked. "Is she the one who opened it?"

This time, the cows just stared at me. They were pleasant enough, I decided, but they weren't half as useful as a horde of magical bees.

"The bees!" I said, remembering. "Arthur!" We hadn't sent him a message since we'd found the worldgate, and if my wildly flashing InterCom was any indication, he wasn't happy about it.

You found something? he'd written. *Are you in another world right now? Is this thing working? Uh-oh. Lucy? I think you should come back. Kip is getting kind of mad. He says he isn't paid to babysit royalty. He says he's leaving. What should I do? I don't think I can stop him. There he goes! He's in the hallway now. He's knocking on your door. He seems a little suspi*

That's where the messages cut off.

"Oh no." I waved my InterCom at Rosemary. "There's trouble. We've got to get back."

Kip was waiting for us in the Travelers' Wing. He obviously wasn't happy. Neither was Arthur, who was standing next to him and looking as though he'd rather be anywhere else. When he saw us running down the hall, though, his shoulders came down from his ears and he broke into a grin. "Here they are!" he said to Kip. "I told you there was nothing to worry about. They're both completely fine."

"No thanks to you," Kip told him. Then he turned his glare on us. "I'd like to know what you thought you were doing."

"We went dancing!" I'd thought of this as Rosemary and I had hustled down the stairs and dragged the construction barrier back into place behind us. "In Centerbury. We were bored, and we decided to sneak out. We're very sorry. It was irresponsible of us."

"Yes." Rosemary nodded solemnly. "We're the worst."

"Dancing?" Kip looked at Arthur. "I thought you said they went out for pastries."

Arthur looked stricken. "I did say that, didn't I?"

"Well," I said, "that's because we got our pastries first. Everyone knows you can't dance until you've eaten some pastries."

"We thought of saving one for you," Rosemary told Kip, "but then we didn't."

This didn't seem to make Kip feel any better. "Mrs. Bracknell isn't going to be happy about this," he said. "It's lucky you both made it home safely."

Arthur was looking around overhead, as though he'd

129

misplaced something in midair. "Ah, Lucy?" he said. "Are the bees still out dancing?"

"The bees?" I shook my head. "The bees didn't come with us. They're here with you."

"No," said Arthur, "they're not. I thought you had them."

"And we thought you did!"

"Maybe they went off somewhere on their own," Rosemary suggested.

"Without telling us? I don't think they'd do that." It was true that the bees didn't like to ask for permission, but they were usually thoughtful enough to let me know what they were up to. "Did you see them go?" I asked Kip.

He shrugged. "I'm supposed to keep an eye on you three. No one said anything about bees."

I pushed past him into Arthur's room. The air should have been buzzing with the beat of hundreds of little wings, but the whole room was silent and still. I started to feel sick to my stomach. The closet door was shut, so I tugged it open. At first I didn't see anything except the few pieces of clothing we'd hung up neatly on hangers. Then I heard a thin, frantic hum.

The floor of the closet was carpeted in bees. They were moving, but barely; some crawled listlessly toward my feet when they realized I was standing there, and others beat their wings, hovering in the air for a moment or two before falling back into the crowd. I wasn't any sort of expert when it came to bees, but even I could tell that something was badly wrong.

I knelt down and opened my hands. A few of the strongest

bees dragged themselves onto my palms. "What's happened to you?" I asked. "Are you sick?"

The bees writhed a little. "They want to talk," said Arthur in a low voice, "but they're not strong enough."

"I think they're trying." Slowly, with enormous effort, the bees in my hands were shuffling into formation. Rosemary and Kip had followed us into the closet by now, and all four of us watched as the bees spelled out a word letter by letter:

F-L-O-W-E-R-S.

Arthur frowned. "You want us to bring you flowers?"

All the bees quivered violently. They didn't like that idea at all.

"Maybe flowers are what made them sick," I said. "Maybe they found a plant that's harmful to bees, or maybe—"

"Oh, worlds," said Rosemary. "The vase!"

"What vase?" I asked, but Rosemary was already gone. She'd run into my room, and when the rest of us followed her, I saw what she'd meant. There on the windowsill was the bunch of bedraggled purple flowers that had appeared in my room that afternoon, drooping in a vase made of green glass. On the sill around the flowers, more bodies of bees were scattered: at least ten, maybe twenty. They lay silent and still, and when Rosemary nudged them with a fingertip, they didn't move.

"Oh no," said Arthur. He sat down on the bed, looking grim.

"Who brought these flowers here?" I spun around to face Kip. He looked as alarmed as the rest of us. "Who put the vase in this room?"

Kip stammered that he didn't know anything about it. "It looks like an otherworld flower to me, Miss Eberslee," he said, "but plants aren't my specialty. I don't know what you'd call it."

"I," said Rosemary, "would call it a warning."

16

It didn't take long for Kip to decide that the three of us were too much for one travel officer to handle. He went to find Celeste, taking the poisonous purple flowers with him and locking all three of us back in my bedroom for safekeeping. While Rosemary told Arthur what we'd found on the eighth floor of Interworld Travel, I knelt by the closet and tended to the bees. The ones who'd died must have come closest to the flowers; the rest were still doing poorly, but when I placed a little saucer of sugar water on the floor, they perked up enough to shuffle over and taste it. If any of the bees knew who'd placed the flowers on our windowsill, though, they were too exhausted to tell me about it.

"There were seven doors?" Arthur was practically bouncing with excitement. "And there are seven worlds besides this one, aren't there? I'll bet each door leads to a different world." He sat down on the bed for half a second, then sprang right up again. "Does one of them lead to East?"

"We didn't get a chance to check," said Rosemary. "Lucy barely had time to put the padlock back on the door to Northeast after we got your messages. But I think you might be right. Seven doors, seven worlds." She walked over to the window, where raindrops from the evening's storm were still trailing down the glass. "Pa is going to lose his mind when he hears about this."

"And Mrs. Bracknell knows about the worldgates?"

"I think she's in charge of them," I said. "That's how the travel officers made it sound, at least. Anyway, no one's going to build any doors to other worlds in this building without her permission."

"I don't trust Mrs. Bracknell," Rosemary said darkly. "I don't trust anyone here."

Even I was starting to agree with her. What if no one at Interworld Travel had wanted our help in the first place? What if they'd only wanted to get us out of their way? They hadn't told us about their secret doors to other worlds, they'd locked us up, and someone in the building was trying to hurt us—or at least to scare us badly. "The thrunt could have come through one of those new worldgates," I said. "The poisonous flowers, too. Anyone who knows about the eighth floor could have brought them over."

A key turned in the lock just then, and all of us went quiet. Kip stalked into the room, followed by Celeste and then, surprisingly, by Thomas. Thomas was the youngest and least imposing of the three, but Kip and Celeste wouldn't quite meet his eyes as they stood back to make room for him.

"All still here?" Thomas said. "No more illegal dancing excursions?" He winked at me and made a show of counting our heads as though we were all back in school. "One, two, three. Well, that's a relief."

I was glad to see Thomas, of course, but I couldn't help feeling wary. "You're not here to hover over us, too, are you?"

Thomas didn't answer my question. He was shifting from side to side again. "Kip came to me and explained what happened to your bees, Goose," he said. "I've been concerned about your safety here since I heard about the otherworld creature that attacked you, and now I'm really worried. I don't think the three of you should stay in this building any longer."

"Finally!" said Rosemary. "Does this mean I can go home?"

Thomas looked apologetic. "Not exactly. There's a place we can send the three of you—an Interworld Travel property up in the mountains. It's very private; hardly anyone even knows it's there, and there's plenty of security. I'd like you to stay there."

"You mean *forever?*" said Arthur.

"Of course not, Your Highness," Thomas said hastily. "Just . . . for now."

The thought of being locked up in the Interworld Travel building any longer made me want to scream, but so did the thought of being sent to the mountains. Right above us, there could be a door that would take me to the Gatekeeper, a door

135

that would bring Rosemary's sisters back to Southeast, and a door that would take Arthur home. Anyway, strange things were happening at Interworld Travel, and if no one would tell me what was really going on, I wanted to find out for myself.

"I don't need protection," I told Thomas. "None of us do. The safer you all try to make us, the more danger we end up running into. And I don't appreciate being shipped halfway across the world like . . ." I thought back to the vast piles of stuff in Mr. Silos's sitting room. "Like a crate of Florida grapefruit!" I finished triumphantly.

Thomas raised an eyebrow at me.

"Lucy's right," said Arthur. "We'll stay here, thanks."

"And I still want to go home," Rosemary grumbled.

"I'm sorry," said Thomas, "but I can't give you a choice in the matter. You'd better collect your things. We'll leave for the mountains in an hour."

It didn't take us long to pack. We hadn't come to Interworld Travel with much, and a lot of what we'd brought with us had gone missing over the past few days. Thomas stood silently in the doorway as Arthur and I pulled our clothes from the closets; Rosemary took a blanket from the back of the couch and tossed it into her bag defiantly, but Thomas didn't say a word about it. When I reached into my rucksack, my hand brushed against the long scarf the Gatekeeper had knitted for me, and my heart sank. It seemed like years ago that she'd passed through that worldgate, and I still hadn't managed to bring her home. Now I wasn't sure I'd ever get the chance.

When we'd finished packing our worldly possessions, we went back to Arthur's room. Arthur had poked holes in the lid of a cardboard box he'd found somewhere, and I knelt down to help him guide the bees inside it. "I know you're not feeling up to traveling right now," I said to the bees, scooping them up by the wriggling handful, "but we're being ordered to leave. There's nothing we can do about it." I lowered them into the shoebox and glanced over my shoulder. Behind us, Thomas was discussing something with Kip and Celeste; I couldn't make out exactly what they were saying, but their voices were low and urgent. "At least, Thomas says there's not."

"He'll say anything," Rosemary grumbled. "He's even less trustworthy than those other two."

Arthur looked scandalized. "He's Lucy's brother!"

"Does it make a difference?" Rosemary sat down next to us. "He's hurrying us out of the building where we've just found a mess of secret worldgates. If you ask me, he wants us gone before we can find out what else Interworld Travel is hiding."

I put the lid on the box of bees and stood up. "All packed up, Goose?" Thomas called from across the room. "Good girl. I knew you wouldn't give me any trouble."

He'd known that when he'd arranged for me to work at the end of the world, too, hadn't he? He'd promised Mrs. Bracknell that I wouldn't make trouble, and so far, he'd been right. I filed and sorted and stamped; I tried to be helpful and I did as I was told. Why should he expect me to stop now? It was my job to shove my questions aside, follow orders, and pretend not to know that all the doors to all the worlds were blowing open just above my head.

I looked down at Arthur and Rosemary. The box of bees vibrated in my hands. "Grab your things," I said quietly, "and get ready to run."

17

Thomas must not have expected us to sprint out of the room: by the time he noticed us leaving, we were already out the door. Arthur slammed it behind us. Then I grabbed one of the chairs Kip and Celeste had been using and wedged it under the doorknob. It wasn't anything a trio of travel officers couldn't push out of the way with a little effort, but I hoped it would slow them down for a minute or two. On the other side of the door, someone jostled the knob.

"The eighth floor," I said to Arthur and Rosemary. They nodded, and we all headed for the stairs.

As we left the Travelers' Wing, I looked back over my shoulder. Mrs. Bracknell's finest had been quicker than I'd expected: Celeste was already throwing a leg over the chair, and I was sure Kip and Thomas weren't far behind. "Oh no," said Arthur, following my gaze. "I think we might be in trouble."

"Less talking," snapped Rosemary. "More running."

For the second time that night, we pulled apart the barricade blocking the stairs to the eighth floor. This time, though, we didn't try to be neat or quiet; we tossed the pieces of plywood behind us and let them smack against the marble floor.

One piece almost hit Huggins, who was coming up the stairs. "Watch out!" Arthur shouted.

Huggins looked at the three of us. Then he looked at Thomas, Kip, and Celeste, who were barreling out the door of the Travelers' Wing. "Is everything all right?" he asked us. "You look like you're in a hurry."

I tore down the last section of the barricade. "We are," I said to Huggins, "but I think this would be an excellent time to ask those travel officers if they can help you with your cows."

"Are you sure?" Huggins looked skeptical, but he waved Thomas down anyway. "Mr. Eberslee?" he called. "I'm glad I ran into you. I've been waiting to talk to someone for days. . . ."

Thomas grumbled something I couldn't hear as we flew up the stairs. I wasn't as fast as Rosemary, and Arthur was even slower than that, but when we reached the long row of otherworld doors, all three of us came to a dead stop. Rosemary shone her flashlight down the hallway, and Arthur, who hadn't seen the place before, drew in his breath. "Where to now?" he asked.

I could hear footsteps on the stairs behind us; Thomas must have dispatched with Huggins by now, and there wasn't time to think. "Not the cows," I said, passing by the barn door. I passed the red door with the bronze knocker, too, and the door with marble columns, but I slowed down when I reached the sleek black door. I didn't have any idea which world it led to, but that didn't matter. As I grabbed the combination lock on the knob, the three travel officers reached the end of the hallway.

It didn't take them long to guess what we were up to. "Stop!" Thomas shouted. "Don't touch that door, Lucy!"

The dials on the lock clicked into place, and I pulled the door open.

"Thank the worlds!" said Rosemary. She dove through the doorway, dragging Arthur with her. I didn't know where they'd gone, but I stumbled after them anyway and slammed the door leading back to my own world behind me.

18

It was nighttime in the other world, too. At first I couldn't see because of the thick darkness all around me. A few moments after that, I couldn't see because someone was shining a beam of light straight in my eyes. It was twice as bright as Rosemary's flashlight, and from the way she was cursing, I guessed she wasn't the one controlling it.

"Mrs. Bracknell?" The voice in the darkness sounded dubious, and the beam of light wavered. "You're not Mrs. Bracknell. And you're an hour early. Who are you?"

"Get that thing out of our faces and we'll tell you," Rosemary shot back.

She must have sounded ferocious enough, because the beam of light dimmed to a mere glow. The boy in front of us was dressed in a white jumpsuit like the ones the travel officers back in Southeast had worn when they'd chased Henry Tallard into the lobby of Interworld Travel. His visor was pushed back on top of his head, though, and he didn't look any older than me. "Did Mrs. Bracknell send you?" he asked, looking at Arthur as though he were the one of us most likely to have something useful to say.

"Yes," I said, jumping in before Arthur could open his mouth. "Mrs. Bracknell is busy, but she sent us in her place. We're also from Interworld Travel. I'm Lucy Eberslee."

As soon as I said my last name, the boy's face relaxed. There was plenty I already didn't like about him, but at least he was predictable. "You'd better get in the pod, then," he said. "And hurry. It's not safe out here."

"You can say that again," said Arthur, looking over his shoulder. I looked, too, but I couldn't see the sleek black door in the darkness, and even though I hadn't managed to lock it behind me, no one was running through the doorway after us. I wondered what was stopping them.

The boy was shining his light on something just beyond us now, a large, transparent orb with doors that stood open and cushioned seats inside. It reminded me of an illustration from a book of otherworld fairy tales I'd had growing up: in one story, a girl had gone to a masquerade ball in a magical carriage made of glass and drawn by four white horses. There weren't any horses in sight here, though, and I didn't think the boy was likely to take us to any sort of party. But the orb—the pod, he'd called it—seemed magical enough to me. Once we'd all taken our seats, the doors closed by themselves, and when the boy pressed a button, the pod started to roll forward, even while our seats stayed upright. "We'll have to take the long way around," the boy said apologetically. "It's better if we're not seen. But I'm sure Mrs. Bracknell briefed you already."

"Of course she did," I said, trying to act like I meant it. "She didn't tell us who we'd be meeting, though. What's your name?"

"Me?" He said the word as though the answer should have been obvious to anyone who mattered. "I'm Michael. I'm Mrs. Bracknell's personal secretary."

"I've never heard of you," Rosemary said with relish.

Michael's expression didn't change, but I could tell he was bristling just under the surface. "I've been out here in West for the past few months," he explained. (Arthur was visibly relieved to hear this; I was sure he'd been wondering which world we'd stumbled into. I hadn't been quite sure myself, but only West had the technology to come up with a traveling contraption like the pod.) "Before that," Michael continued, "I worked out of the Interworld Travel building. That must have been before your time. And before that," he said importantly, "I was the Gatekeeper's deputy at the Eastern end of the world."

"Really!" I said. So *that's* what had happened to the deputy before me: he'd been plucked up by Mrs. Bracknell. That was strange. From the way the Gatekeeper had spoken about my predecessor, I'd always assumed she'd eaten him whole and washed him down with a glass of milk. Then again, maybe being eaten was preferable to working as Mrs. Bracknell's personal secretary. As we rolled through the darkness, with the claws and teeth of otherworld creatures scrabbling just outside our pod, I wondered what she was up to here in West. Why had she planned to come through a secret worldgate in the middle of the night? Why had she sent her secretary to another world? And what was she going to do when she showed up an hour from now and Michael wasn't there to meet her? More likely, I realized, she'd be here sooner than that: Thomas had probably run off to find her as soon as we'd passed through the doorway.

At least the pod was making good time. The first inkling of dawn was lighting the sky, and I could see now that we were on the outskirts of a city. The vast black shapes of buildings rose up on the horizon. Lights—more lights than I'd ever seen in one place—twinkled in the windows and along the roads that twisted toward the city, running over and under one another like yarn in a knotted skein. But our pod kept to the far edge of civilization, and soon we plunged into a stand of trees, where everything was more or less dark again.

At the end of the world, I'd learned to keep certain things to myself, but if the Gatekeeper had tried to pass this lesson along to Michael as well, it hadn't stuck. Maybe we hadn't been as impressed with him as he'd hoped, because he wanted us to know all the daring and important things he'd been up to in West, and how he was the only one who could be trusted with Mrs. Bracknell's most important projects. "She had me catch her a thistle-backed thrunt yesterday," he said proudly. "I'm not sure if you know this, but those little creatures are nasty. Getting it into the thrunt-proof box wasn't as easy as you'd think."

Michael looked around the pod a little anxiously. "Do you happen to know if everything went well? With the thrunt, I mean? She never said what she wanted it for."

Rosemary almost stood up right there in the pod, but Arthur pulled her down. Both of them were staring at Michael, and I suppose I was, too. *Mrs. Bracknell* had put the thrunt in the archives? When she'd been the one going on and on about how important it was to keep us safe? I knew there was plenty she hadn't been telling us, but even I hadn't expected that.

"It went wonderfully," I said, forcing out a grin. "Didn't it?" I asked the others.

"Oh, yes," Arthur agreed. "We loved the thrunt. Very spiky."

Rosemary gritted her teeth. "Does Mrs. Bracknell need to transport dangerous animals from other worlds very often?"

"Not from West," said Michael. "At least, not lately. She's been busy with her work, and of course she can't come to West too often these days. Now that all the worldgates are supposed to be closed, it'd look awfully funny if anyone spotted her here." He frowned. "Is that why she sent you three? And why you're not in uniform?"

"Exactly." I smoothed my rumpled sweater. "We're in disguise. No one would ever suspect we worked for her."

"Ah," said Michael knowingly. "I was wondering why she didn't come herself. It shouldn't take three people to do, er . . . what needs to be done."

"Yes! About that." Arthur leaned forward. "I'm awfully forgetful, and when Mrs. Bracknell gave us our orders, I wasn't

146

quite paying attention." He fiddled with his glasses. "Would you remind me what we're here to do?"

He'd taken things too far; I could tell that in an instant. Michael sat up straight, and all his muscles looked stiff. I could practically hear the rusty gears creaking to life in the shallows of his mind. "Don't be silly," I said to Arthur. "I can remind you later. Michael is Mrs. Bracknell's *personal secretary*. He's extremely important, and he doesn't have the time to explain our job to us all over again."

This seemed to be enough to calm Michael down, or at least to distract him as the pod rolled out of the trees and turned a corner into a circular drive. It was light enough now for me to see we'd reached a tall, narrow house painted the same sleek black as the worldgate I'd opened, with stone steps at the front and two stone-faced men standing guard on either side of them. They were both dressed in white jumpsuits like Michael's, but unlike Michael, they held otherworld devices that looked heavy and dangerous. I hadn't seen anything like them when we'd gone to visit Mr. Silos.

Rosemary looked out at the house and narrowed her eyes at the guards. "Does this place belong to Interworld Travel?"

Michael made a small, exasperated noise through his nose. "Not officially," he said. "This is Mrs. Bracknell's personal residence, where she stays whenever she needs to do business in West. It's extremely secure."

The pod rolled to a stop, and the two guards stepped forward, as if they'd heard what Michael had said about security and decided to emphasize the point. "Stay here while I talk to them, please," said Michael, pressing a button to open the pod door. "They've been told to blast any trespassers on sight, and they take their jobs seriously. I'm sure Mrs. Bracknell would be upset if you three were blasted."

"I'm not so sure she would be," Rosemary said once Michael was out of earshot. "She's the one who planted that thrunt! And I'll bet she poisoned the bees as well."

"I don't understand why," said Arthur. "She must think we're a danger somehow." He eyed the guards' weapons. "And now we've accidentally gotten ourselves into her *extremely secure* house."

"She's not going to like that," I agreed. I was starting to wish I'd picked the door that led to the world full of cows. "Should we make a run for it?"

"And get blasted?" Rosemary gave her curls a shake. "I'd rather not, thanks."

"Then we'll have to keep pretending we know what's going on." I lowered my voice as Michael turned back to the pod. "If we can get in and out of this place without making anyone too suspicious, we might have a chance of escaping before Mrs. Bracknell finds out we were here."

The others nodded, and Michael stuck his head through the open pod door. "Come on out," he said. "I've told the guards you're here on Mrs. B's orders." With his chin held so high that I wondered how he could move forward without tripping, he led us past the guards and up the stairs. "Open," he said in imperious tones, and the front door of the tall black house obeyed. Even Rosemary looked impressed.

On the inside, everything was glossy white: the floors, the walls, the hovering globes that cast light on all of us as we stepped into the foyer. There weren't any doors leading out of the little room, or any windows, and as soon as we were all inside, the front entrance slid shut behind us. I saw Arthur swallow; I hoped he wasn't afraid of close quarters.

"Stairs," said Michael briskly, and the room changed around us. On both sides of us, sections of wall slipped away to reveal narrow white staircases, one leading up, the other leading down. "Er, *down*stairs," Michael amended. The upward-leading staircase disappeared again behind its wall. "The house recognizes my voice, and Mrs. Bracknell's," Michael told us, "but it won't know yours, so you'll have to give a shout for me when you're done with the interrogation."

Interrogation? Arthur mouthed at me. I didn't like the sound of it, either, but all I could do was follow Michael down the stairs, trying not to notice my stomach sinking a little more with each step I took.

The staircase ended abruptly in a blank white wall. "Here's where I leave you," Michael said. "I've got work to do upstairs, but I'll be here if you need me." He sounded very much as if he hoped we would. "And this should be obvious, but please don't get too close to the prisoner. It would be inconvenient if anyone got hurt. Open."

This last command was directed to the wall in front of us,

149

which slid away without a sound. Rosemary, Arthur, and I all looked at one another. Then Michael made his small, exasperated noise again, and the three of us filed through the doorway. I wasn't eager to meet whoever Mrs. Bracknell had locked away in the underbelly of her house, but I couldn't think what else to do. "Close," said Michael behind us, and the wall slid back into place, cutting us off from him completely.

The room beyond us was as stark as the rest of the house: white walls, white ceiling, white tile floors, white globes of light illuminating our surroundings. Mrs. Bracknell clearly didn't spend a lot of time here; the only furnishings were two straight-backed white chairs set at opposite ends of the room, and they didn't look comfortable. One chair was empty. In the other sat a man—a tired-looking man who lifted his head as though his shoulders couldn't quite stand the weight of it.

"You two again?" said Henry Tallard. His eyes moved from me to Arthur, and then on to Rosemary. "You've grown a third head since I saw you last. There aren't enough chairs for all of us, I'm afraid, but you won't need to sit down." He let out a short bark of laughter. "I'll tell you exactly what I told *her*: nothing at all."

19

Henry Tallard was in a bad mood. Anyone who'd spent hours locked in a stark white room would have felt the same, I reasoned, but that didn't make it any nicer to be in his company.

"She's sent mere infants to question me," he said, casting his eyes up to the ceiling. "She doesn't even respect me enough to come herself." Then he pulled his gaze downward and stared straight at the three of us. "Don't waste my time, children. Go back to Clara Bracknell and tell her I've come up with thirty-seven new ways to make her miserable. I'm looking forward to trying them out one by one."

"You think we work for Mrs. Bracknell?" Rosemary made a face. "I'd rather hop on one foot backward through all eight worlds. Trust me, we don't work for her."

"You're here in her private residence," said Tallard. "And I saw your two friends at Interworld Travel this morning, and at the end of the world a week before that, so I hope you can understand why I'm not inclined to *trust you*." He leaned forward—there didn't seem to be anything keeping him in the chair, I realized unhappily—and pointed straight at me. "That girl's the Gatekeeper's deputy."

I couldn't argue with that. "I *do* work for Interworld Travel," I admitted, "but Rosemary's telling the truth. We're not here to interrogate you. We're in trouble with Mrs. Bracknell ourselves, and we escaped through a door—"

"Doors, doors, doors!" Tallard shoved his chair back, making it squeak against the white tile. "I don't want to hear about doors. I've seen enough doors for a dozen lifetimes. I knew she was opening them, but I didn't dream she'd be bold enough to do it in her own building. If I'd guessed it earlier, I could have spared myself a lot of pain in the fire pits of Pitfire."

Arthur edged closer to me. "Is he all right?" he whispered. "I'm not sure he's all right."

Tallard's hearing, at least, was impeccable. "If you were the most renowned explorer in eight worlds," he said to Arthur, "and you were confined to a room where the only thing worth exploring was your own navel, I'm not sure you'd be all right, either." He paused and tilted his head slightly, as if he were listening for something. "Do I hear bees?"

I'd stowed the box of bees in my rucksack back in Southeast, and in all the excitement, I'd actually forgotten about them. They must have been feeling better, though, because even through the layers of cardboard and canvas, I could hear them buzzing with fury at the sound of Tallard's voice. "I don't like bees," he was saying now.

"I'm sure they feel the same about you," I told him, "but you're just going to have to stand one another while we work things out." Henry Tallard was the worst kind of explorer: the kind who's so convinced of his own importance that he can't be bothered to fill out his travel papers correctly, or to explain himself clearly to anyone. If we wanted useful information from him, we'd have to extract it carefully. "I'm going to need you to start at the beginning," I said in official tones. "I want to know what you've done to upset Mrs. Bracknell."

"So you *are* here to interrogate me." Tallard looked a little smug. "Though I'm sure you already know the answer to that question. Didn't she give you anything more interesting to ask?"

I opened the top of my rucksack so Tallard could hear the bees more easily.

"All right, have it your way." Tallard edged away from the rucksack. "I suppose it all started at that museum gala. The Explorers' Ball. You've heard of it?"

We hadn't.

"They hold it every year at the Southern Museum of Magic and Industry. It's got all the usual trappings: champagne, canapés, self-playing violins, miniature fireworks you can hold in your palm, that sort of thing. And it's always an awful bore, but all the most notable explorers from all the worlds are expected to be there, and it wouldn't look nice if I dodged the invitation. This year, I stayed at the ball much longer than I'd intended.

I'd been dragged into a conversation with a tedious little person who wanted to write a new biography about me. The staff was cleaning up all around us, and the other guests had left, but that man wouldn't stop talking. He followed me out the door and into the street, which is where we both were when the alarm went up from the museum. Someone had stolen Aunt Arabella's gatecutters." He grinned, showing teeth that were yellower and more higgledy-piggledy than they looked in his official portraits. "Do you know who that person was?"

By now, I thought I did. "Mrs. Bracknell?" I asked.

"That's always been my guess. She was at the museum that night, and it's not a task she'd want to entrust to her underlings, though I'm sure she had their help." He scanned our faces. "Were all of you there? Dressed as waitstaff, perhaps? Did she pass you the gatecutters once she'd taken them and waltzed off into the night? I'd really like to know. I've been wondering about it for months."

"We weren't there," Rosemary told him. "Mere infants don't generally attend museum galas. What happened next?"

"The Southern authorities promised to look into the theft, but I didn't have an ounce of faith that they'd learn anything useful. I wanted to know who took the gatecutters and what they planned to do with them, so I decided to look into the matter myself—to avenge my aunt Arabella, you might say. I went from world to world, asking questions of anyone I could find. As I've already told your employer, I won't breathe a word about my sources. I can tell you it's not hard to find a few souls willing to share gossip with a worlds-famous explorer, though, especially if you ease it out of them over a few glasses of Northwestern triple-aged ale. It didn't take me long to piece together the general shape of Mrs. Bracknell's plan."

"And what was that?"

"She wanted to seal up the worldgates." Tallard sounded almost bored by this, as though it were a lesson he'd been asked to recite for the hundredth time at school. "She'd come up with a way to close them all. With the gatecutters missing, she knew no one would be able to open them again."

"That doesn't make sense," I told him. "Mrs. Bracknell is the last person who'd want to close up the doors between the worlds. Helping people travel through the worldgates is her job; she'd have no good reason to close them."

"Especially if she was just going to turn around and open them again," Arthur pointed out. "Mrs. Bracknell wouldn't go to all that trouble for nothing. No one would!"

At this point, something funny happened to Henry Tallard. Ever since we'd entered the room, he'd been wearing the same disdainful expression I'd seen on his face at Interworld Travel. Now, though, his eyes opened wider, his jaw relaxed, and his mouth came unstuck from its sneer. He looked at the three of us again, one at a time, slowly. "Either you're the best pack of liars I've met in any world," he said, "or you really don't have the faintest idea what's been happening."

"I'm extremely bad at lying," Arthur said helpfully. "Ask anyone."

Tallard nodded. "I believe you. And yet here you are. You came through one of the doors at Interworld Travel?"

"It wasn't entirely on purpose," I admitted. "We meant to go through the door, of course, but we didn't know where we'd end up."

Tallard almost smiled at this. "You three are astoundingly ignorant," he said cheerfully, "but at least you've got an explorer's instinct. That will get you far—unless, of course, it gets you killed." He shrugged, as if it didn't really matter which way things went for any of us. "If you truly don't know Mrs. Bracknell's plans, then I'm not surprised you can barely tell which way is up."

"It would be nice," Rosemary said icily, "if you could direct us."

Tallard scratched his beard while he thought this over. "All right," he said. "I'll tell you what I know, but I'm going to need a favor from you in exchange. Is that fair?"

"Absolutely," said Arthur at once, before Rosemary or I could ask any questions. The more time I spent with Arthur, the less surprised I was that he'd managed to fall into another world by accident. I was beginning to wonder if everything that happened to him was more or less accidental.

"Excellent." Henry Tallard leaned forward, resting his elbows on the singed patches of his canvas pants. He looked right at me. "When you said Mrs. Bracknell didn't have a good reason to close all the worldgates, you were only half right. You're from Southeast, aren't you?"

156

"I am." I couldn't imagine why it mattered.

"And what can you tell me about Southeast?"

"Um . . . It's small. It's got meadows and mountains. Centerbury is pretty nice." I thought hard, trying to come up with something else to say. "The weather's usually clearest on Tuesdays."

"In other words," said Tallard, "it's a pass-through."

"It isn't!" I said.

But Rosemary was nodding again. "He's got a point, Lucy. Southeast hasn't got any magic of its own, or any decent technology. It doesn't have much industry, and it's not a particularly interesting place to go on vacation. You've met a lot of travelers, haven't you? When was the last time you met someone who was visiting Southeast because they wanted to?"

I shot her a glare. "It's *scenic*."

"Exactly." Henry Tallard looked pleased with us. "Not many people come to Southeast to begin with, and the ones who do are usually trying to find their way out again. They'll go to Northeast for crops, or to South for spell-casting tools, or even to Northwest for a week's vacation in the Ungoverned Wilderness, but they've got no reason to spend their money in Southeast. Simply put, it's bad for business. The House of Governors has been worrying about the whole situation for years, and now it seems Mrs. Bracknell has finally decided to do something about it."

"By sealing all the worlds off from each other?" Arthur asked. "I don't think it's going to help Southeast attract any visitors.

How would they get into the world in the first place?"

"If you saw all those doors Mrs. Bracknell's been making with the gatecutters she stole," said Tallard, "then you already know the answer to that. The original worldgates are closed now, and the leaders of the other seven worlds are certainly starting to worry. I imagine their local Interworld Travel offices are in a panic. Some won't mind the change so much—East, for example, has always been obnoxiously independent—but others can't survive on their own for long." Tallard smirked. "Enter Mrs. Bracknell. She's just *happened* to build a whole new row of worldgates, and they all *happen* to be located conveniently in the scenic little city of Centerbury. If you're a Southern mage in need of a Northwestern night-blooming toadflower, you'll have to travel into Southeast to get it. If you're a Northeastern farmer selling eggs at a market in West, you'll have to journey to Southeast first. And do you think Mrs. Bracknell will let visitors hop out of one world and into another? No, no; they'll need to wait their turn, file their papers properly, and have their baggage inspected. Maybe they'll spend some money at Mrs. Bracknell's new Interworld Travel Hub while they're waiting. Maybe they'll even stay in Centerbury for a while."

"She could sell rooms in the Travelers' Wing," I said, puzzling it out aloud. "And dinners in the café. She could charge people to use the worldgates."

"She'll have no trouble catching smugglers," Rosemary said gloomily. "Silos and Daughters is doomed."

"And if someone from another world upsets her," said Henry

Tallard, "she can shut that world off from the others as punish-ment. It's a nice little racket, isn't it?" If I hadn't known how much Henry Tallard disliked Mrs. Bracknell, I would have thought he was genuinely impressed. "As soon as she throws those worldgates open to the public, Clara Bracknell is going to bring Southeast more wealth and power than it will know what to do with."

"To be fair," said Rosemary, "she'll probably keep plenty of both for herself." She glared at Henry Tallard. "If you've known all this for months, why haven't you stopped her?"

"For worlds' sake, I *tried*. I went to both ends of the world to try to catch her lackeys in the act of sealing up the doors, but both times I was too late. Then I searched every corner of Southeast for the new worldgates she was opening. I don't mind telling you that was no picnic, especially once someone told Mrs. Bracknell what I was up to and she set fifty travel officers on my trail."

That, I realized, had been my fault. It was probably best to change the subject. "Won't the other worlds be angry with her?" I asked.

"I imagine they'll be grateful, at least to start with," Tallard said. "They don't know Mrs. Bracknell is the one who caused all this trouble in the first place, and she's going to great lengths to make sure they never find out. Which is why I'm here." He gestured at the white walls all around him. "She's kept me alive because she wants to know who else I've told about her little project, but she'll find a creative way to dispatch me soon enough. If she suspects you three are getting close to the truth, she'll do the same to you as well."

"She already tried to have us eaten," Arthur volunteered. "And sent to the mountains."

Henry Tallard nodded. "I wonder if you would have returned from that trip."

All of us shuddered. I felt sure he was right. And then I realized it: strictly speaking, Mrs. Bracknell didn't try to send us to the mountains. My brother, Thomas, did. Did he know she'd been trying to *dispatch* us? Was he helping her do it? Of course not, I thought; he couldn't have known about her plans. But I couldn't stop thinking about Thomas standing at the other end of the eighth-floor hallway, shouting at me not to go through the worldgate. We weren't particularly close—he'd started his first job at Interworld Travel when I was only three—and I knew how loyal he was to his work. Would he do whatever he was told? Did he actually have a choice in the matter?

"All this time," Rosemary mused, "when Mrs. Bracknell said she was trying to keep us safe, she was actually keeping us captive. Waiting for the moment she could polish us off."

"Oh, don't!" I said. It was too awful to think about. "We're not polished off yet. There must be something we can do. Does Mrs. Bracknell still have the gatecutters?"

"I assume so," said Henry Tallard. "Once she's done opening doors, she'll probably hide them away somewhere to make sure no one else can open a door she hasn't authorized. When I turned myself in to Interworld Travel, I was hoping to catch a glimpse of them—or even steal them myself if I could. But the gatecutters aren't in her office, I'm sorry to say, and she's not an easy woman to outrun. Did you know she dragged me through that worldgate into West herself?"

"So you were never locked up in a cell in the House of Governors?" I asked.

"Never," said Tallard. "The travel officers took me straight to Mrs. Bracknell, and Mrs. Bracknell brought me straight here. Every officer in that building knows what the governor is up to. They're helping her do it."

Including Thomas, of course. I shoved the thought aside. "We need to let the otherworld leaders know what Mrs. Bracknell is doing," I said. "Her worldgates are still under construction. They'll never let her finish them."

Arthur nodded. "Good thinking, Lucy."

But Henry Tallard didn't look so impressed. "They won't listen to you," he said. "You or I could walk into the Western Interworld Travel branch right now and accuse Mrs. Bracknell of conspiracy, but it wouldn't do any good. She may not be as well known as *some* of us"—here he gestured to himself, of course—"but she's respected all around the worlds. Even worse, people actually seem to like her. If we didn't bring evidence to support our case, they'd laugh us out the door. That's where the favor I asked for comes in."

Right. The favor. I thought I could guess what it was. "You need us to steal the gatecutters?" I asked. "To use as evidence?"

"Oh, no; that's a hopeless task, too. Mrs. Bracknell probably keeps them strapped to her waist or tucked under her pillow. If *I* couldn't retrieve them, *you* certainly can't. And as I was saying, the other seven leaders of Interworld Travel might not care what a group of questionable children has to tell them—"

"Questionable!" said Rosemary. "Ha!"

"—but they'll certainly listen to their own senior officers," Tallard finished. "When they closed the doors between the worlds, Mrs. Bracknell and her team made sixteen gatekeepers disappear in the process. I'm sure at least a handful of those sixteen must remember what happened to them. If you can find those gatekeepers, and they share what they know about Mrs. Bracknell's project, that should be enough to catch people's attention." He grinned at us. "I'd go looking for them myself, but I don't think the guards outside would let me get very far. It's appalling how little respect they have for famous explorers."

"About the missing gatekeepers," I said. "You don't think they've already been . . . ?" I couldn't finish the question. If Mrs. Bracknell had harmed my own frizzy-haired, heavy-footed Gatekeeper, I didn't want to think about it.

But Henry Tallard only shrugged. "I don't know what's happened to them. If I were Mrs. Bracknell, I wouldn't want to lose the knowledge that sixteen worldgate experts could give me, but who's to say whether she'd feel the same? I only know that *if* they're alive, someone really should find them. Don't you agree?"

Before any of us could answer, one of the white walls slid open.

162

None of us had asked Michael to return, but there he was anyway. He'd changed out of his white jumpsuit into a standard-issue travel officer suit and tie, though his pants were an inch too long and his tie was an inch too short. Just behind him stood Mrs. Bracknell's two guards, still holding their weapons. They looked grim, but guards always did, as though constant grimness was a requirement of the job. Michael, on the other hand, looked furious.

"I'd never seen you three before," he said, "so I called up your Interworld Travel personnel files. Lucy Eberslee, your employment was terminated last week. And as for the other two"—he glared at Arthur and Rosemary—"the system's got no record of your faces. I haven't had a chance to search the database of known otherworld criminals, but it wouldn't surprise me if you both turned up there. What I know for sure is that none of you work for Mrs. Bracknell."

"I was *terminated?*" I said.

"That's better than blasted," murmured Henry Tallard, "which is what you may be soon."

The guards grabbed the three of us by the shoulders and marched us up the stairs. They made me go first, so I couldn't see Rosemary or Arthur behind me. "Close!" Michael snapped, and I heard the door in the wall slide shut, locking Henry Tallard on the other side of it.

Even at a time like this, Arthur couldn't help himself from making conversation. "I hope I'm not being too curious," he said, "but where are you taking us?"

163

Michael let out a long sigh, the kind people produce only when they've been having a very bad day. "To Mrs. Bracknell, of course," he said. "She'll be waiting for me at the worldgate by now, and I'm sure she'll know what to do with you."

20

None of us spoke much as the pod rolled us back the way we'd come. Michael's gaze never wavered from the driving controls, and the rest of us literally couldn't move: Mrs. Bracknell's guards had strapped us into our seats with some sort of tough metal cord to make sure we couldn't escape. I didn't recognize the landscape around us, but when the morning sky began to crackle with jagged blue lightning, I could tell we must be getting closer to the worldgate. Birds were gathering overhead, bright-feathered ones with long, curved beaks and earsplitting cries. "They sound like ambulance sirens," Arthur said, mostly to himself.

"They're yellow-winged wailers," Rosemary told him. "There'll be more on the way if the weather keeps up. They adore being zapped by lightning; I think it gives them a sort of rush. When Pa brought me to West for the first time, a whole flock of them chased us down the street during a storm, trying to haul us away and feed us to their young." She looked a little wistful at the memory. "It was very exciting."

We rolled down a hill, past a stand of trees, and into a green clearing. In the damp, matted grass in front of us stood Mrs. Bracknell, looking a little damp and matted herself. She was yawning—it couldn't have been daylight yet in Southeast—and checking her wristwatch. As the pod came to a stop, she looked up and gave Michael a tight smile. *You're late*, she mouthed.

Then she saw us, and the smile dropped straight off her face.

I didn't envy Michael one bit as he stepped out of the pod to explain the situation. I could only hear snatches of their conversation, mostly from Mrs. Bracknell—"What are they doing here?" and "You let them speak to him?" and "Extremely disappointed"—but it didn't sound as though the news was going over particularly well.

"I wouldn't want to be him right now," Rosemary said, tilting her head toward Michael. "She's hopping mad."

"I wouldn't want to be *us*," said Arthur. "What do you think she'll do to us?"

"I'd rather not imagine it, thanks," I said.

Once Michael's back was turned and Mrs. Bracknell was busy shouting at him, Rosemary started digging through her pockets. The guards had wrapped their metal cords around our waists, but they hadn't bothered to secure our hands or arms. I'd overheard one of them asking the other how much damage the three of us could possibly manage to do. Now I could tell

Rosemary was looking forward to answering their question.

She found her double-edged defense ray and got to work cutting herself free from the cords. A strange metallic smell filled the pod. "Ah," said Rosemary, breathing it in. "That's much better." She made a few strategic gashes in the side of the pod before aiming her defense ray at the cords around me. "Try not to breathe for a few seconds, Lucy. I'd rather not cut your ribs in half."

Once all of us were free, I looked toward Mrs. Bracknell. She'd finished reprimanding Michael, and now the two of them stood close together, talking in low, urgent tones. I knew there must be a worldgate just beyond them, but there was no door hovering in the clearing and no sign to indicate we were anywhere near the end of the world. No sign except for the yellow-winged wailers, that is: the lightning strikes were coming more quickly now, and so were they, screeching furiously enough that I couldn't overhear what Mrs. Bracknell and Michael were saying. "Does anyone see the door?" I asked. "If Mrs. Bracknell just came through it, it can't be far from here."

Arthur scanned the landscape and frowned. "Will it look the same on this side as it did at Interworld Travel?"

"I don't know," I told him. "It was dark when we came through the first time. I suppose it could look like anything."

There was another flash of lightning. In the electric blue brightness, something caught my eye: a thin, dark line that grew up from the ground just behind Mrs. Bracknell's left foot and traced a rectangular path through the grass and trees and sky, as though someone had cut a tidy piece out of the scenery and tried their best to stick it back into place. The rectangle looked just big enough for a person to pass through.

"I see it," I said. "I see the worldgate. It doesn't look like anything, though. It looks like *nothing*." I cinched up my rucksack. "Now all we've got to do is get through it."

Rosemary squinted, trying to make out the outline of the door. "And what do we do once we're through?"

"We go through another one of the doors on the eighth floor," I said. "We do Henry Tallard's favor. We find the Gatekeeper—and Florence, of course, and the others—and we help them stop Mrs. Bracknell from taking over the worlds."

I waited for Rosemary to say that she wasn't interested in doing Henry Tallard any favors, that she'd run back to Silos and Daughters and leave the problems of Interworld Travel behind for good. Then I waited for Arthur to agree that although he'd be sad to miss the fun, he'd really better be getting home to East. Neither of them had known the Gatekeeper; neither of them was responsible for protecting the door at the end of the world. If they stayed out of sight for a while and kept their mouths shut, there was a chance Mrs. Bracknell would be willing to leave them alone. But I, for one, wasn't interested in staying out of sight any longer.

Then Rosemary nodded, and Arthur nodded, too. "Right," said Rosemary. "It's a good plan, Lucy. But I think I'm going to need that defense ray again."

We never really had a chance of making it through the worldgate unnoticed. Mrs. Bracknell was standing right in front of it, and when she saw us running out of the pod, she shook her head as though she'd been badly disappointed. "Honestly, Michael," she said, "can't you do *anything* right?"

I would have liked to spend a minute or two enjoying the look on Michael's face, but I didn't have the time: Rosemary was brandishing her double-edged defense ray in Mrs. Bracknell's direction, and Arthur was waving a long branch he'd picked up off the ground. I grabbed a branch of my own and started waving it, too. "Out of the way!" Arthur shouted. "We're going through that door, and you're not going to stop us!"

Mrs. Bracknell pulled Michael out of the way and stepped in front of the worldgate herself. "You two look ridiculous," she said to me and Arthur. "And you"—she scowled at Rosemary—"are going to get somebody killed. You're swinging that ray so wildly, someone is bound to lose an earlobe or a bit of nose."

I walked forward, still holding my branch. Mrs. Bracknell was right: I *did* look ridiculous. "Let us through, please," I said. I wasn't sure what to do after that, though; this wasn't the sort of situation I had much experience with. I was used to being the person guarding the worldgate, not the person trying to get through it.

Now it was my turn to get a disappointed look from Mrs. Bracknell. "I expected better from you, Miss Eberslee," she said. "What can you be thinking? This behavior is entirely inappropriate for a gatekeeper's deputy."

"I'm not a gatekeeper's deputy anymore, though," I told her. Lightning crackled somewhere nearby, and the yellow-winged wailers howled. "You had me terminated, apparently."

"Did Michael tell you that?" Mrs. Bracknell sighed. "I'd meant to break the news myself, but you've seen how busy things have been around the office. I'm sorry, Miss Eberslee. You were a tolerable employee—until now, at least—but if the door at the end of the world is closed and there's no gatekeeper to guard it, there's certainly no need for a gatekeeper's deputy." There was another crackle of lightning, right above us this time, and her gaze flicked up to the sky. "Why don't you all get back in the pod, and we'll talk things through?"

"Not a chance," said Arthur. "You tried to have us *eaten*."

As the lightning faded away, the yellow-winged wailers rushed over. Rosemary had been right about them: there were at least fifty by now, and more kept flapping in from the tree-tops. They circled overhead, calling to each other. With each call, Mrs. Bracknell looked more concerned. "You really should put the weapon away, at the very least," she said to Rosemary. "It's the birds—"

But the birds didn't give her time to explain. They'd spotted the double-edged Western defense ray, and its golden beam must have been even more thrilling than lightning, because they plunged into a nosedive, wailing so loudly that I couldn't hear the rest of whatever Mrs. Bracknell had to say.

They were bigger than I'd realized from the ground, the tips of their beaks were sharper than I wanted to think about, and they smelled awful, like a pan left too long on a hot stovetop. The first one to reach us dove straight into Rosemary, knocking her down. She swung her defense ray at the bird, but it didn't seem to bother him at all; he just wailed more loudly than ever. "This isn't good!" Arthur shouted over the noise. "They're going to feed us to their young!"

I pushed through the flock to Rosemary and pulled her to her feet. The birds were all around us now, raking their claws through Michael's hair and chasing Mrs. Bracknell across the grass as she ran toward the pod. I went in the opposite direction, toward the worldgate. Arthur had managed to fling it open somehow, and it looked like a gaping black mouth ready to swallow us whole. *Better than being swallowed by a yellow-winged wailer*, I thought as the three of us ran through it.

21

We ran straight into Thomas.

"Lucy!" he said. I wondered how long he'd been waiting there in the eighth-floor hallway. "Thank the worlds you're back. I'm sure you've got hundreds of questions, but if you'll come with me—"

We pushed right past him. Arthur and I had dropped our branches back in West, but Rosemary still had her defense ray drawn, and that was enough to keep Thomas a safe distance away from us as I fiddled with the lock on the next worldgate over, the one with marble columns. The door swung open, and a warm, salty breeze filled the hallway.

"I know what you're doing for Mrs. Bracknell," I told Thomas. "I'm not going anywhere with you."

"If you'll only—" Thomas said, but I'd already gone through the worldgate by then, and I couldn't be bothered to hear the rest.

22

If I'd taken another step forward, I would have been soaked. We were standing at the end of a long pier reaching out into the sea, with massive waves breaking around the piles below us and the sun beating down from above. On this side of the worldgate, the door back to Southeast was just a thin black outline against the horizon, with nothing except the roaring sea to suggest that an entrance to another world was nearby. Mrs. Bracknell must have wanted to keep her worldgates secret until the time was ripe, because she'd chosen a lonely place for this door, too. In the distance, I could see ships and a bustling shoreline, and a few people were taking in the air farther down the pier, but I didn't think any of them had noticed us hurrying out of the sky and into their world.

"Where do you think we are?" I asked Rosemary over the rush of waves. "North?"

She nodded, shielding her eyes from the sun as she looked around. "Better than West, at least," she said, starting to march down the pier as if she owned it. "We might get blown up or sunk, but I don't think anything here will try to eat us."

Arthur and I hurried after her. "How do you know it's North?" Arthur asked once we'd finally caught up. "Don't other worlds have seas in them, and piers? Mine's got both. Couldn't we be in East?"

Out on the water, there was an echoing boom. Flames and smoke rose up from a ship far in the distance, and people on the shoreline began to cheer.

"See that?" Rosemary pointed toward the flaming ship. "No one else in the worlds loves their ocean battles as much as Northerners."

We reached the end of the pier and started walking toward the busier part of the shoreline, where there were shops and houses and crowds lined up waiting for steam ferries to transport them to other islands. "We're on Omegos, I think," Rosemary said. "It's the island that's farthest away from anything interesting. I've been here before, though; the old worldgate from Northeast was on Omegos, too. At least there's a ferry that goes straight to Sigmos. We'll have to get in line for tickets."

"Hold on." I caught her by the elbow. "Why are we going to another island? Shouldn't we search this one for the gatekeepers first?"

"By knocking on doorways and asking if anyone's seen sixteen people wandering around looking completely confused?"

Rosemary shook her head. "North is huge, Lucy. There are twenty-four major islands and probably hundreds of minor ones. And we've got no guarantee that the gatekeepers are even in North! We can't search every inch of all eight worlds; it'll take us centuries."

"I wasn't planning to try that," I said. "I've been thinking about where I might keep a group of gatekeepers hidden if I were Mrs. Bracknell. We know she was holding Henry Tallard at one of her own houses in West, but I don't think the gatekeepers were there, too. She wouldn't have risked keeping them so close together."

"And she'd have needed more than two guards," Arthur volunteered.

"Right. But what if Mrs. Bracknell owns more property? She might have other houses in other worlds. Maybe she's keeping the gatekeepers at one of those houses."

"Maybe." Rosemary twisted a curl around her finger. "Assuming they're still alive."

"They *are* alive." I was sure I was right; I had to be. I'd been to three new worlds in the past few hours, but I still couldn't imagine any world where the Gatekeeper wasn't stomping around, complaining about slugs in the radish beds and explorers in the begonias. Getting rid of the Gatekeeper would have been as impossible as trying to pull up a tangled mess of deep-rooted weeds, and I didn't think Mrs. Bracknell was much of a gardener.

"We'll look for Mrs. Bracknell's property, then," said

Rosemary, "but we can't go around asking if anyone knows her. She might have travel officers here, and if they're anything like that awful secretary, I'd rather not run into them. We've got to be discreet—which is why we still need to get to Sigmos." She paused, looking at us, waiting.

I nudged Arthur. "I think she wants one of us to ask what's on Sigmos."

"Ah. You're right." At least Arthur was game for it. "What's on Sigmos, Rosemary?"

Rosemary grinned. "A smugglers' den."

From the otherworld coins jumbled in the pockets of Rosemary's bag, we were able to scrape together enough Northern change to buy three return tickets on the Sigmos ferry. The ship was crowded; all the seats were taken by the time we got on board, so we found a patch of deck near the stern where we could sit without getting tripped over too often. A horn blew above us and the ferry pulled away from Omegos.

Off the port side, I could see the pier where we'd arrived. If anyone had followed us through the worldgate—Thomas or Mrs. Bracknell or a yellow-winged wailer—they weren't there now. I should have been happy about that, I supposed, but I couldn't help wondering. Thomas had seen us go to North. Why hadn't he run after us? He hadn't followed us into West, either. Maybe he agreed with Mrs. Bracknell's guards that his little Goose wasn't likely to do much damage, or maybe he didn't think chasing us down was worth the effort. In any case, he must have known we'd have to go back through the worldgate eventually. I wasn't looking forward to seeing him when we did.

The ferry trip took a few hours, and at first I tried to sleep. I was jolted awake more than once, though, by a bang from a nearby cannon or a whistle from a steamship's horn. The bees, who seemed to be feeling better, had ventured out of their cardboard box and filled the air with low, anxious hums. WE'VE NEVER BEEN ON A SHIP BEFORE, they told me when I peeled one eye open to glare at them. WE'RE NOT SURE WE LIKE IT.

I gave up on sleep altogether and wandered over to the railing, where people were leaning into the wind to watch the battles taking place off our starboard side. "What's going on?" I asked a fair-haired woman clutching a pair of binoculars.

"That's Omegos's fleet," she told me. She lowered her binoculars and pointed to a few ships flying green and white flags. "They're going up against Thetos—the ships with red flags. That battleship there, in the orange and gold, is from Alphos. It's here to support the Omegans, who haven't had a win in months. And the ships with black flags are privateers, of course. They're fighting for Thetos at the moment, but you know how fickle they can be."

I had no idea what the woman was talking about, but it seemed wiser not to mention that. "How about all those ships with blue flags?" I asked. "The ones straight ahead of us?"

"That's the Northern worldwide navy," the woman said. "They're doing their military exercises. Didn't you read about it in the paper?" She narrowed her eyes, as if she wasn't sure what to make of me. "They're preparing for war with the other worlds."

The ferry lurched just then, and I grabbed on to the railing. "Which other worlds?"

"Any of them. All of them. Does it matter?" The woman raised her binoculars again. "The chief admiral says as soon as he finds out who's closed our worldgates, he'll blast their whole world off the map, and I say good riddance!"

"Good riddance!" the crowd around me cheered.

My stomach churned—whether it was from seasickness or nerves I wasn't quite sure—and I made my way back to my companions. Arthur, I discovered, was that maddening sort of person who can fall asleep in any situation. He was leaning against the ferry railing, snoring softly, with his head tipped back and his glasses dangling dangerously off one ear. At least Rosemary wasn't sleeping. She was sitting with her knees pulled up to her chest, typing furiously on her InterCom.

"Rosemary!" I whispered. "What are you doing?"

She didn't look up. "Writing to Pa. Telling him I'm safe." A cannon boomed off the starboard side, and Rosemary raised her eyebrows. "Relatively speaking."

"I thought you could only write to me and Arthur with those things."

"You can write to anyone," said Rosemary. "I mean, *you* can't, because I'm not going to show you how. But *I* can write to anyone. So I'm writing to Pa."

"Have you told him what's going on? With Mrs. Bracknell, I mean?"

She nodded.

"Well, what did he say? Is there something he can do?"

"I don't know." Rosemary finally looked up from the Inter-Com. "He hasn't written back yet. It's not even morning yet in Southeast."

"I thought smugglers loved the dark of night."

Rosemary laughed. "I'll let you know if Pa has any idea where all the gatekeepers might be," she said. "Meanwhile, though, we'll ask around at the smugglers' den. Someone there is bound to have noticed something unusual."

23

The smugglers' den on Sigmos wasn't anything like I was expecting. When we got off the ferry, with Arthur still yawning and the bees saying WHAT A RELIEF!, Rosemary led us away from the docks and down twisty lanes of houses. The buildings looked similar to the ones I'd seen on Omegos: tall redbrick homes squeezed together side by side, some stately, some crumbling, and lots with marble columns flanking the doorways. The streets were all paved in brick, too. On Omegos, green and white flags had flown from windows and lampposts; here the flags were red and yellow. On the ferry, I remembered, I'd seen a few badly wounded ships with red and yellow flags limping by.

"Here we are!" said Rosemary. She stopped in front of a brick house with a tidy lawn in front. There was no flag flying from a windowsill, but over the doorway, between the marble columns, someone had hung a sign. Interworld Institute for the Study of Extralegal Commerce, it said in official type.

"The sign is a sort of joke," Rosemary explained. She knocked on the door, rapping out a quick pattern I couldn't quite follow. The door opened a crack, cautiously.

Then someone inside the house squealed, the door swung all the way open, and a girl with curls just as bouncy as Rosemary's flew out of it. "You didn't tell me you were coming!" the girl cried, wrapping Rosemary up in a hug. "I had no idea you were in North!"

"And I had no idea you were *here!*"

"I only came on the ferry last night. Thank goodness you made it here, too. I've been worried sick about everyone." The girl looked up and caught sight of me and Arthur standing a few feet back, like unexpected houseguests. "Oh, Rosie," she said, "have you made friends? I can't believe it!"

Rosemary wriggled out of the girl's arms. "This is Lucy," she said, pointing to me. "She's just gotten fired from Interworld Travel, so you know she's all right. And this is Arthur, who says he's a prince, and these are some bees." She turned back to us. "This is my sister Sarah."

We all shook Sarah's hand, except for the bees, who buzzed around it as politely as they could. "I thought your pa said you were stuck in East," I said.

"That's our other sister, Tillie," Sarah said cheerfully, showing us into the house. "Poor Till. She's in a place called Iceland, apparently, and she just hates the cold. Rosie, I thought you

181

were stuck in Southeast with Pa!"

"I was." Rosemary slipped me and Arthur a hint of a smile. "We all were. But we found a door."

Sarah stopped in her tracks. "A worldgate?" she asked. "What do you mean, you *found* one? No, wait, don't tell me yet. The others will want to hear this."

The others turned out to be a hodgepodge of about twenty people gathered in stairwells and perched on shabby-looking settees, talking together in low voices or hunched over Inter-Coms. As Sarah led us through the house, they all looked up, and the talking stopped. In the large, bright kitchen, a woman in work gloves was fixing a pipe under the sink. When she saw us, she put down her tools, stood up, and pushed the hair out of her eyes. "Rosemary!" she said. "And company. Hello." The smile she gave us was quick but friendly. "Sarah didn't tell us to expect you."

"I didn't expect them, either," said Sarah. "They say they found a worldgate."

The woman in gloves looked wary. "One that works?"

"Yes," I said, "a new one. We just got here a few hours ago from Southeast."

All the people in the house were crowded into the kitchen now, and they all started talking at once. "Hold on, folks!" called the woman in gloves. "I'm Tam," she said to us as the voices died to a low rumble. "I'm not a smuggler—not anymore. This is my home, and I let folks stop by when they need a place to stay in North. As you can see, we're close to bursting at the

182

moment. If you're here to tell us there's a way to get out of the world, I'm sure everyone in this house wants to hear what you've got to say."

Arthur, Rosemary, and I told the smugglers everything we knew, starting with the day the Gatekeeper disappeared and going right up to the moment we'd knocked on their door. A lot of them smirked at the beginning, especially at me when they heard I'd used to work at the end of the world, but that changed when I told them about the doors Mrs. Bracknell was building.

"I don't believe it," a man in mud-crusted boots said. "South-east isn't next to North. You can't build a door from here to there."

"You can," I said, "if you bunch up the fabric of time and space. That's what Mrs. Bracknell's done. At least, that's what it looks like to me."

"Is that really possible?" a redheaded woman asked. "Is that safe?"

"Can you prove the door exists?" the man in boots asked us. "If we all go down to Omegos right now and walk off the pier, will we end up in Southeast?"

"I'm not going anywhere," said an older man. "If they're right, we'll end up in a nest of Interworld Travel officers, and if they're wrong, we'll end up in the sea. I'm not much of a swimmer, so I'd rather take their word for it."

Some of the smugglers laughed, but Tam looked serious. "All the worldgates are in one place?" she wanted to know. "That seems dangerous. At any end of the world, there are bound to be side effects, but when you put seven ends of the world all in a row . . ." She shook her head. "To start with, I can't imagine what the weather must be like."

"It's not as bad as you'd expect," I said. "I think it's getting worse, though, and the worldgates are still under construction."

"Some of them are fraying at the edges," Rosemary added.

"You're sure?" Tam sat down at the kitchen table. "If your Mrs. Bracknell isn't careful, she's going to unravel the universe."

As the smugglers talked, I began to realize that getting them all to agree on anything would be close to impossible. A few of them didn't see much wrong with Mrs. Bracknell's plan; they'd hated trekking hundreds of miles from one door to the next, and a central location would make traveling between the worlds much more convenient, even if that location *was* a complete pass-through. Others didn't think it would be possible to smuggle anything at all through a building crawling with travel officers. And a third group—the people who'd been stuck in North the longest, I was willing to bet—just wanted to go home. "We're trying to fix everything," Rosemary told them, "but to do that, we need to find the gatekeepers, and we need your help. Do any of you know where they might have gone? We think Mrs. Bracknell might be keeping them at one of her houses; can someone find out where those are? The quicker the better."

"Who put these kids in charge?" the man in boots muttered.

Tam shot him a look that closed his mouth. "This situation is serious," she said. "All our worlds and our livelihoods have

184

been thrown off balance, and I see only three people in this room who are doing anything about it. If you're not willing to help them, you can find somewhere else to stay." She looked around the kitchen. "That goes for everyone."

As the smugglers tapped away on their InterComs to find out what they could from their friends in other worlds, Sarah pulled the three of us aside. "Tam's sticking her neck out for you," she murmured, "so you'd better be on your best behavior while you're here. Especially you, Rosie."

Rosemary straightened her spine. "What do you mean, especially me?"

"Remember what happened at the Northern embassy?" said Sarah. "With the chocolate cake? Remember what happened with the techsand supplier in Southwest?"

"That was all *years* ago," Rosemary said, "or *months* ago, anyway."

Sarah shrugged. "I don't want you bringing any trouble here to Tam's house. That's all."

"I like Tam. I would never—"

"I know you wouldn't mean to," said Sarah, "but, Rosie, maybe you could try not to be quite so much . . . *yourself?*"

Rosemary blinked hard and walked out of the kitchen without a word.

I'd never seen Rosemary leave without firing off a retort before, and I wasn't sure what to do. Neither was Arthur. "Should we go after her, do you think?" he asked.

"Not yet," I said. "Let's wait a minute."

"All right." Arthur looked up at the clock on the kitchen wall, as though he intended to time every second of that minute. "I joined a running club once," he said after a while. "A few years ago. In school."

I wasn't sure exactly what that had to do with Rosemary. "Oh?" I asked.

"I wasn't a member very long. All my brothers had been champion racers, so I thought I might be one, too. I thought I might have a knack for running." He laughed. "I didn't, of course. In my very first race, I came in dead last, tripped over my own feet at the finish line, and fell in the mud in front of everyone. My brothers still like to remind me of that. They're always challenging me to footraces whenever we're all at home. It puts them in an awfully good mood." He shrugged. "What I mean to say is that families can be tricky things."

In the warm air over our heads, the bees hummed. YOU'RE RIGHT ABOUT THAT.

A while later, we found Rosemary on the staircase. She was leaning against an old grandfather clock on the landing, staring hard at her InterCom. "Don't ask me what happened with the techsand supplier," she said without looking up. "And *definitely* don't ask me about the chocolate cake."

"We wouldn't dream of it," said Arthur.

"Promise," I said.

"Good." Rosemary waved her InterCom in our direction. "It must be morning at home, because I've heard back from Pa.

186

He says the House of Governors has just announced it's found a solution to the 'terrible trouble of the broken worldgates,' and Governor Clara Bracknell will be sharing more information with the people of Southeast in a statement soon." Rosemary made a face at the InterCom. "I assume that means she wasn't eaten by a yellow-winged wailer."

"The House of Governors made the statement?" I asked. "Then they know what Mrs. Bracknell is planning?"

"Of course they do," said Rosemary, "and I'm sure they're all falling over themselves with excitement. But there's more news, according to Pa, and I don't think you're going to like it. The announcement says that a team at Interworld Travel has identified the people responsible for sealing the worldgates and causing havoc across all eight worlds. 'Those four people,'" Rosemary read grimly, "'are the explorer Henry Tallard; the notorious lawbreaker Rosemary Silos; Lucy Eberslee, unemployed; and a criminal mastermind from East known to authorities only as Prince Arthur.'"

I sat right down on the stairs. "You've got to be kidding me."

DISGRACEFUL! said the bees. THEY DIDN'T MENTION US?

"A criminal mastermind," said Arthur thoughtfully. "I like the sound of that."

Rosemary kept reading off the InterCom. "'Henry Tallard has been captured, but his three accomplices remain at large and are believed to be in hiding in another world. The House of Governors is currently working to alert all citizens to the danger posed by these individuals. Anyone suspected of assisting, harboring, or fraternizing with them will be brought in for questioning and possible arrest.' In other words," said Rosemary, looking up, "we're fugitives."

"Oh, worlds," I said. "Do you think my parents have seen this?"

"It's all over Southeast, apparently," said Rosemary. "They're offering a reward for our capture. Do you think we should turn ourselves in? I could sort of use the money."

"That's not funny." I couldn't stop thinking of my mother and father at the breakfast table, unfolding the morning newspaper and nearly choking on their toast. I wondered whether it would horrify them more to read that I was an accused criminal on the run or that I was currently out of work. "Everyone will believe this, too. I was standing right next to the worldgate when it closed. Even I thought I'd broken it."

"And I *am* a notorious lawbreaker," Rosemary said proudly. "I can't deny it. It won't look good for me at the trial."

"It won't look good for any of us," said Arthur. He must have realized that the life of a criminal mastermind had its downsides after all. "We ran away from Interworld Travel. We lied to Mrs. Bracknell's secretary and conspired with Henry Tallard. We left Mrs. Bracknell to be attacked by enormous birds—though, in our defense, she did try to have us eaten. And now we've gone to ground in a *smugglers' den*."

"You make it sound so scandalous!" Tam had come up behind us while none of us was looking. She was still smiling, though, so I guessed she hadn't overheard too much. "I wanted to let you know that Zenna's got some of that information you were asking for. I can't say if it'll be useful or not, but you ought to have it in any case." She paused, studying our faces. "You three look a little shaky. Did one of those cannonballs land in the harbor again? It's been happening so often lately that I hardly notice it anymore."

"No cannonballs," said Rosemary. "Not yet, anyway. Thanks, Tam. We'll come and take a look."

24

Zenna, a woman about my mother's age, was waiting for us at the kitchen table, along with half a dozen other smugglers. She gave us a wide, warm smile. "I've got a lot of friends in a lot of worlds," she said, "and most of them owe me favors. I do my best to keep it that way. One of my friends happens to work in Southeast at the records bureau, so I asked him if he could send me Clara Bracknell's address." Her smile grew even wider. "He sent me five. That woman's got more houses than she knows what to do with."

Rosemary whistled. "Must be nice to be in the House of Governors."

"Anyway, I wrote down the addresses for you." Zenna handed us a piece of paper with five addresses scribbled in purple ink. Two of them were in Southeast—the Interworld Travel building, where I guessed Mrs. Bracknell kept an apartment, and a house close by in Centerbury. One of the addresses was in West. "We've been there already," I said, picking up a pen from the table and making a little x next to the Western address. I made another one next to the entry for Interworld Travel. "Mrs. Bracknell might have the gatekeepers at her house in Centerbury," I said, tapping the end of the pen against the second Southeastern address, "but it would be risky for her, and it would be even riskier for us if we tried to go there. We'd better look somewhere else first."

There were two more addresses on the list: one in Northeast and another in Northwest. "It's too bad Mrs. Bracknell didn't want to build a seaside home on a Northern island somewhere," said Arthur, looking over my shoulder. "We're going to have to go back through the worldgate. It doesn't sound like they'll be too happy to see us again at the Interworld Travel building."

The redheaded smuggler looked up from her InterCom. "There's a Northwestern address on that list, isn't there?" she asked. "I'm from Northwest, and I've just heard from a friend back home. He's a ranger in the Ungoverned Wilderness, and he saw a large group of people wandering around near one of the worldgates last week, just before it closed. He assumed they were tourists back then, of course."

"But they might have been gatekeepers." I put down the pen. "Did one of them have frizzy hair and a tendency to stomp?" The redheaded smuggler didn't know. "We'd better check the Northwestern address first."

The promise of a trip to Northwest was enough to coax a smile out of Rosemary. I was excited, too; I'd been longing to visit Northwest ever since I was a little girl. True, none of us knew how we'd get past the travel officers who were bound to be waiting for us by the worldgate, and true, we had no idea how to sneak a group of hungry, irritable gatekeepers out of Mrs. Bracknell's house once we'd found it, but it felt good to know where in the worlds we were going. In fact, everything felt good around the kitchen table that morning. Tam offered to cook us breakfast, Arthur made everyone laugh by telling them how he'd fallen out of a library into another world, and even the bees were feeling healthy enough to spell some of their favorite words, elaborate ones like PULCHRITUDI-NOUS and BOURGEOISIE. Tam's bacon and Northquail eggs tasted even more delicious than they smelled, and I realized I hadn't had a meal so good since the Gatekeeper had disappeared.

"You three." The smuggler in mud-crusted boots walked into the kitchen, pointing at Arthur and Rosemary and me. He held up an InterCom in his other hand. "You didn't tell us there was a reward out for your capture. And you didn't tell Tam that Southeast will throw us all in jail just for the crime of being in your company, did you?"

Around the table, conversation stopped. Tam set down her spatula. My eggs went suddenly cold.

"Oh dear," said Arthur. "Word spreads fast in a smugglers' den."

"Of course we don't *believe* you did anything wrong," Sarah said as she hustled us out the door, "and none of us minds breaking the law. We do plenty of that every day. But we try not to give Interworld Travel any extra reasons to notice us, and it'd be just awful if they shut Tam's place down for good. I hope you understand."

Tam herself had wanted us to stay at least long enough to finish our meal, but none of the other smugglers had looked particularly happy about the idea. We could tell we'd overstayed our welcome when the man in boots started talking about all the things he'd do with his share of the reward money; Tam promised us he was only joking, but he'd looked awfully serious to me. After Sarah shooed us out of the smugglers' den, we hurried back to the docks and squeezed on board an outbound ferry just before it weighed anchor.

The trip back to Omegos seemed to take forever. Arthur kept looking backward to see if the smuggler in boots was chasing us, Rosemary kept looking forward to see if Mrs. Bracknell and her officers had tracked us down, and I kept watching the ships of the Northern worldwide navy preparing for war. Soon enough, the House of Governors' statement would spread, and everyone in all eight worlds would believe we were criminals. If the Northern navy didn't blast us off the map, someone else would certainly try to.

I'd half expected a legion of Interworld Travel officers to meet us on Omegos, but no one in white jumpsuits was waiting to apprehend us at the ferry terminal or along the shore. There weren't any officers waiting for us near the worldgate, either; the pier was empty. "*Too* empty," Rosemary said as we walked down it. "I don't like this. It doesn't feel right."

"It feels good to me," said Arthur, swinging his arms. The water below us was growing rougher as we got closer to the worldgate; every time a wave slammed against the pilings, it sent a little shiver through the pier. "We'll be through the doors and off to Northwest before Mrs. Bracknell can do anything about it."

I hoped Arthur was right, but it was a lot easier for me to believe Rosemary. "There's nobody here right now, but we don't know who'll be waiting for us on the other side of the door," I pointed out. "At least we've still got Rosemary's defense ray."

Rosemary nodded and reached into her pockets. Then she frowned and started searching through her bag. "It's not here," she said. "I know I put it away, but now it's missing. Ugh; that's the end of the world for you."

We'd reached the end of the pier, where the thin outline of the worldgate was traced on the sky in front of us. Arthur stared up at it. "Are we still going to open the door?" he asked. "Do you have a plan, Lucy?"

A large wave broke below us, and an even larger one followed right on its heels, sending salt spray into our faces and making our legs tremble. The Gatekeeper had told me once that she enjoyed all the mess and chaos at the end of the world; the challenge of it made her mind more nimble. Now, as I looked down into the rumbling sea, I wondered if mine had gotten nimbler, too. "Yes," I said finally, wiping the salt from my eyes. "We'll open the door. But we won't go through it."

25

This time, when I opened the door between the worlds, I found Michael on the other side of it. He looked just awful.

"Hello," I said. "That's a terrible scratch you've got over your eye. Did a yellow-winged wailer give it to you?" I gave him an administrative smile. "You should have someone take a look at it before it gets infected."

Michael couldn't help noticing me this time. "She's here!" he shouted over his shoulder. "I've found her!"

"I think it's fairer to say that *I* found *you*," I told him, "but you'll take credit for anything, won't you?"

A squad of travel officers ran to Michael's side. There were five in all—Kip and Celeste, plus three more I didn't recognize, all decked out in protective gear and staring at me across the worldgate threshold. At least Thomas wasn't anywhere in sight. Neither was Mrs. Bracknell.

196

"I heard you all are supposed to arrest me," I said. "You might as well try. I'm not looking forward to it, but it should make Mrs. Bracknell happy." I took a step backward on the pier. "You're not supposed to cross into another world without all your papers in order, but I promise I won't mention it to anyone."

Michael scowled. "Why don't you come here?"

"I already told you I wasn't looking forward to being arrested. Do you really think I'm going to make it easy for you?" I took another step backward and held up my hands. "If you're as talented as you pretend to be, it shouldn't take you long to round us up."

I guess Michael didn't appreciate my jokes, because his scowl only grew deeper. "She's talking nonsense," he said to the travel officers. "Go and get her."

The travel officers nodded and ran through the doorway. They were all carrying huge nets, like something a kinder person might use to scoop up a butterfly. Celeste, who was first through the worldgate, raised her net over her head and started to swish it through the air toward me.

Then Rosemary dashed out from behind the open door and grabbed Celeste by the ankles. They both fell to the pier in a mess of knees and elbows, and the net fell into the sea. Arthur, still behind the door, threw whatever he could grab from our open bags at the travel officers; shoes and books and balled-up sweaters whizzed through the air. So did the bees. They swarmed at the officers, who flinched behind their protective visors and waved their nets in self-defense. One lost her balance and slipped off the pier.

I made my way through the tumult as quickly as I could, climbing over squirming travel officers, dodging flying night-gowns and undergarments. Kip scrambled after me. He reached out a hand to grab my ankle, but I pulled away just in time and he grabbed the frayed edge of the worldgate instead. Then I heard him swear. "We've got threads coming loose!" he shouted to the others. "Get out of the sea and find a maintenance kit!"

I stumbled through the doorway, praying I wouldn't trip on a loop of fabric and pull all the worlds down with me. Michael must have lost his nerve and run off somewhere, because the eighth floor of Interworld Travel was deserted. "Northwest," I murmured to myself, looking up and down the row of doors. "Which one of you goes to Northwest?"

It didn't take me long to spot the door at the far end of the row, painted pale green and carved with a pattern of leaves and vines. It wasn't locked, but the doorway was crisscrossed with strips of construction tape. I ran down the hall, ripped the tape away, undid the padlock, and turned the knob.

Behind the door was a plain wooden wall.

It wasn't Northwest; it wasn't any other world but our own. Mrs. Bracknell's team had put up the doorframe, but they hadn't yet snipped the gatecutters through the fabric of time and space, and I couldn't exactly wait for them to do it. I kicked at the construction tape that lay balled up at my feet. If the gatekeepers were stuck in Northwest, I had no idea how we were going to reach them.

"We're here!" called Arthur, running into the hallway from North with Rosemary right behind him. Arthur had pieces of butterfly netting in his hair, and Rosemary was scraped and scratched from head to toe, but both of them were smiling, and the bees surrounded them in a triumphant halo. "We got all the travel officers into the sea!"

"Except for Kip," Rosemary corrected. "But he's holding on to that worldgate to keep all the worlds from falling to pieces, so we decided we could spare him."

Arthur nodded. "You should have seen us, Lucy! One of the officers almost scooped me up, but her net had a hole in it and I scrambled right through."

"Then I knocked her off the pier," said Rosemary. "It was glorious. I'm sure they'll all come after us once they reach shore, but we'll be far into Northwest before then."

"Not Northwest." I pointed at the pale green door. "The worldgate's not open yet. This door doesn't go anywhere."

Rosemary made a face. "Honestly! We'll have to go to Northeast, then. At least we know that worldgate works."

We started jogging down the hall toward the barn door at the other end. Before we got anywhere close, though, there was a rush of footsteps on the stairs, and Michael turned up at the end of the hall, breathing hard, with a crowd of travel officers behind him. He must have pulled them out of some sort of meeting, because they didn't have nets, and they weren't wearing visors. Instead, they all wore suits. One of them still had a marking pen clutched in his hand.

"Don't move!" Michael shouted at us. "I'm taking all of you to Mrs. Bracknell. The bees, too!"

The travel officers raced toward us. We had no chance of reaching the Northeastern door; they'd catch us long before we could manage to get to the end of the hall. I lunged for the nearest door, the red one with a bronze knocker. In half a second I'd unlocked it, and the three of us tumbled through.

26

This time, the travel officers followed us.

We were in a narrow, dirt-paved lane spotted with rainwater. High stone walls rose up on either side of us, and men and women in suits spilled through the worldgate behind us, blinking in the sudden sunlight. There was nowhere to run but forward.

"We've got to get away from those officers!" I called to Rosemary and Arthur. Rosemary nodded and sprinted down the lane, but Arthur was the one I was worried about. Hadn't he said just a few hours before that he wasn't any good at running? What if the travel officers caught him? We couldn't leave him behind; we'd have to go back. . . .

"Sorry about the mud!" Arthur cried.

He splashed through a mud puddle and blazed straight past me. In a matter of seconds, he was shoulder to shoulder with Rosemary, and I was the one who had to scramble to keep up.

"I thought you didn't have a knack for this," I said between breaths.

Arthur glanced over his shoulder at me. "I've never been running for my life before!" he called back. "It's fantastic motivation. And anyway," he said, leading us around a corner, "I know where we are."

"We're in East?"

Arthur nodded. "Not only that, we're in my hometown. I'd know these lanes anywhere."

"Then for worlds' sake," said Rosemary, "stop chattering and take us somewhere safe!"

The lane ended without warning, and we found ourselves in a busy street. Cars rolled by us, going much faster than the traveling contraption we'd borrowed from the Gatekeeper. The street was covered in hard gray pavement and lined with shops. Parents dragged children past bakery windows, street performers made music on strange stringed instruments, and colored electric lights hung on wires above us, flashing green and yellow and red.

"Turn left!" called Arthur. We ran after him down the sidewalk. The travel officers thundered out of the alley behind us, and they turned left, too. We wove through the crowds, apologizing to people carrying shopping baskets or walking their dogs. "Excuse us!" Arthur kept saying. "Step aside, please! So sorry for the inconvenience!" By the time we'd run a few city blocks, traffic had slowed to a crawl, and everyone on the street was gawking at us.

Some of the travel officers had fallen behind, but most of them were still too close for comfort. At the front of the pack was Michael himself. I hadn't thought he'd be able to keep up with us, but he must have been fueled by sheer annoyance, because he was almost close enough to grab my arm. "This," he shouted, "is not the sort of behavior I'd expect from an Eberslee!"

"I wouldn't expect it, either," I called back, "but here we are!"

I wove around a child teetering on a pink bicycle and narrowly missed a lamppost. Arthur had run into the middle of the street now, dodging automobiles left and right; I took a deep breath and plunged after him. The travel officers tried to follow, but they weren't as familiar with otherworld traffic as Arthur was, and they started to fall behind. "Maybe it's a parade," I heard a woman say to her friend, "or a work of performance art."

Her friend sighed. "Whatever it is, it's extremely annoying."

We turned another corner and ran up the street toward an enormous pale brick building surrounded by an iron fence. Flags waved from the fence posts, and rows of men in neat uniforms stood at attention in front of the gate. "Where are you going?" Rosemary shouted at Arthur. "You can't go in *there*. That's a *palace!*"

"I know!" Arthur ran straight up to the rows of men in uniforms, stopped, and gave a hurried salute. To my surprise, the men in uniforms saluted back.

"I need you to let the three of us in," Arthur told them, "but lock the gate behind us, and don't let any of those people in suits get inside." He pointed behind us at the travel officers, who were rushing down the street toward us, all looking extremely out of breath.

"Certainly," said one of the uniformed men. As Rosemary and I stared at each other and then at Arthur, the man hurried us through the gate. "Will there be anything else, Your Highness?"

"That's all for now, thank you," said Arthur, and all the men in uniforms saluted him again. Then they turned their attention back to the street, ordering all the travel officers to halt in the name of the king. I could hear Michael trying to argue his way into the palace grounds, but none of the uniformed men seemed particularly impressed.

Arthur had sat down on the grassy lawn in front of the palace to catch his breath. "We should be safe here," he said. "Even Mrs. Bracknell isn't a match for my father's royal sentries." He took a long breath in and lay back on the grass. "It's lucky we turned out to be so close to home."

Rosemary was still gaping at him, so I had to be the one to ask. "Arthur," I said carefully, "are you actually a prince?"

"Of course," said Arthur. "I told you that ages ago."

"I didn't realize you were telling the truth!" I said, sitting down next to him. "I thought you were pretending."

"You did?" Arthur sounded genuinely surprised. "But you've called me 'Your Highness' before."

"I was joking!"

Arthur frowned. "It's not a very funny joke."

WE BELIEVED YOU, the bees assured him. BEES CAN TELL THESE THINGS.

Maybe they could, but I wished they'd told the rest of us. "Your father's really a king, then?" I asked.

"Not a very important one," said Arthur. "Our country is so small it doesn't even get printed on maps. I'm sure you've never heard of it."

I looked over his head at the enormous palace. Being in charge of a whole country, even one I'd never heard of, didn't sound so unimportant to me. "Will you be a king, too, then, someday?"

"Oh, no. I've got seven older brothers. When there are seven princes already, no one gets particularly excited about the eighth."

Rosemary was excited, though. "Do you have bodyguards?" she wanted to know. "And someone to taste your soup in case it's been poisoned? Do you wear a crown? Does everyone kneel when you walk into a room?"

Arthur laughed. "It's not really like that. The crown is only for special occasions, and no one ever kneels, thank goodness. I'd feel awful about it if they did." He stretched his arms over his head and yawned in a very un-royal way. "Anyway, I'm not at the palace very often anymore. I'm usually at school on the other side of the kingdom. My father says my tutors will prepare me for the future, but they never mentioned anything to me about other worlds, so I'm not sure they're quite as smart as Father thinks."

The sentries had turned all the travel officers away from the gate now. "You can't stay in there forever," Michael shouted to us over his shoulder as a guard marched him back down the street. "Don't think I won't tell Mrs. Bracknell about this!"

"Oh, I'm sure you will," Rosemary called back. "Please send her our best!"

We all waved cheerfully as Michael disappeared the way he'd come. "He's right, though, you know," I said, sitting down next to the others. "We *can't* stay here forever. We're supposed to be looking for the gatekeepers, and I don't think they're likely to be anywhere in this world. Mrs. Bracknell doesn't own any property in East."

"Even if the gatekeepers were here, we'd have an awful time trying to find them," said Rosemary, flopping back into the grass. "East is huge. Sarah said our sister Tillie is in a place called Iceland. Is Iceland anywhere near here?" She sounded hopeful, but Arthur said it wasn't.

"Well, we've got no chance of getting to Northwest," I said, "since the door that leads there isn't opened yet. We could try to get to Northeast, but all those travel officers will be waiting to arrest us as soon as we walk back through the worldgate. Maybe we *are* stuck here forever."

Arthur assured us that there were worse places to be stuck. "You can all come back to school with me," he said. "My tutors can teach you how to solve equations and read things in Latin. The bees could live in the school meadow!"

Rosemary stuck out her tongue at the suggestion. "Maybe

princes go to school," she said, "but smugglers don't."

As nice as East seemed, I wasn't sure I was ready to live the rest of my life there. "You were supposed to be meeting your tutor when you came through the door at the end of the world, weren't you?" I asked Arthur.

"That's right. I was at the library, avoiding him, and I found a little doorway I'd never seen before."

"And you fell through it."

"Right," said Arthur. "And then you were there, and the bees . . ."

I remembered all that well enough. "Could you take us there?"

"To the library?" Arthur asked. "Of course, but there won't be much to see. I'm sure the door at the end of the world is just as broken on this side as it is on the other one." He lowered his voice. "Especially since I snapped that key in the lock."

"You did *what?*" said Rosemary.

"We'll tell you the whole story later," I promised her. "And I know we probably won't be able to get through that door, but I'd like to see the library anyway. It's where the Gatekeeper was going when she disappeared. Someone there might know what happened to her."

"This isn't going to work," Rosemary grumbled as we trudged across a green park toward the old stone library. It was autumn in East, and dried leaves covered the grass. Two of the king's sentries had driven us here, and now they walked a respectful distance behind us in case we happened to need protection from any suit-clad travel officers or furious private secretaries. "I don't want to crush your spirits, Lucy, but no one in East ever notices anything. I've been through this worldgate a few times myself, and I can tell you that even if ten of Mrs. Bracknell's finest officers had tackled the Gatekeeper right there in the middle of the library, no one would have looked up long enough to wonder what was going on."

"We're not as bad as all that," said Arthur. "I'm sure I would have noticed someone getting hauled away by Interworld Travel."

Rosemary crunched through a pile of leaves. "You didn't even know a door to another world was right in front of your face until you fell through it."

"That," said Arthur, "is because I'm farsighted!"

I couldn't imagine how anyone hadn't known about a worldgate built in such a public place, but when we stepped inside the library, I began to understand how Arthur could have missed it. The building was old and vast, with winding back staircases, secret nooks carved out of the walls, and endless shelves of books. Although the worldgate was closed now, it wasn't easy to make our way from room to room without getting hopelessly lost.

"I hope I can find that door again," said Arthur. "I think I was near the astronomy encyclopedias, or maybe it was the Portuguese dictionaries. . . ." He trailed off, leading us up the main staircase, through a reading room lit by crystal chandeliers, and into a thicket of reference materials. I wondered how many books had vanished from the library stacks over the years, and how the people who lived nearby had accounted for all the rainstorms and cyclones that must have passed through the area. "Maybe they rounded up some scientists and told them to study the weather," Rosemary suggested when I asked. "That's the sort of thing Easterners would do—assuming they noticed it at all."

Easterners really *didn't* notice much, I realized: even though a prince, two bedraggled girls with rucksacks, and some royal sentries were parading through the library, the other patrons hardly bothered to look up. They must have watched plenty of explorers, tourists, smugglers, and diplomats pass through the door at the end of the world, all without batting an eye.

"The door is this way," said Rosemary at last. She pointed toward a darkened back hallway. "This is the exact place where my pa once dropped all the glass jars of powdered hot pepper we were bringing home to sell, and everyone in the building started to sneeze. It was a miracle we weren't caught in the act." She shook her head. "Poor old Bernard. I hope he's all right. He wasn't a very good gatekeeper."

We followed Rosemary into the hallway, where the only sounds were the hiss of a furnace and the quick footsteps of distant librarians. The air was thick with the smell of old books, and the walls were papered with flyers taped up by people who'd lost things at the library: jewelry, umbrellas, winter hats. Most of them, I assumed, had never found what they were looking for.

209

At the end of the hall was a door painted green. "This is it," said Rosemary. A sign nailed to the doorframe said Special Collections, and a metal folding chair rested against the wall. I wondered if that was where Bernard used to sit.

Arthur looked around and nodded. "This is where I was standing right before I met you, Lucy. Isn't it funny to think your gatehouse is on the other side of this door?"

"It used to be, at least," I said. I wondered what was there now—just a blank wall like the one I'd seen behind the door at Interworld Travel? Whatever it was, I didn't feel anywhere close to home.

The door was stuck shut, of course. It didn't open when I pulled on it, or when Rosemary pushed it, and certainly not when Arthur knocked politely, but I hadn't really expected it to. Even the bees were thwarted when they tried to fly through the gap under the door. NO USE, they reported back. THE WORLDGATE IS GONE.

There was a squeaking noise behind us, and we turned around to see a woman rolling an empty metal cart down the hall. According to a pin on her shirt, she was a reference librar-ian. "May I help you?" she asked.

Arthur's face lit up. "Actually, I think you can. Do you have a moment to talk about the end of the world?"

"What he means," I said quickly, "is that we're wondering if you've seen anything strange happening near this door recently."

The librarian made a little humming noise as she thought. "Bernard would be the best person to ask about that," she said.

"He's in charge of the collection back there. I haven't ever seen it myself. Bernard is very particular about who he allows in."

"And Bernard is here right now?"

"Well, no," said the librarian. "I haven't seen him for a while, as a matter of fact. I think he must be on vacation."

"That's one way of putting it," Rosemary said under her breath.

The librarian's brow creased, as if it bothered her to give an unsatisfactory answer to anyone's question. "Would you like to arrange a time to see the collection when Bernard comes back?"

"No, thank you," I said. Rosemary had been right after all: this wasn't going to work. No one in this world knew what had happened to the gatekeepers, and even if they had, we wouldn't have been able to do anything about it. All the royal sentries in the king's palace wouldn't be defense enough if we tried to go back through the open worldgate while everyone still believed the stories Mrs. Bracknell was telling about us.

"I'm sorry I can't be more helpful," the librarian was saying. "I wish Bernard had let us know he was planning to take time off. He didn't even leave his keys behind. All the patrons who've stopped by to see the collection have been so disappointed."

Rosemary nudged me with her elbow. "We're not the only ones you've spoken to?"

"Not at all," said the librarian. "I've turned at least five people away, and some of them were very angry when I did it. One gentleman actually threw a compass at me, if you can believe it!" (I could.) "And there's an old woman who turns up every day to shout at the door and whack it with her cane. I've asked her more than once to stop, but she keeps coming back." The librarian smiled a little. "I suppose I *have* seen a few strange things happening here, now that I think about it."

"An old woman," I said. "With frizzy white hair?"

"Extremely frizzy," said the librarian.

"And she comes here every day?" I was trying to stay calm, but my words rushed out in spite of themselves, and the bees began to clamor above us.

The librarian glanced up at them. "Every day for the past week or so, and always precisely at noon. How did those bees get in here?"

"They're friends of ours," Arthur reassured her. "Lucy, are you all right?"

"What time is it?" I asked. "Is it noon yet?"

The librarian glanced at her watch. "It's two twenty-three." There was that crease in her brow again. "But if you're looking for the woman with the cane, I've seen her walking sometimes in the school meadow. Does that help you solve your problem?"

"Oh, yes." I beamed at Arthur and Rosemary. Rosemary's jaw was in the process of dropping, and Arthur looked totally mystified, but that made sense: he'd never met the Gatekeeper. "It helps more than you know."

27

In the school meadow, a wiry woman in a witchy black cloak stomped through the grass. I would have known that stomp in this world or any other.

"Gatekeeper!" I called as I ran toward her. "Gatekeeper, are you all right?"

The Gatekeeper looked up and squinted at me in the autumn sunlight. Then she leaned forward on her cane and squinted some more. "Lucy Eberslee? For worlds' sake, my girl!" She let out a loud, crackling laugh as the bees swarmed around her and I gave her a hug. "Now, there's no need to get sentimental," she said, but she didn't push me away or thwack me with her cane. Her cloak was damp and caked in dirt, and she looked bonier than ever. "How did you get here?" she asked, looking me up and down. "And what do you think you're doing in East? Don't tell me you've forgotten our rules!"

"Don't leave the end of the world for any reason?" I couldn't help laughing. "I'm sorry, Gatekeeper. I broke that one ages ago. And I haven't been eating many vegetables, either. No wonder Mrs. Bracknell terminated me."

I could see the Gatekeeper's hair frizzing on the spot. She thumped her cane three times on the ground. "Stop right there," she said, "and reverse course, and tell me everything. I'd like to hear from the people standing behind you, too, once they've stopped gawking."

The three of us told the Gatekeeper as much as we could remember, and the bees filled in what we couldn't. If anything surprised her, she didn't show it, but she did shake her head when we told her how we'd gotten to East. "A new worldgate only hours from here," she said, "and I've been wasting my time shouting at that door in the library?"

"There's no way you could have known," I told her.

"Don't be kind, Lucy. I can follow the thunderclouds as well as anyone." The Gatekeeper glowered. "I complained years ago, you know, when Clara Bracknell was chosen to lead Interworld Travel. Her only interest in other worlds has always been what she can take from them if they won't give it willingly. Never wanted to hear what we gatekeepers had to say about things, either. Well, she'll be hearing from me now, whether she likes it or not."

The Gatekeeper had been living in the meadow all this time, she told us, sleeping on the matted grass under a stand of trees, ducking into the library when it rained, and hitting the glass-fronted snack dispensers with her cane at mealtimes until a packet of something crunchy or spicy jogged free. Arthur was so horrified to hear this that he told the royal sentries to drive us all back to the palace at once. "We've got real food there," he assured her, "and a very nice roof, and beds with sheets. I'm sure you'll enjoy it." The Gatekeeper harrumphed, but she didn't say no.

Rosemary hadn't said much since we'd found the Gatekeeper. Maybe she didn't want anything to do with the woman who'd once sent her pa to prison, I thought, or maybe she was just in awe. I'd seen plenty of people go suddenly quiet in the Gatekeeper's presence. Once we'd all piled into the palace car, though, she leaned over and nudged me with her elbow. "Isn't anyone going to *ask* it?"

I had no idea what she meant. "Ask what?"

"What's happened to the other gatekeepers!" said Rosemary. "Didn't Henry Tallard say there are sixteen missing? I thought we'd find them all together somewhere, but I didn't see anyone else wandering through that meadow."

I hadn't seen anyone, either. I'd been so happy to see the Gatekeeper that I'd barely noticed anything else, and I certainly hadn't remembered to look for fifteen more people. "You're right," I said. "There's Florence, and Bernard. . . ."

"Poor Bernard." The Gatekeeper sighed. "What a fool."

Arthur looked pale. "Is he—"

"Alive? Dead? I've got no idea." The Gatekeeper laid her cane down by her feet, and the bees settled on her lap. "I don't know where they took him. All I know is that if it hadn't been for the glue, they would have taken me along with him." She closed her eyes and leaned back in her seat, as though this explained everything.

I put a hand on the Gatekeeper's shoulder. "I know you must be tired," I said, "but you're going to have to tell us what happened to you once you went through the door at the end of the world."

Her eyes flicked open again, and she peered at me. "Lucy Eberslee," she said again. "You've changed. I like it." She stifled a yawn. "Do you remember those two travel officers who went through our worldgate on Maintenance Day?"

"I think so," I said. "A man and a woman, right?" They'd gone to East on business only an hour or so before the Gatekeeper had left, and I'd stamped their government passports without a second thought.

"That's right," said the Gatekeeper. "The man met me on the other side of the door. At first I thought he'd come to help us work on the worldgate, but then he grabbed me by the elbows and marched me out of the building like I was some sort of lawbreaker." The Gatekeeper scowled. "He had one of these Eastern traveling contraptions parked nearby, and he had me get inside. That's where they'd stashed Bernard, too. He was a sorry sight."

"They'd hurt him?" I asked.

"Oh, no. Bernard is always a sorry sight. His clothes are all too large or too small, and nothing matches; he claims all the laundry gets jumbled up at the end of the world. Anyway, there sat Bernard, looking half an inch from death, along with the other travel officer. She wasn't looking well, either. From what I could gather, she was supposed to go back into the library to stick the door shut, but she'd lost the tube of glue somewhere along the way."

"I'm sorry," said Arthur, "but do you mean it's possible to seal a worldgate shut with *glue?*"

"Oh, not just any glue," said the Gatekeeper. "Most of them won't do the trick. But Southern repair-all glue will keep a door closed for good if you dab it on the latch or squirt it around the frame."

"Of course." Rosemary shook her head. "I should have thought of that myself. Southern repair-all glue sticks to *anything*. My pa says he knows a man who used it to fix a broken teacup thirty years ago, and the man's still walking around with a teacup stuck to his hand."

The Gatekeeper nodded. "It's dangerous stuff. But the officers' tube had gone missing at the end of the world, and they were all in a tizzy about it. Bernard and I had to stay locked in that awful car all night while they searched the grounds. The man kept shouting about how they were already late, they'd gotten the gatekeepers, anyway, and if they didn't leave soon they'd be in trouble with *her*."

"He must have meant Mrs. Bracknell." I wondered what she'd told her travel officers to scare them all so badly. If any of them disapproved of her plans, they certainly hadn't shown it.

"Now, Bernard and I didn't know where we were being taken," the Gatekeeper said, "but we were sure we didn't want to go wherever it was, and being locked in the car gave us a chance to plot. When the officers came back and unlocked the doors, Bernard would create a distraction and I'd climb out. I was supposed to go back to Southeast for help if I could, and if I couldn't, I'd go to the Eastern branch of Interworld Travel to sound the alarm. That's more or less what happened, too. They found that awful glue at last, but when they came back to us, Bernard shouted something about poisonous spiders in the car, and I gave the travel officers a few good whacks with my cane on my way out the door. Then I hid in the library stacks. The officers came looking for me, of course, and they got close once or twice, but once they'd sealed the worldgate, I don't think their hearts were in it. By the time I crawled out of hiding, the door at the end of the world was closed, the car was gone, and I realized Bernard hadn't given me a single cent of Eastern money." Her eyes closed again. "The Interworld Travel office is on another continent. I thought at first that I could swim there, but do you know how big this ridiculous world is? And almost three-quarters of it is water! I can't imagine what Easterners do with it all."

The Gatekeeper looked as though she might fall asleep at any moment, and after hearing what she'd been through, I couldn't blame her. "And you don't know what's happened to Bernard?" I asked. "Do you think he's still somewhere in East?"

218

"I've got no idea," said the Gatekeeper. "All I've been doing is trying to get home and waiting for those travel officers to come back and grab me. They must have been too frightened to tell Mrs. Bracknell they'd lost me, or she would have come to get me herself by now. I imagine she'll be here soon enough."

The bees roused themselves from the Gatekeeper's lap. NOT IF WE STOP HER FIRST.

The Gatekeeper opened one eye to give them a skeptical look. "And how do you suggest we do that?"

I'd been thinking about it, and I didn't see why we had to give up on the task Henry Tallard had set for us in the first place. True, we'd only found one of the missing gatekeepers, but surely one would be enough. "We go to the Interworld Travel office here on East," I said, "and we tell them everything we know about Mrs. Bracknell and the doors at the end of the world, and the whole problem will be out of our hands. Henry Tallard said no one at Interworld Travel would listen to us, but they'll listen to you, won't they?"

"They'd better," the Gatekeeper muttered. "But I don't see how we're going to get there. Didn't you hear what I said about the water? Even if we can find a way to pay our fare on a ship, it will take us days to cross the sea, and days to cross back."

I looked over at Arthur. "Is she right about that?"

"There *is* a lot of water here on East," he admitted. Then he smiled. "But we princes have ways of getting around it."

28

"I don't like this at all," the Gatekeeper said. "Do I look like a bird to you, young man? Should I be in the air?" She didn't give Arthur any time to answer. "No! Of course I shouldn't! It's extremely unsafe. Is this how people behave in East these days? Swooping through the clouds without any regard for gravity?"

After a warm meal, a hot bath, and the best night's sleep I'd had in weeks, I'd woken up in one of the palace guest rooms that morning and found Arthur outside the door. His father, the king, was out of the country, Arthur had said, but he'd left behind the royal airplane. "And I'm sure he won't mind if we fly it to Interworld Travel," Arthur had told me as I'd yawned at him. "We'll be there and back so quickly, he probably won't even know we've used it."

I'd rubbed my eyes. "Did you say *fly*?"

The flying contraption turned out to be even noisier than

Eastern cars, and much larger, too, with the insignia of Arthur's family painted on its flanks. At least Arthur wasn't the one in charge of flying it. The king's pilot sat at the front of the airplane, directing it through the sky and chatting with the sentries Arthur had convinced to join us. The Gatekeeper didn't like this, either. "How can they joke at a time like this?" she asked as the pilot chuckled at something a sentry had said. "There should be absolutely no laughter allowed until everyone's feet are back on the ground."

"They have flying machines in South, too," Rosemary said from across the airplane, looking up from her InterCom. "I've always wanted to zip around in one."

"I haven't." The Gatekeeper crossed her arms. "In any case, those Southern machines run on magic. What's keeping this one in the air? Nothing but metal bolts and hope, that's what!"

I squeezed the Gatekeeper's hand and left her to fret while I went to talk to Rosemary. "Any news from your pa?" I asked.

She shrugged. "Not much. He says there's an announcement planned in the lobby of Interworld Travel tomorrow evening. The governors are asking everyone in Centerbury to come. He didn't want to set foot in the place, but I told him he'd better go anyway." She flicked a switch on the InterCom and set it aside. "If Mrs. Bracknell has something to tell the whole world, I'd like to know what it is."

The airplane had to land to refuel more than once, bumping and rumbling its way to a stop each time while the Gatekeeper groused. Eventually, we all filed off the plane and into a massive, crowded building where the Eastern travel officers who checked our documents didn't know quite what to make of our otherworld passports. ("You'd think they'd never seen one before!" the Gatekeeper said in horror.) Once they realized that Arthur was a prince, though, they were only too eager to let the rest of us through. The sentries had gotten a car for us, and the Gatekeeper passed them a little black book from the folds of her cloak. The page she'd turned to was full of addresses. She tapped her finger on the one for Interworld Travel, Eastern Division, and the sentry at the wheel nodded.

The road we followed was wide and flat, with low buildings planted on both sides and taller ones on the horizon. Beyond that were snow-peaked mountains much higher and grander than anything I'd seen in Southeast. I couldn't see a duck pond or sheep meadow anywhere. "Where did you say we were again?" I asked the Gatekeeper.

She squinted at the page of addresses. "Colorado," she said, "in someplace called America."

Arthur looked out the window at the strange landscape as we rolled through it. "It doesn't seem like a natural place to put an Interworld Travel office."

"No," the Gatekeeper agreed, "but it's precisely halfway between East's two worldgates. Equally inconvenient for everyone, I suppose. It's their own fault their world is so enormous."

When the car came to a stop, I didn't realize at first that we'd arrived. We'd left the main road and were in a city now, on a busy street lined with golden-leafed trees. "Here we are," said the driver to the Gatekeeper. "This is the address you requested." He pointed to a squat one-story building in front of us. It had a faded blue awning and wide glass windows where someone had posted worn-out pictures of landscapes: a sun-bleached sandy beach, a forest that might have been green, some gently rolling hills a little torn at the corners. A piece of paper taped to the door read, simply, Eastern Travel Service, and a little red sign just underneath it cheered, We're Open!

"It's not much like our Interworld Travel building, is it?" said Rosemary.

Even the Gatekeeper looked uncertain. "You're sure this is the place?" she asked the sentries. They said they were positive, though, so we gathered our bags and went inside.

I'm not sure the Eastern branch of Interworld Travel had ever seen so much activity. A middle-aged man in a blue sweater sat behind a desk reading a magazine, and when the little bell on the door handle jangled, he looked so startled that he almost fell off his chair. His eyes darted over us: a Gatekeeper, a smuggler, a prince, two royal sentries, a passel of bees, and a former gatekeeper's deputy (currently unemployed). It was a wonder all of us fit in the room.

"Good morning?" said the man, as though he wasn't quite sure it was. "May I help you? Is your group . . . planning a trip?" He pushed his magazine aside and started fiddling with a stack of brochures just as faded as the pictures in the window. "You might be interested in our special fare to Beijing."

The Gatekeeper stomped to the front of the group. "We need to speak to whoever is in charge here. I oversee one of the Southeastern worldgates, and I have extremely urgent information about a plot against your world and others."

This captured the man's interest enough that he put down his brochures. "We don't do much otherworld business these days, but whatever there is, I'm in charge of it. Claude Wilson, head of Interworld Travel." He stood up and held his hand out to the Gatekeeper, who shook it. "And you are?"

"Alarmed," the Gatekeeper said. She looked around the office. "Where is your staff?"

"At home." Mr. Wilson shrugged. "It's eight o'clock on a Sunday morning, ma'am."

Weekends had never been of much interest to the Gatekeeper. "Well, call them in, then!" she said. "The worlds are in crisis!"

Mr. Wilson came out from behind his desk, giving the Gatekeeper's cane a wide berth. "If you've come to tell me the worldgates are shut," he said, "you don't need to bother; I'm already aware of that. The field team in Auckland called to tell me the news as soon as it happened. We're short-staffed at our worldgate in the kingdom of Mellora, unfortunately, and I haven't been able to reach Bernard, but I'm sending an officer there next week to look into things at that end of the world."

TOO LATE! said the bees.

Mr. Wilson backed away from them. "As you can see," he

said, "the Eastern bureau is small." He gestured to the office around him—a floral-patterned sofa, a coffee maker, a bulletin board on the plain white wall. "We're not equipped to solve problems like this. When complications with the worldgates crop up, we prefer to let our otherworld neighbors address them. I agree the situation is concerning, but unless you've got a pair of gatecutters with you, I'm not sure there's anything I can do. I'm very sorry to disappoint you."

I recognized that pinch of irritation in his voice, the one that hinted he'd really prefer it if we all left him in peace to finish his magazine. I'd sometimes hinted that myself, back at the end of the world, but now I wished I hadn't. "What would you say," I asked him, "if we told you that the Southeastern Interworld Travel Commission is responsible for shutting all the worldgates and kidnapping the gatekeepers? And that they're opening new worldgates themselves, all so Southeast can control everything and everyone that passes from one world to another?"

"I'd say that sounds extremely unlikely," Mr. Wilson said. "Isn't Clara Bracknell in charge of Southeast? She's a respectable person." He gave me a long look. "And who did you say you were?"

I hadn't mentioned that yet. "I'm Lucy," I said carefully.

"You're not a gatekeeper, are you?"

"She's not," the Gatekeeper said, "but I am, and I trust Lucy implicitly." She put a hand on my shoulder. "If you care about this world of yours at all, you should trust her, too."

Mr. Wilson didn't say anything. He picked up a white ceramic mug from his desk, walked across the waiting room, and filled it with coffee. Then he sat down on the sofa and drank the whole mugful in one long gulp.

"All right," he said at last. "You'd better tell me more."

29

Mr. Wilson's staff turned out to be a group of five youngish men, all wearing short-sleeved black shirts, and all named Dave. After he'd listened to the Gatekeeper's accounting of events, Mr. Wilson called the Daves in to work and switched on an Eastern computing machine, which whirred and beeped so furiously that I wondered if it might explode. I wasn't the only one worrying, either. "I keep telling Claude that old clunker is gonna blow any day now," one of the Daves told us, "but Claude doesn't care. He's not really a computer guy."

With all of us looking over his shoulder, Mr. Wilson tapped at a few keys on the computer, and an image flickered onto the screen: a map of the eight worlds, a two-dimensional version of the sculpture we'd seen back in Southeast. The circles hadn't moved from their usual positions, but the familiar lines connecting them weren't there any longer. "That's how it looked when

I logged in last week," said a Dave. "No gates open anywhere." He leaned in for a closer look. "No, wait. That's different." He pointed at the pattern of thin lines crossing the space at the center of all the worlds. "Either your screen's got some cracks, Claude, or someone's cut at least five new gates through the world-fabric."

"Whoa," said the other Daves.

One of them nudged Mr. Wilson aside and pressed a few more keys. The image on the screen grew bigger. All the Daves stared at it. "Look at that," a Dave said, jabbing his finger at one of the lines. "And that, near Southeast. Oh man, that one's bad."

I leaned closer. I had to squint to see what he was pointing at: a series of faint, irregular squiggles branching off from the lines representing the worldgates. One of them, coming from the place where Mrs. Bracknell had built her doorway to North, was growing larger even as we watched, inching its way across the screen. "That's the place where Kip said threads were coming loose," I told Rosemary and Arthur.

All the Daves wore identical expressions of worry. "It looks to me like these gates are starting to unravel," one of them said. "What do you think, Claude?"

"I think I'd like to hear Mrs. Bracknell explain exactly what's going on in Southeast." Mr. Wilson stood up from his chair. "And I'm sure my colleagues in other worlds would like to hear the same before the fabric of space and time disintegrates and all of us go with it." He pressed a button on the computer, and the screen went black. "Book us all seats on the next flight to Mellora, please, Dave."

"Oh," said Arthur, "don't worry about that. We brought our own plane."

Word was spreading fast about Mrs. Bracknell's upcoming announcement, Rosemary told us on the trip back to the end of the world. "Pa has been talking to some of his friends in South," she said. "They asked him if it was true that someone in Southeast has a plan to save the worlds. Pa tried to tell them Mrs. Bracknell wasn't opening worldgates out of the kindness of her heart, but all his friends wanted to talk about was his no-good daughter who sealed the worldgates in the first place. So I guess word has been spreading fast about that, too."

"We'll set the record straight," Arthur promised her. "By this time tomorrow, the only crimes you'll be suspected of are the ones you actually committed."

Rosemary smiled and closed her eyes. "That's a nice thought."

The Gatekeeper wasn't any happier about being up in the air than she had been before, but when I sat down next to her, she reached out and patted my hand. "I'm glad you came to find me, Lucy," she said, pulling her cloak more tightly around her shoulders. "It's exactly what a deputy should do in a crisis."

"Former deputy," I reminded her.

The Gatekeeper snorted. "We'll see about that. I have a few things I'd like to say to Mrs. Bracknell the next time I see her, and none of them are very nice."

By the time we got back to Arthur's kingdom, we were all bleary-eyed and stiff. I hadn't gotten much sleep as the airplane zoomed through the sky, and all I'd had to eat that day were the little packets of crackers and nuts one of the Daves had found stashed in a storage bin. At least everything at the end of the world was quiet. There weren't any angry travel officers protesting outside the palace fence or lying in wait for us as we made our way back down the dirt-paved lane, retracing our steps back to Southeast. Just like the worldgates we'd seen in West and North, the door at the end of the world was almost invisible. If I hadn't passed through it myself, I'd have mistaken it for a few irregular cracks in the high stone wall. But it was snowing in two-minute spurts in the lane, followed each time by a brief, blistering heat wave, so we knew we'd come to the right place.

The Gatekeeper looked at the door and shook her head. "Not quite as grand as I'd expected," she said. "And no gatekeeper? The skin crawls to think of it."

"It's a *secret* worldgate," I reminded her.

"Not for much longer," said Rosemary darkly. "If we don't get back home before Mrs. Bracknell's announcement, we might run into a wave of tourists on the other side of the door."

"Better than a wave of people with nets!" said Arthur.

He had a good point. Even with the royal sentries, the Gatekeeper, Mr. Wilson, and the Daves by our side, I wasn't sure what we'd find when we opened the worldgate, or whether we'd all be able to escape from whatever it was. The Gatekeeper didn't seem concerned, though. She blew on her hands to warm them—it was snowing again—and ran her fingers along the cracks in the wall until she'd pried the door open. "Nets or not," she said, "I want to go home, and Clara Bracknell and her officers won't stop me." She stepped through the doorway. "Well? Are the rest of you coming?"

30

There was no one waiting in the eighth-floor hallway. Not travel officers with nets, or Mrs. Bracknell with some unpleasant otherworld weapon. Even Michael was nowhere in sight. I stood in the middle of the hall, looking from one end to the other, but the whole place was empty. No one leaped out at us or tried to have us arrested.

Rosemary blinked as she came through the worldgate. "Where is everybody?"

"I've got no idea," I said. In the dim light, I was starting to notice that other things had changed, too. The floor had been swept. The piece of construction tape I'd left outside the Northwestern door was gone. As a matter of fact, *all* the construction tape was gone, and so were the combination locks on the worldgates. More quilts hung on the walls between them, and above each door, someone had affixed metal labels engraved in tasteful script. The one over the door we'd just walked through said East. Directly across from us, lying on its side and waiting to be hung, was a much larger sign. Welcome to Southeast, it said. Center of the Worlds. When the Gatekeeper saw it, she snorted.

Mr. Wilson had lingered on the Eastern side of the door to study the fraying fabric around its edges. Now he hurried through the worldgate, looking angry. "They've rushed the work, and it shows," he said. "If someone tugged at one of those threads hard enough, they could start pulling the worlds apart." He opened the Northern doorway and glanced at the damage Kip had done during our scuffle, shaking his head. "Get a message to as many of the other Interworld Travel offices as you can," he said to the Daves. "They're going to want to take a look at this place. But tell them to be careful, or they'll tear up the worlds."

All the Daves nodded. Each one disappeared through a different worldgate.

"The rest of you," said Mr. Wilson, "need to take me to Mrs. Bracknell." He rolled up the sleeves of his sweater. "Quickly."

With the bees in the lead, we wound our way down the staircase. Somewhere between the sixth floor and the fifth, rounds of applause started to swell up from the lobby. "What time did your pa say Mrs. Bracknell was going to make her special announcement?" I asked Rosemary.

"Six o'clock." Rosemary glanced at her watch. "Oh, worlds. It's ten past six. That's why none of the travel officers were waiting to meet us. Everyone in Centerbury is supposed to be in that lobby."

"Then they'll all hear what we've got to say." I was starting to get dizzy from going around and around the staircase, and the applause was getting louder by the minute, but I tried not to pay attention to any of that. At the end of the world, it's important to stay as calm as possible.

Not that you'd know it from talking to the bees. HURRY! they said, zooming down the staircase and flying back up to urge us on. HURRY! And then, suddenly: STOP!

I did. Rosemary, Arthur, the Gatekeeper, and Mr. Wilson all staggered to a halt behind me. Below us, only a few steps away, was the lobby of the Interworld Travel building. Even on its busiest days, I'd never seen the room so full of people. The crowd covered every inch of the marble floor and flowed out into the street; if Mr. Silos was in there somewhere, or if my own parents were, I couldn't pick them out. I could see Thomas, though. He was standing in a long line of gray-suited travel officers right at the front of the crowd. Kip and Celeste were there, too, to my dismay, looking just as though no one had ever tried to push them into the sea. I recognized a few of the others who'd chased us into East, and I didn't have to look very hard to find Michael: while the officers on either side of him were scratching their necks or trying not to yawn, he was standing at attention and looking as proud as if he was the head of Interworld Travel himself.

Mrs. Bracknell stood with her back to us at a lectern that

234

someone had set up on the wide staircase landing. If the bees hadn't told me to stop, I'd have crashed straight into her. She must not have heard us over the applause, though, because she didn't seem to know we were standing behind her. In fact, I wasn't sure anyone had noticed us yet. Most people's gazes were glued to Mrs. Bracknell, and anyone who wasn't watching her was staring up at the sculpture of the eight worlds. The beams of light that joined the glass spheres together had gotten brighter since I'd seen them last, and all of them radiated from the golden-green Southeastern globe. Once you'd seen it, it was hard to look away.

"In a matter of days, the Southeast Worldhub will be fully operational," Mrs. Bracknell was saying to the crowd. "Our old worldgates may never be repaired, but misfortune can open the door to new possibilities, if you'll forgive the expression, and I'm proud of my team for coming up with an ingenious solution to our interworld crisis. They've been hard at work since the moment our first worldgate was sealed, developing the technology to open new pathways between the worlds in a convenient central location. For hundreds of years, travelers have had to cross enormous distances to get from one world to the next. They've had to endure dangerous weather conditions, cope with unpredictable circumstances, and submit to frustrating regulations that turn travel from a pleasure into a chore."

"Ha!" The Gatekeeper nudged me. "She's talking about us."

"But now?" Mrs. Bracknell waved her hand. "Interworld travel will be as simple as taking a few steps down the hall.

235

While we can't completely eliminate the side effects of placing several worldgates in one location, our engineers have developed a unique insulation material that should protect us all from danger and disruption."

Arthur shot me a questioning look. "Those enormous quilts, I think," I whispered.

"And with one central checkpoint run by experienced travel officers, we'll be able to cut down on time-consuming paperwork and expensive staff. Our whole organization mourns the loss of our beloved gatekeepers, and we'll continue trying to find out what's happened to them, but we can't deny any longer that gatekeeping itself has become a relic of an outdated system."

"Relic?" The Gatekeeper had heard enough. With her hair all afrizz and her cloak swooping behind her more witchily than ever, she stomped up to the lectern and whacked it with her cane. "I'm no relic, Clara Bracknell, and you'd better take care to remember it!"

The crowd stopped clapping and started murmuring instead. Mrs. Bracknell stepped away from the lectern and spent a good long while staring at the Gatekeeper. "I thought you were *gone!*" she said loud enough for all of us to hear it. "They were supposed to make sure—" She stopped midsentence. "Ladies and gentlemen," she said, returning to the lectern, "I'm sorry for the interruption, but it seems we've had an unexpected stroke of good fortune. One of our missing gatekeepers has returned to us."

"No thanks to you!" said the Gatekeeper. She faced the

crowd and waved her cane in Mrs. Bracknell's direction. "This woman is the one who made sure we all went missing in the first place!"

Michael was already halfway up the stairs. "You all!" he shouted, catching sight of us. "What do you think you're doing here?"

Mrs. Bracknell wheeled around to look where Michael was pointing. If the expression on her face was any guide, she wasn't too pleased with what she saw. The murmurs in the crowd had grown to a low roar now, and I could hear snippets of conversation here and there: "Who's the witch with the stick?" and "Aren't those the criminals? The ones who sealed the worldgates?" and "He doesn't *look* much like a prince." In the long row of travel officers, Thomas stood frozen, staring straight at me.

"Excuse me, everyone!" I said, but no one seemed to notice. I could barely hear my own voice over the noise of the crowd. *Shout,* I told myself. *Scream. Make a general ruckus. You've got two strong lungs, and you know how to use them.*

"Hey!" I hollered as loudly as I could. "Pay attention!"

That seemed to do the trick.

"We're not criminals," I called out. "We didn't seal any worldgates at all. Mrs. Bracknell did that—or at least her officers did. She's not solving your problems; she's the one who caused them!"

"You tell 'em, Lucy!" Mr. Silos shouted from somewhere in the back of the crowd.

Mrs. Bracknell and Michael strode toward us, with a growing

gaggle of travel officers close behind them and the Gatekeeper still trying to trip everyone with her cane. "Lower your voice, please," Mrs. Bracknell snapped at me, "or you'll wish that thistle-backed thrunt had eaten you days ago."

"Excuse me, Clara," said Mr. Wilson, stepping forward. "I hate to interrupt, but threatening our patrons with carnivorous beasts is a serious breach of protocol."

Mrs. Bracknell blinked at him. "Claude Wilson?" she said. "From East?"

"I can have him arrested if you'd like," Michael offered.

"No, don't do that. He's the head of the Eastern commission." Mrs. Bracknell looked at Mr. Wilson with his rolled-up sweater sleeves, and then at the royal sentries who stood on either side of him. If they were at all confused by the situation they found themselves in, they were well trained enough not to show it. "I think there's been a misunderstanding," Mrs. Bracknell said calmly, putting her hands in her pockets. "I'm not sure what these people have been telling you, Mr. Wilson, but I can promise you that none of it is true."

Mr. Wilson gave her a mild smile. "It seems accurate enough to me. Center of the Worlds, eh, Clara?"

Mrs. Bracknell said nothing. She wasn't blinking anymore.

Mr. Wilson shrugged. "The heads of the other branches will be on their way soon to repair the damage you've done. I'm sure Josie Santos over in South will be relieved to find out where Arabella Tallard's gatecutters have gone."

"I don't know what you're talking about," Mrs. Bracknell said carefully. "As I've just been saying to the others, my team has developed a new technology—"

This was when the cows came down the stairs.

The clatter of hooves was loud enough to drown out whatever Mrs. Bracknell had planned to say. The cows were moving slowly, stepping carefully; they obviously didn't want to trip. There must have been at least twenty of them. "I thought cows couldn't go down stairs," Arthur murmured as the first one stepped onto the landing and let out a long, low moo.

"They're Northeastern cows," Rosemary told him. "Very talented. I guess one of the Daves left a worldgate open."

"Betsy! Euphemia! Fern!" shouted Huggins from somewhere in the lobby. He pushed through the crowd and climbed up to the landing. "What are you ladies doing here?" The cows trotted over to him and rubbed their heads affectionately against his stomach.

Everyone had stopped gawking at us and started gawking at the cows instead. "What in the worlds is happening?" Mr. Wilson cried. "Where did these animals come from?" The cows were wandering through the lobby now, and Betsy or Euphemia or Fern was trying to eat his sweater. "Do they have valid passports?"

"I'm really not sure—" Mrs. Bracknell started to say, but she was cut off again by a new wave of visitors coming down the stairs.

These, at least, were human. In the lead was Zenna, one of the women we'd met in North. She was followed by a pack of other smugglers, only some of whom I recognized. Zenna caught sight of us and waved furiously in our direction. "We wanted to see if we could find that new worldgate you were talking about," she called over the ruckus. "Looks like we did!"

"Is that Mrs. Bracknell?" one of the other smugglers asked, pointing. "The one with all those travel officers behind her?"

Mrs. Bracknell glared up at the smugglers. Even she couldn't stay calm anymore. "You're not allowed to be here!" she shouted. "Who let you through that worldgate? You're all in extremely serious trouble."

Zenna frowned at her. "Rosemary and her friends told us all about you," she said, "and I think *you're* the one who's in trouble."

From somewhere behind her, a trumpet blew. "Make way for the chief admiral!" someone bellowed. "Make way or be blasted!"

"Oh, for worlds' sake," snapped Mrs. Bracknell.

The pack of smugglers parted, and a very short man in a brass-buttoned uniform and a wide hat marched imperiously down the stairs. "I am here," he announced, "to make a declaration of war against those who closed our worldgates! My Northern fleet will not relent until Southeast lies in ruins!"

Mrs. Bracknell stared at him. "Has this turned into a costume party?"

By now, the crowd in the lobby was in a frenzy. Some people were running after the cows, who were munching on decorative ferns and going around and around in the revolving doors. Others were yelling about criminals and smugglers and going to war with North. And most of the rest were jostling each other, trying to get a better view of the commotion behind the lectern. Travel officers were chasing after smugglers, smugglers were chasing after travel officers, someone in the crowd was telling the chief admiral of North that Southeast didn't even have a sea, cows were treading on the royal sentries' feet, and the Gatekeeper was still trying to give Mrs. Bracknell a piece of her mind.

"If you've harmed the other gatekeepers," she shouted, "if you've touched so much as a hair on Bernard's useless, infuriating head—"

"Careful!" shouted Arthur. "She's reaching for something!"

But the Gatekeeper didn't hear him. "Did you really think you could fool everyone in eight entire worlds, Clara?" she asked. "When I tell them what happened to me—"

"You won't tell them anything!" Mrs. Bracknell shouted. She was holding something now: a gleaming pair of scissors, small and sharp. As the Gatekeeper charged toward her, Mrs. Bracknell bent over and snipped at the air down by her ankles. A gash of bright light opened up in front of her.

The Gatekeeper fell through it.

"Stop!" cried Mr. Wilson, too late. He reached out to grab the Gatekeeper's cloak. But he leaned too far, or maybe he tripped, or maybe the light had a pull all its own. Whatever the truth might have been, all I knew was that within half a second, both of them had vanished.

31

We stared down into the light.

"What is that?" Arthur asked.

I shook my head. "*Where* is that?"

Mrs. Bracknell didn't move. She was still clutching the gate-cutters.

"I'll take care of it for you, ma'am," said Michael, running to her side. He had something in his hands, too—a bright pink tube, half rolled up. Rosemary moved toward him, but she wasn't fast enough; with a few squeezes of the tube, he'd glued the light shut. "There you go," he said to Mrs. Bracknell. "Good as new." Then he looked around at all of us on the landing. The smugglers had stopped chasing the travel officers, and the travel officers had stopped chasing the smugglers. Even the cows stood still. "Whatever you think you just saw," Michael said, "you didn't. Is that clear?"

In that moment, I swore I could have lifted him over my head and tossed him clear across the building. "Clear as bog-water!" I said. "What happened to the Gatekeeper? And Mr. Wilson? Where did they go?"

Mrs. Bracknell fiddled with the gatecutters in her hands. "I don't know, exactly," she said, "but it's *possible* . . ." She cleared her throat. "It's possible they're no longer in any of the eight worlds."

"What do you mean? What else is there?"

Mrs. Bracknell wouldn't answer.

Rosemary, though, was looking at the sculpture floating above us. "There's the space beyond the worlds," she said, pointing. "The emptiness that's all around us."

"Have you been there?" I asked her.

Rosemary swallowed. "Lucy, I don't think anyone's been there."

"I'm not sure," said Mrs. Bracknell slowly, "that it's possible to survive it."

My face felt hot with worry. "Then hurry up and bring them back! Go ahead. Use those gatecutters and open up a door to let them through."

Mrs. Bracknell and Michael exchanged a look. "I don't think that would be wise," Mrs. Bracknell said at last. "I didn't mean to send them out of the worlds. It was an impulse; I was hasty, but I needed them gone. They wanted to shut down the world-hub we've *all* done *so much* to create." She was speaking to her travel officers now, and some of the vigor had come back into her voice. "No one in the crowd will have noticed. I don't see any reason to alarm them. It's probably best if none of us mention the incident again."

I looked out into the lobby, where the scene was messier than ever. Mrs. Bracknell was right: it wasn't likely that anyone would have noticed the Gatekeeper and Mr. Wilson falling into nowhere, and even if they had, they wouldn't understand what they'd seen. It had all happened so quickly.

"You think we won't talk?" Zenna looked incredulous.

"You're smugglers," said Mrs. Bracknell. "Who would trust a smuggler's word? Or a farmer's? Or a . . ." She turned to the royal sentries, who looked more than a little uncomfortable. "Well, I don't know who you are, but it doesn't matter. You've entered Southeast illegally, which means you've committed a crime. I'll have you brought to trial in the House of Governors. And *you*, Chief Admiral, can keep your mouth shut or I'll seal that door to North right back up again." She put the gatecutters back in her pocket and brushed her hands on her jacket, as though she'd solved a particularly thorny problem. "There's no point in any of you making trouble. My officers will vouch for me."

I looked over at the travel officers, who had reassembled themselves into a long, gray-suited line. Their faces were grim. One woman clasped and unclasped her fingers nervously. "Is that true?" I asked them. "You won't tell anyone what Mrs. Bracknell just did?"

They stood there in infuriating silence: Celeste, Kip, Michael, even JEANNE. And as for Thomas—

"It's not true." Thomas took a step out of line. He'd turned almost as gray as his suit, but he wasn't swaying from side to side anymore; he was standing firm, and for a moment I filled up with pride. Then I remembered he'd tried to *dispatch* me, and the weight of the memory made me deflate.

But Thomas kept speaking. "I've had enough," he said. "I can't vouch for you anymore, Mrs. Bracknell. The House of Governors will want to know what happened here, and I'm going to tell them the truth."

Mrs. Bracknell gave him a long stare. "The truth won't be kind to us," she said. "To *any* of us."

"I know that, ma'am." Thomas didn't meet Mrs. Bracknell's eyes. Instead, he looked straight at me. "It seems to me that I should be at least half as brave as my sister has been."

After all that had happened between us, I wasn't sure whether to cheer or scream. "Oh, you Eberslees!" Rosemary whispered to me. "You just love to be noble!"

"All right, Thomas." Mrs. Bracknell's hands were in her pockets again, and her voice was still calm. "If you must, you must. Now, if you'll all excuse me . . ."

To her credit, Mrs. Bracknell was quick. By the time I saw the glint of metal in her hand, it was already too late: she ran up half a flight of stairs, snipped the gatecutters through the air, and disappeared into whatever was beyond.

We all ran toward the hole in the world. Huggins, who was closest, got to it first. He peered through it, which—for a horrifying moment—made him look as though he'd lost his head. "She's off and running," he said, pulling himself back from the hole.

I pushed my way to the front of the crowd. "In the space beyond the worlds?"

"No, no. *That* was over *there*"—Huggins pointed to the spot where the Gatekeeper had disappeared—"and *this* is over *here*. Looks like she's headed toward another world. She's slicing through all that fabric as she goes." He took another look through the hole. "Wouldn't have expected her to be so fast!"

Michael had uncapped his pink tube of repair-all glue again, but as he ran toward the hole in the world, Rosemary stuck out her foot and tripped him. "Oh, no you don't!" she said, snatching the glue out of his hands and tossing it halfway across the lobby. "Mrs. Bracknell's not getting away that easily. We're going after her."

"We are?" Arthur gave me a nervous look. Rosemary was looking at me, too, as though she was waiting for my answer before she went anywhere.

"Of course we are!" I didn't have time to think about it. "But if we don't hurry, we'll lose her."

Rosemary didn't need to be told twice. She dove through the makeshift worldgate and started running across the tattered fabric of space and time, with Arthur right behind her.

VENGEANCE!

cried the bees as they swarmed through the hole.

The royal sentries hesitated, as though they weren't sure what was expected of them in such an unusual situation. "Stay here, please," I told them, "and stop those travel officers from chasing us, if you can." I thought of glancing over my shoulder to see what Thomas was up to—would he try to stop me?—but then I thought better of it. I ran into the other world without looking back once.

32

The first thing I noticed was the scent. Everything smelled green and growing, like a permanent springtime. Thousand-year-old trees formed a canopy above me, and their roots sprang up under my feet, making me lose my balance more than once as I clambered after Rosemary and Arthur. Not far ahead of us was Mrs. Bracknell, a gray-suited curiosity in the leafy forest. She'd been wearing businesslike black shoes, but when she saw us chasing after her, she kicked them off. Huggins had been right: she *was* fast.

We'd only been running for a minute or two before Rosemary slowed to a stop. "We'll never catch her if we don't unload," she said, dumping her bag on the ground. Then she reached inside it and pulled out her InterCom. "Just in case. You both still have yours?"

Arthur nodded, and I fished my own InterCom out of my

rucksack. I grabbed my passport, too, and stuffed both things into my pocket. I felt a pang in my stomach as I left the rest behind—my books, my clothes, everything I'd brought with me from the end of the world, all lying in a heap somewhere in an otherworld forest.

We were in Northwest, or at least I thought we were. Other worlds had forests of their own, but none had quite so many baffled-looking campers looking up from their cook fires as we thundered past. Waterfalls rumbled pleasantly in the near distance, and the air was full of birdsong, faint music, and the constant whoops of tourists swinging through the Ungoverned Wilderness on vines. "I've always wanted . . . to come here . . . ," I said between breaths, "but I'm not sure . . . I can really . . . enjoy it. Duck!" A vine-swinging tourist had missed us by mere inches.

Rosemary watched the tourist as he swooped away. "Now *that's* how to get around," she said. We were coming to the crest of a hill, and when we reached the top, she grabbed a vine of her own and sailed out into the air. "Come on!" she hollered. "It's faster this way!"

"I've never traveled by vine before," Arthur said skeptically. "How do you steer it?"

I tugged at the vine next to Rosemary's; it seemed sturdy enough. "I don't think you *do* steer it," I called back to Arthur as I ran down the hill. "I think you just . . . *go!*" I hadn't even finished my sentence before my feet were off the ground and the green-scented wind was in my hair. Arthur was right behind me, and for once, the bees had to hurry to keep up.

The vines were Northwest's idea of public transportation, I realized; when you reached the end of one, there was always another hanging just a few feet ahead. In a matter of minutes, we'd nearly caught up to Mrs. Bracknell. We'd entered a busier part of the forest, though, and it was getting harder to weave through the growing groups of hikers and birdwatchers. "Coming through!" Arthur hollered as we swung over a pack of children who looked as if they were on a school trip. "Could someone down there lend us a hand and stop that woman?"

The kids didn't need to be asked twice: they took off after Mrs. Bracknell like a yellow-winged wailer after a lightning bolt. When she looked over her shoulder and saw the whole lot of us coming after her, her eyes went wide. She reached for a vine, then hesitated and reached into her pocket instead. I jumped to the ground and ran after her, but I wasn't fast enough: before I'd gotten close enough to reach her, she'd cut a hole in the world and disappeared through it.

The schoolchildren gathered around the hole, poking at its unraveling edges and sticking their heads through it until their teacher pulled them away. "Don't yank those threads!" I shouted to them as we ran past. I had no idea what was on the other side of the hole, but I barely had time to wonder where it might take us before I was diving through it.

33

Tall grass stretched for miles all around us. Blue sky stretched for days above us. Mrs. Bracknell was only a few strides in front of us.

"I don't think those bulls are happy to see us," Rosemary said, pointing.

BULLS? said the bees.

The bulls charged.

"Oh, *worlds*!" said Mrs. Bracknell. She bent down, snipped the gatecutters along the grass, and jumped through. . . .

34

I was falling, but not for long. Then my eyes stung fiercely, the air went out of my lungs, and my limbs felt heavy and cold. The sea was in my mouth; it was everywhere. I paddled to the surface and gasped for breath.

Arthur was there, clinging to a log. His glasses were splattered with water, and the bees formed a cloud just above his head. "Where's Rosemary?" I asked him.

"Here!" called Rosemary as she sailed through the hole in the sky and landed in the sea. She sputtered and shook the water from her ears. "Are you both all right? Do you know how to swim?"

"Yes," I said, "but so does Mrs. Bracknell." She was treading water a few strokes ahead of us, reaching up with the gate-cutters. As she snipped at the air, a hole between the worlds opened just above the surface of the waves.

We started swimming toward it. In front of us, Mrs. Bracknell grabbed on to the edge of the hole and pulled herself out of the water. Behind us, a bull careened through the air and landed with a splash. Somewhere close—too close!—a cannon went off. . . .

35

We were running through a city in the wind and rain. Brightly colored electric signs blinked on and off in a language I didn't recognize, screens flashed everywhere, and lights shone down on us from buildings that stood taller than any forest tree. People rushed toward us and away from us across the pavement, and I almost lost Mrs. Bracknell in the crowd. . . .

36

We were running on hard-packed sand in a place where nothing grew. The air shimmered with heat, and the ground began to shake. Cracks were opening up in the ground below us. . . .

37

We were running across a narrow rope bridge that swung dangerously from side to side with every step we took. The bees whirred with delight. Far below us, something vast and purple glowed in the darkness. I thought it might have been a lake, but it looked as though it was breathing. Behind me, I heard Arthur shout. . . .

38

I tumbled through the hole in the world and landed hard on my back.

The sky was bundled up in low gray clouds, and for more than a minute, all I could do was stare up at them. They made me think of the Gatekeeper's hair, the color of it, and how it had billowed around her face as she'd fallen into the space beyond the worlds.

Then my breath came back to me, and my head stopped spinning, and I could hear Rosemary coughing on the ground next to me. I forced myself to sit up. "Are you all right?" I asked her.

"Perfect," said Rosemary. She didn't *sound* perfect. "Just choked on some road dust." She coughed again. "I don't suppose there's anyplace near here where I could get a glass of water?"

I looked around. We were by the side of a narrow, empty road that someone had carved through a stand of trees. I wasn't sure which world we were in by now; we could have been anywhere. The ground here was beginning to tremble, too, the way it had done in the hot, sandy world. The wind was picking up, making me shiver in my damp clothes. And we'd lost Mrs. Bracknell. She must have run around the bend in the road or slipped into the trees while we'd been staring up at the sky.

"Where's Arthur?" Rosemary asked, and the breath went right out of me again. I stood up and looked all around us, but Arthur wasn't there. A hole in the air behind us glowed faintly purple, and the bees hovered around it making faint, worried hums.

"He was behind me on the bridge," I said. "I heard him shout, but I didn't see why. Do you think he fell?"

Rosemary drew in her breath. "It was a long way down."

We both scrambled back to the hole in the air and looked through it.

There, on the other side of the ragged world-fabric, was the rickety bridge swaying back and forth. Arthur was lying on the planks. He didn't look up when we shouted his name, or when the bees buzzed in his ears. His legs were dangling over the side of the bridge, and one of his shoes had fallen off. "Grab his left arm," I told Rosemary. "I'll take his right, and we'll pull him through."

Rosemary nodded, and both of us pulled. At the end of the world, I'd never lifted anything much heavier than the boxes of old books the Gatekeeper stored in her attic, but I couldn't leave Arthur to fall into whatever that pulsing purple thing might have been. The fabric of space and time made a horrible tearing sound as we dragged him across it, and I worried we might all tumble back through the hole together, but Rosemary and I gave one last good tug, and Arthur flopped facedown on the ground in front of us.

We stared down at him, hoping.

"Ow," he said faintly into the pavement. Then, slowly, he rolled over and blinked up at us. "You could have put me on my back, you know. I *am* a prince."

"Oh, thank the worlds." Rosemary started to pull him to his feet, but Arthur shook his head.

"I don't think I'm quite ready for that," he said, "if it's all the same to you."

"What happened?" I asked. "Where are your glasses?"

Arthur sighed. "Someone bumped into me in that city—the rainy one, with the lights—and they fell off. I was all right for a while, but it was so dark in that last world, and I couldn't quite see, and I tripped." He squinted up at us. "Did I miss everything? Have you caught Mrs. Bracknell yet?"

SHE ESCAPED, said the bees. FOR NOW.

"We're not sure where she's gone," I said. "Rosemary and I fell, too."

"I *would* have stayed upright if it weren't for this ridiculous ground," Rosemary added. "It's moving all over the place. I've never felt anything like it."

I hadn't, either. We'd had occasional earthquakes at the

259

end of the world before, but this felt different, as though the ground beneath our feet were being tugged in a hundred different directions. The wind was stronger than ever, too; it seemed to be coming from the hole in the world. Above us, the clouds were darkening, and the sky behind them was turning an eerie shade of green. If we were anywhere in West, there was sure to be a flock of yellow-winged wailers somewhere nearby. "It's all the holes in the worlds," I said, "all the worldgates Mrs. Bracknell is opening so close to each other. She's made at least six."

"Didn't she say something about insulation?" Arthur sat up slowly. "To stop all these side effects?"

"That's what all those quilts back at Interworld Travel were for, but she doesn't have any insulation now." There was a loud rumble, and the ground seemed to tilt below us. Behind us, the worldgate we'd pulled Arthur through was growing wider by the minute as its edges unraveled. "Mrs. Bracknell's been slicing the fabric of space and time to shreds," I said. "The more holes she cuts, the worse things will get."

"Then we'd better go and stop her," said Rosemary. "At least, we've got to try. Come on." She helped Arthur to his feet, and we walked around the bend in the road.

The ground was even shakier here; tree branches were snapping in the wind, and the sky had turned from green to mustard yellow. I put a hand in my pocket: my passport had disappeared. Rosemary's bandanna vanished off her head even as I stared at her. The bees flew down the road a few feet, then pulled back with a start and spelled one word, over and over: DANGER. DANGER. DANGER.

"Look." I pointed past the bees. Above the road, three worldgates gaped open: one leading left, one leading right, and one leading straight ahead.

"*Three?*" Rosemary swore. "No wonder the sky is yellow."

"And there's no way to tell where Mrs. Bracknell's gone?" Arthur asked.

"I don't think so," I said. "We don't even know for sure that she went through any of them at all."

We stared at the gates without saying a word.

"We'll just take them one at a time," Arthur said at last. "Maybe we'll choose the right one the first time around."

"Or maybe we won't." The wind whipped my hair into my eyes, and I couldn't see much more clearly than Arthur could. "I think we should each go through one of the gates. We still have our InterComs, right?" Arthur and Rosemary both said that they did. "One of us will find Mrs. Bracknell, and that person will tell the others where she is. And the bees—"

WE'LL STAY HERE, the bees said quickly.

"Splitting up?" said Arthur. "Are you sure we should?"

"Lucy's right. It makes sense." Rosemary looked down at her feet. "Mathematically, I mean."

"And it won't be for long," I said, hoping I was right. "If none of us finds anything in the next ten minutes, we'll all meet back here." I ducked as a tree limb flew by overhead. "Assuming *here* still exists."

"All right," said Arthur. He walked over to the gate leading right, and Rosemary walked to the one leading left. I stood in front of the one leading straight ahead. Then the ground jolted beneath us, and all three of us jumped.

39

I was in the hot, sandy world again. I shielded my eyes from the sun and looked around me: no Mrs. Bracknell, at least not that I could see. The ground was still shaking here, too, and sand was sliding down from the dunes on either side of me. I started walking fast, heading for higher ground.

My InterCom flashed: it was Arthur. *Any luck?*

Not yet, I wrote back, *but I'm still looking around.*

I'm on an oslamd! said Arthur.

I frowned. *Oslamd?*

Island, he said. *Sorry. Can't see very well. Wush I had my flasses.*

Rosemary didn't say anything.

From the top of the dune, I could see the world around me: tall machines off in the distance, sand stretching to the horizon, and cracks spiderwebbing across the ground. Not far away, a dark spot blotted out a piece of the horizon. It was the worldgate we'd run through earlier, the one that led to the swaying bridge where Arthur had fallen. *Mrs. Bracknell's not here*, I wrote on my InterCom. *She might have run into another world. I don't know for sure.*

She isn't here euther, said Arthur. *But lots of coconuts!* There was a pause while he typed out another message. *Where is Tosemury?*

I'd been wondering that, too. *Rosemary? Are you okay?*

The cracks in the ground were growing larger now, especially near the worldgates. I started running back the way I'd come. Just as I reached the bottom of the dune, my InterCom flashed again.

I'm fine, said Rosemary. *I found her. Come here now!*

40

The world where Rosemary had gone was dim and full of noise. At first I couldn't see well enough to tell where the noise was coming from. It sounded like the thrumming engine of an otherworld car, or like the beating heart of a storm. Then the world came into focus, and I could see waves breaking on a rocky shore. There were rocks beneath my feet, too, damp and slippery ones that made it difficult to walk. Something dark and shimmering stretched above us, and I wondered if it was the sky, or if this place was cocooned somehow in the fabric of space and time. "Rosemary?" I called.

Straight ahead! she wrote on the InterCom. *Hurry!*

I did my best to make my way over the rocks, but I slipped twice, and there were other obstacles, too: the wind, the trembling ground, the piles of strange objects the waves had brought in and left to dry on the shore. Mixed in with the usual kelp and sea glass were pencil stubs and inkwells, eyeglasses and key chains, crumpled-up school assignments, mismatched mittens, and singleton socks. I nearly tripped over a box full of pink customs declarations, each page printed with the Interworld Travel logo. If I searched long enough, I wondered, would I find everything I'd ever lost at the end of the world washed up on these rocks?

Arthur appeared through the worldgate behind me. He was holding a coconut, but he didn't say why. "It's windy out there," he said instead, squinting at me. "Windy in here, too. I think the sky is shaking."

He was right. That thrumming, rumbling noise wasn't from the waves alone, I'd realized; thin cracks of light were unspooling across the darkness above us, and the darkness was trembling. "Rosemary's that way," I told Arthur, pointing.

He set down his coconut, and we walked forward together. The land grew narrower around us, as if it was about to run out altogether, and mist rising up from the water clouded our view. "If I didn't know better," said Arthur quietly, "I'd think this place was the end of the world." Then he stopped and grabbed my shoulder. "Is that Rosemary?"

I stopped, too. "Oh, worlds."

It *was* Rosemary standing in front of us, with her jaw set firmly and her shoulders squared. Behind her, with one hand gripped on Rosemary's collar and the other hand on Rosemary's InterCom, was Mrs. Bracknell. And in front of them both, illuminating the place, was a gash of bright light in the ground—a hole into the space beyond the worlds.

"I'm sorry," said Rosemary miserably. "She grabbed me as soon as I got here. She cut that awful hole in the ground and said if I tried to warn you to stay away, she'd push me through it." Rosemary kicked at a pebble, which rolled into the gash of light and disappeared.

Mrs. Bracknell looked exhausted. Her clothes were damp and torn, and there was a streak of mud across her forehead and a long red welt on her arm. She was strong enough to keep Rosemary from moving, though. I shouldn't have been surprised: anyone who could keep a thistle-backed thrunt under control and fight off a pack of yellow-winged wailers wasn't likely to be weak. If she'd ever felt guilty about sending the Gatekeeper and Mr. Wilson into the space beyond the worlds, the sting of her conscience had long since worn off.

"Lucy. Your Highness. I'm glad you're here," Mrs. Bracknell said crisply, as though she were addressing her travel officers. "I don't know where *here* is, exactly, but that's beside the point right now. Rosemary tells me you both have these smugglers' devices?" She waved the InterCom in our direction. "You must, since you responded to my messages so promptly."

I nodded. So did Arthur.

"Excellent," said Mrs. Bracknell. "Drop them through the hole, please."

Arthur took a step back. "We can't. Rosemary said her pa would sell our ears on the black market."

"That sounds gruesome," Mrs. Bracknell admitted, "and

likely to be very painful. I'm sure you won't enjoy it. Drop the devices, please." She tightened her grip on Rosemary's collar, and Rosemary yelped. I glared at Mrs. Bracknell, but I let go of my InterCom. So did Arthur.

"Thank you." Mrs. Bracknell's knuckles relaxed a fraction of an inch. There was a rumble above us, a sound more dangerous than thunder, as if the whole sky was about to tear itself loose. "Now, here's what we'll do. The three of you will stay perfectly still. If you try to leave"—she was looking at me and Arthur now—"I'll send Rosemary out beyond the worlds. Do you understand?"

We nodded again.

"In the meantime," said Mrs. Bracknell, "I'm going to send a note to Rosemary's father. Mr. Silos, isn't that right? Do you think he can get a message to the House of Governors?"

Rosemary narrowed her eyes. "That depends on the message."

"Oh, it's going to be persuasive. It *has* to be persuasive. The other governors didn't ask too many questions when I told them about my Worldhub—they prefer not to know things, really— but now, with the Gatekeeper gone, and poor Mr. Wilson, too, they'll feel obliged to investigate. It won't look good for me. The head of Interworld Travel stealing magical tools, making gatekeepers disappear, sending an old woman to goodness-knows-where . . ." Mrs. Bracknell shook the thought out of her head. "No. I can't allow it. There would be a trial; there would be a sentence. I'd be banished to the fire pits of Pitfire, most likely. It would be horrible for everyone."

I stared at her. "It's already horrible for the Gatekeeper!"

"And for me," said Rosemary. "I'm not especially enjoying myself."

"Don't be selfish," Mrs. Bracknell told her. "I'm going to explain to the House of Governors that I've got the three of you here with me. I won't ask for much. If they agree to let me come home quietly, without any legal fuss or publicity, I'll bring you safely back to Southeast. If they won't agree . . ." Mrs. Bracknell looked contemplatively into the gash of light. "No, they *will* agree. The governors won't risk losing you. Your families would be furious."

Rosemary laughed. "If you mean you're holding us hostage, you've made a bad miscalculation. The three of us aren't worth a thing!"

"She's right!" Arthur beamed. "Princes are valuable captives in most situations, but you won't get very far with my family. They might not even notice I'm gone!"

"And I'm not a very good smuggler," Rosemary confessed. "I'm always being too bold. The whole smuggling community will probably be relieved once I'm out of the way."

"My parents will be disappointed when they hear I've lost my job," I said. "Who knows? They might send me out of the worlds themselves. I'm just an inconvenience." I met Mrs. Bracknell's gaze. "You think so yourself, don't you?"

Mrs. Bracknell looked impatient. "There's no point in trying to convince me the three of you are useless," she said. "You've given me nothing but trouble for days—especially you, Lucy

Eberslee. Thomas swore you wouldn't cause problems, but look what you've done! As soon as you asked me if I knew where the gatecutters were, I knew you had to go. But you got past my best officers somehow, and you *refused* to be eaten." The ground rolled beneath us, and the sky trembled. Mrs. Bracknell frowned up at it. "I'd better write that message. We need to finish our business here before the worlds fall apart."

I hoped for all our sakes that they wouldn't. "When we go home," I said, "if you're not banished to a fiery pit, will you close your new doors between the worlds?"

Mrs. Bracknell barely looked up from the InterCom. "Close the Worldhub? Oh, no."

"But the other worlds are furious!"

"Of course they are. I always expected they would be. They'll learn to appreciate the new system, though, and if they don't"— she shrugged—"well, I'm not sure there's anything they can do. They're not the ones with the gatecutters, are they?" She tucked the InterCom under her arm and patted her pocket.

Then she frowned. "The gatecutters," she said. "They were here just a minute ago. Where are they?" She turned Rosemary around and pulled her close. "Did you take them?"

"Of course not." Rosemary held up her empty hands. "I would have loved to, but I was too busy trying not to fall through that awful glowing hole you made."

"People do often lose things at the end of the world," Arthur said helpfully.

"You think I don't know that?" Mrs. Bracknell snapped. She

was rummaging through her pockets again. I looked around, too, but I couldn't see anything glinting from the cracks between the rocks. If she hadn't dropped the gatecutters, then they'd probably disappeared all on their own, just like the socks and gloves and spare change that tended to go missing near the worldgates.

And if that was the case, then I knew where they'd gone.

Generally speaking, of course. There were more little piles of objects on the shore than I could count. The mist made it hard to see most of them clearly, and some of the objects fell back into the water each time the ground shook. I took a few cautious steps toward the closest pile and knelt down to sort through it: some soggy unopened letters, a postcard from somewhere called Nairobi, three pearl-drop earrings, and a crab that scuttled over my fingers on its way to the sea.

"What are you doing?" said Mrs. Bracknell.

"Yes, Lucy," said Rosemary, "what *are* you doing?" Mrs. Bracknell was holding her closer than ever to the hole in the world, and her voice was tense.

"I'm organizing." I sorted the letters into a neat stack and the earrings into another, but there wasn't anything more underneath them. "At the end of the world, it's important to be organized."

Rosemary gaped at me. "Have you lost your mind?"

"People do often lose things at the end of the world," Arthur said again. This time, though, he sounded worried.

"I don't have time for this!" Mrs. Bracknell turned back to

the InterCom. "I'm sending that message now."

It's hard to keep things sorted neatly near a worldgate in the best of circumstances. In this place, though, it was practically impossible. The wind kept blowing over my stacks of objects, mixing everything together and burying half of what I'd uncovered. But I didn't look up. I moved from pile to pile, pulling out ribbons and bits of string, thumbtacks and thimbles, keys missing their locks, locks missing their keys. I put pink customs declarations to the left, green returnee reports to the right, and blue applications for otherworld travel straight ahead. If she'd been there to see it, the Gatekeeper would have been thrilled.

"Um, Lucy?" said Arthur. "Are you sure you're all right?"

"I'm sure." I placed three lone socks in a bundle together. "I was the Gatekeeper's deputy. I've gotten very good at this sort of thing."

"I'm sure you have," said Arthur, "but—"

Something that had been hiding underneath the socks shone up at me through the mist. I wrapped my hands around it: a gleaming pair of scissors, small and sharp.

I stood up carefully, trying not to slip on the rocks as I made my way back to the others. The gatecutters shuddered in my fist, as though they were intent on getting lost again. "I've found them!" I called over the roar of the waves. I walked up to the edge of the gash of light and held up the gatecutters for Mrs. Bracknell to see. Underneath my feet, the ground began to rumble.

Mrs. Bracknell stared hard at the gatecutters. "Give those to me, Lucy," she said. "That's an order."

"I don't work for you anymore." I dangled the gatecutters over the gash of light. "And I don't think you should be opening any more doors between the worlds. You've done enough damage already."

"You wouldn't drop them," said Mrs. Bracknell. She let go of Rosemary. "You can't!" She scrambled across the ground and reached across the gash of light. Her fingertips brushed the gatecutters' handles.

The House of Governors never could figure out exactly what happened next. Arthur says Mrs. Bracknell slipped on the rocks, and Rosemary says the ground jolted under us. Neither of them will say I pulled my hand away from Mrs. Bracknell's, but that's how I remember it. What I know for sure is that first she was standing across from me, and then she was falling, and then she was gone, swallowed up in the space beyond the worlds.

I looked into the light until my eyes hurt. Arthur came up behind me and took the gatecutters from my fist. Rosemary put a hand on my shoulder.

"We'd better go home," she said. "The bees will be worried sick."

None of us wanted to use the gatecutters, so we went back the way we'd come, down the empty road, across the bridge, through the sand and the city and the sea, past the bulls and the wide-eyed campers in the Ungoverned Wilderness. All along our path, the wind blew, the ground rumbled, and the sky shook. By the time we finally stepped out of the forest into the Interworld Travel building, dark clouds had formed up near the lobby ceiling, and it was starting to snow on the gathered crowd. The first face I saw was Thomas's.

"Goose!" he cried.

"Do you have any Southern repair-all glue?" I asked him. "We've got a lot of damage to fix."

41

The House of Governors didn't like to do anything quickly if it could help it, but when the governors saw the size of the mess Mrs. Bracknell had made across all the worlds, even they agreed it had to be cleaned up at once. They appointed a new head of Interworld Travel, an energetic young governor named Miss Harrison, who wasted no time in clearing the snow out of the lobby and the cows out of the revolving doors. Most of the travel officers were sent out to seal the holes Mrs. Bracknell had snipped so carelessly in the worlds, carrying tubes of repair-all glue and bolts of thick fabric to patch up the gaps. One officer, however, stayed in Southeast: Miss Harrison had taken quick stock of Michael and given him the special task of removing every last trace of cow dung from the Interworld Travel building. Rosemary, Arthur, and I all agreed that we liked Miss Harrison a lot.

She'd asked the three of us to lend the travel officers a hand with their repairs, which is how I found myself, later that week, in a Northeastern meadow with Thomas. Once we'd penned off the area to keep out the roaming bulls, I cut out squares of fabric and Thomas glued them in place. These patches would be weak, but at least they'd keep the worlds from coming apart until scientists and magicians could find a more permanent solution.

"I've been looking for you in the Travelers' Wing," Thomas said as we worked. I knew he had; I'd been ducking through doorways and slipping around corners every time I'd seen him coming. I'd had a feeling he wanted to talk, and that was the last thing I was interested in doing. "I wanted to tell you that Miss Harrison invited me to stay on as an officer, but I'm not going to do it. I'm leaving Interworld Travel at the end of the month."

I set down the fabric I'd been cutting. Thomas had always worked for Interworld Travel! I couldn't imagine him doing anything else. "I guess you'll run for a governorship, then," I said, "or would you rather be a diplomat? I think either job would suit you." I should have stopped there, but I wasn't much good at biting my tongue anymore. "Both are perfect for a bald-faced liar."

Thomas was so startled that he almost dropped his glue. "When did I lie to you, Goose?"

I counted on my fingers. "You pretended you hadn't asked Interworld Travel to hire me. After the thrunt tried to eat us, you acted like you didn't know anything about it. And you said you were sending me to the mountains to keep me safe, when all you really wanted to do was help Mrs. Bracknell get me out of the way. She wanted to *kill* me, and you didn't even care!"

"Oh, Lucy." Thomas looked horrified. "You really thought . . . No wonder you haven't wanted to see me!" He put down his tube of repair-all glue. Then he pulled off his crisp gray suit jacket, laid it on the grass, and sat down on top of it. "I knew about Mrs. Bracknell's project. Most of the senior staff did. She told us she'd come up with a way to make going between the worlds simpler and faster, and better for Southeast. Better for everyone, Mrs. Bracknell said. It had to be a secret, of course. We knew the heads of the other Interworld Travel offices wouldn't be pleased. But there were parts of the project I didn't know about, too. I didn't realize she was planning to close the other worldgates until you showed up. She was rattled that afternoon, Lucy, after she spoke with you. I thought it was because someone was going around closing the doors between the worlds, but now I think it was really because she hadn't expected anyone to raise the alarm so quickly. She had to find someone to blame it on."

"Henry Tallard."

"That's right. It was lucky for her that you'd seen him skulking around. He'd been giving her trouble for months. I didn't realize she was going to lock him up, though. And I didn't know anything about the thrunt." Thomas cringed a little. "I kept thinking about it—how it had to have come from West, and how only someone who worked for us could have known how to get there. By the time the bees were poisoned, I was sure someone at Interworld Travel was responsible, but I didn't know who. I thought if I could get you out of the building, away from the worldgates, you'd be safe." He shook his head. "You didn't need my help, of course. I should have realized that years ago."

I looked down at him. "The gatekeepers. All the ones who went missing. Do you know where they are?"

"Not exactly," said Thomas, "not yet. But don't worry; we'll find out. Once Mrs. Bracknell was gone, I cornered that awful secretary of hers and made him tell me everything he knew. She'd apparently sent teams of travel officers out into the worlds. Each team was assigned to retrieve two or three gatekeepers and keep them out of the way until all the old worldgates were closed and the new ones were opened. Then they were all supposed to come back to Southeast to help run the Worldhub."

I imagined the Gatekeeper sitting at a little desk on the eighth floor of Interworld Travel, greeting tourists and handing out maps, and I couldn't help grinning. "That would never have worked."

"I think Mrs. Bracknell was starting to realize that," Thomas agreed. "She didn't expect them to put up much of a fight. And she didn't even consider the deputies."

"Not many people do."

"Anyway, Goose, I'm sorry. I could tell something at Interworld Travel wasn't quite right, but instead of doing something about it, I ignored it and told myself everything was fine. That's why I'm leaving. And I'm not going to be a governor or a diplomat. A friend of mine from school owns a bakery in Centerbury, and she needs someone to take the early morning shift."

"I don't know about that." I sat down next to Thomas. "No Eberslees in the Interworld Travel building or the House of Governors? What will our parents say?"

Thomas laughed. "You know what, Goose? For once in my life, I don't think I care."

Thomas wasn't the only one leaving Interworld Travel. I woke up one morning to find the lobby full of former travel officers who'd been asked to depart. I recognized most of them as the people who'd chased us through the streets back in East: Kip and Celeste were in the crowd, and so was Michael, although he was making it clear to anyone who'd listen that he was by far the most important person Miss Harrison had fired. (The next morning, the lobby was full again, this time with people who'd heard the Interworld Travel Commission had plenty of jobs available.) Huggins and his cows eventually went back to their pasture, the smugglers snuck away in the night, and the chief admiral of North returned to his fleet after receiving a generous payment from the House of Governors. Even Henry Tallard wandered through the Interworld Travel building on his way back from West, though he was in a hurry to meet his biographer to write up the latest installment of his life's adventures. Miss Harrison had promised to shut down Mrs. Bracknell's Worldhub as soon as everything had been restored to normal, but for the moment, the eighth floor of Interworld Travel was bustling with travelers. One evening, without any warning, Florence and her deputy, Ophelia, came soaring through the Southern doorway on the back of a magic carpet. I was glad they were safe, of course, but I was even gladder when they'd flown back up to their gatehouse in the mountains. Every time I saw Florence's black robes swishing around a corner, a gash of bright light ripped open somewhere inside me, and I had to look away.

I didn't stay much longer in Centerbury. We never did manage to retrieve the Gatekeeper's car from the roadside, so Arthur and Rosemary and I took the train as far as we could, and then we went on foot. The Ungoverned Wilderness had swallowed up our old bags, but Miss Harrison had given us each a set of clothes and enough food for the journey, plus a new pair of glasses for Arthur. It was a shorter walk than I remembered, now that the door at the end of the world was sealed. Soon, through the trees, the roof of the gatehouse came into view. AHHH, said the bees, racing ahead of us. HOME.

I hadn't even been gone a month, but the garden was already overgrown, and a thin layer of dirt and dust had settled on the gatehouse windows. The door at the end of the world was just as Arthur and I had left it, though: jammed shut, with half a key wedged in its lock. Rosemary burst out laughing when she saw it. "I can see why you two thought this was all your fault," she said. "It takes a lot of talent to break a lock that badly."

"*Lucy* thought it was all her fault," Arthur corrected, grinning at me. "I felt sure we were unwitting victims of a vast interworld conspiracy."

"You'd better hope Rosemary can fix it," I told him. "If she can't, I'll make you try, and then we'll all be stuck here forever."

Arthur didn't have to worry, though; Rosemary had wiggled the broken key out of the lock in under a minute. "You'll need to get a new one made quickly," she said, pressing the key into my hand, "so don't lose it."

"I won't." I pulled out the little pair of scissors I'd been carrying all the way from Centerbury. "Are you ready?"

"I suppose I am." Arthur looked around the garden. "You know, I'm not sure Southeast is a pass-through after all. It may not have made a name for itself yet, but I think it will someday." He sighed. "I'm going to miss it."

"You say that as though you're not coming back in a month!" said Rosemary. "And as though I won't be bothering you all the time we're away."

"Well, a month is a long time," said Arthur, "and anyway, I'll miss Lucy." After days of making his case to the Daves, Arthur had gotten himself appointed as East's very first otherworld ambassador. He was going to spend most of his time traveling from now on, returning home occasionally to tell the people of East about how interesting it was to visit other worlds, and to have dinner at the palace.

Rosemary was going to East, too, against Mr. Silos's express wishes. He'd wanted her to take a few months off to recover from our adventures, but Rosemary had ignored him. "I may not be as sneaky as Tillie or as well connected as Sarah," she'd told us on the train, "but I don't see how I'll get to be either of those things unless I keep working at it, and there's an enormous stash of Eastern chocolate I'm dying to get my hands on. Everyone in Southeast goes wild for that stuff."

Rosemary and Arthur both stood back as I slipped my fingers into the gatecutters. The blades cut crisply through the places where the door had been glued shut. When I'd guided them around the final corner, I put them back in my pocket, and Rosemary picked the lock. (Much too easily, in my opinion. I'd have to warn Miss Harrison.) Slowly, holding my breath, I pulled open the door at the end of the world.

"Oh! Hello again!" On the other side of the door, the librarian we'd met in East looked up from pushing her cart down the long, dim hallway. "You three were looking for Bernard the other day, weren't you?"

All of us blinked at her. We looked one way, into the sun-dappled gatehouse garden, and then the other, into the library. I wasn't sure I'd ever get used to the sensation. "Yes," I managed to say finally. "That's right."

"Well," said the librarian, "you'll be pleased to know he's just gotten back from his vacation. He should be back at work shortly. If you've already gotten into the special collection, though, I suppose you don't need his help anymore."

"Oh, we do," I told her. "I'm sure we'll always need Bernard."

When the librarian had rolled her cart out of sight, Rosemary and Arthur stepped through the doorway, and the bees flew over to say goodbye. "We'll see you soon," Rosemary promised, "although now that you've got that new job, I'm sure you'll be even busier than we are."

"Don't open any illegal worldgates, Lucy," said Arthur. "At least, not without us."

"I won't." I leaned over the threshold to hug them both. Then I watched as they walked down the library hallway, turned the corner, and disappeared.

WHAT NOW? the bees asked.

"I'm not quite sure." I felt for the piece of key in my pocket. "I should probably find a locksmith." I took one last look down the Eastern hallway, pushed the door shut, and—

"Hold that door!" the Gatekeeper shouted. She barreled through the worldgate in a swirl of black robes, almost knocking me over. "You're not going to keep me out of my own garden, Lucy Eberslee!" She thumped her cane against the ground with relish, sniffed the air, and sighed. "The tomatoes are ripe already. I've been away too long."

The bees flew around her in a frenzy, and I couldn't stop staring. "How did you get home?" I asked. "Are you all right? I thought you were . . . well, I don't know *what* I thought you were, exactly, but it didn't seem—"

"I'm not dead," said the Gatekeeper, "but I've been better. I never want to see another of those Eastern flying contraptions as long as I live. I wouldn't have even set foot in one if Mr. Wilson hadn't gotten me a ticket."

"Mr. Wilson's back, too?" I put both my hands on the Gate-keeper's shoulders. "You've really got to tell me how you made it back here."

"From the space beyond the worlds?" The Gatekeeper shuddered a little. "It wasn't easy, Lucy; I'll tell you that. I'm not sure how long we were wandering there. It was awfully bright, and horribly cold, and sometimes we were right side up and sometimes we were upside down, and Mr. Wilson kept complaining that his nose felt funny. Every so often, I thought I could hear the sea. Just when I thought I might be losing my mind, I looked up and saw another worldgate right there above our heads. I still don't know how it got there."

I had some idea, but I kept it to myself, at least for now.

"I made Mr. Wilson climb on my shoulders," the Gatekeeper said, "and he poked at the thing with my cane. Eventually, we managed to pull ourselves through onto a rocky sort of beach. We were lucky, though. Some Interworld Travel fool was in the middle of gluing the worldgate shut! If we'd come along any later, we would have missed it."

"I'm awfully glad you didn't." I hesitated. "When you were in the space beyond the worlds, did you happen to see Mrs. Bracknell there?"

The Gatekeeper raised her eyebrows. "Is that where she ended up? No, we didn't see anyone else. We could barely see ourselves! And the worldgate's shut now, anyway. I suppose there might be another way out, but if Mrs. Bracknell ever makes her way back from the space beyond the worlds, I suspect she'll be a much different person for it." She leaned on her cane. "But what about you, Lucy? What are you doing back at the gatehouse?"

"Oh, I'm not here for long. I'm just supposed to watch the door until the new gatekeeper comes . . . although, now that you're here, I think I'd better tell Interworld Travel not to send anyone."

"Please do," said the Gatekeeper. "And after that? You won't be my deputy anymore? No more pink forms and green forms and blue forms?"

I shook my head. "Miss Harrison asked me to be in charge of the team that's opening up all the worldgates again. There are going to be lots of us, people from South and West and everywhere. We'll cut open the old doors and put up those insulating quilts Mrs. Bracknell invented so there won't be so many side effects at the ends of the world. We might talk about building new doors, too—ones that all the worlds can agree on, made carefully so they won't unravel. It's going to be total chaos to organize," I said, "but I think I'll be good at it. And I don't have to leave until next week."

"Thank the worlds for that," said the Gatekeeper. "I've got hundreds of tomatoes to pick, from the smell of things, and I could use a helping hand. Come with me, Lucy, if you'd like." She gave a little cackle and thumped off into the garden with a cloud of bees behind her. "We'd better get to work before the hailstorms blow in."

Acknowledgments

A heap of gratitude, as always, to Toni Markiet, who believes in stories down to her bones and always knows just the right threads to tug in order to pull a book—or a universe—into shape.

Thanks also to Megan Ilnitzki, to the rest of the remarkable publishing team at HarperCollins Children's Books—including Amy Ryan, Kathryn Silsand, and Jacqueline Hornberger—and to Poly Bernatene for his brilliant artwork.

Sarah Davies kept my own world from unraveling at least twice during the writing of this book. Enormous thanks to her and to everyone at Greenhouse and Rights People.

A number of wonderful people gave me writing time when I needed it most: Maureen and Leo Pezzementi, Jane and Chris Carlson, Jonathan Carlson and Kelsey Hersh, and Kerry Jo Green. Nora Pezzementi gave me new stories to tell and a new love for telling them. And I owe all the thanks in all the worlds to Zach Pezzementi, without whom this book simply wouldn't exist.

To all the librarians, teachers, and booksellers who share stories with young readers, and to the kids who crawl into those new worlds reluctantly or dive in headfirst: this one's for you.

Books by Caroline Carlson:

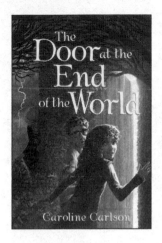

The Very Nearly Honorable League of Pirates series:

HARPER

An Imprint of HarperCollinsPublishers

www.harpercollinschildrens.com